A Song of Secrets

A Spirited Spinters Sweet Regency Romance

ROBYN CHALMERS

Copyright © 2020 by Robyn Enlund

All rights reserved.

No part of this book may be reproduced in any form or by any electronic or mechanical means, including information storage and retrieval systems, without written permission from the author, except for the use of brief quotations in a book review.

Cover Art by Carpe Librum Book Design

Edited by Jenny Q @ Historical Editorial & Lisa Lee

~

For T, P and the Lulus
I'm eternally grateful you all hung in there with me.

I started many Once Upon a Times, but could not have gotten to The
End without you all.
My love and thanks...always.

CHAPTER 1

PERFORMANCE OF 'THE MAGIC FLUTE'
LONDON, 1811

Sarah Hayworth stood behind the towering velvet curtains, head bowed, waiting for her entrance into act two.

Breathe.

The King's Theater and Opera House was raucous tonight, filled to capacity for the performance of The Magic Flute. Guineas would burst from the coffers, although getting her fair share was another story.

She closed her eyes and listened to them chant her name, letting the excitement swell inside, imagining a perfect performance. In front of the curtain, the opera was in progress, but that didn't stop them. They knew the Queen of the Night's vengeance aria was next, and they were ready to be thrilled. Eight hundred people, and the Prince of Wales himself, waiting for this one performance. Waiting for her.

Luckily, she was born to thrill them. If they weren't on their feet at the end, hearts racing, faces flushed, and hands creating a crescendo of applause, Sarah would consider the evening a failure. She needed to give them value for those guineas, as much as she needed their ovations in return. Accolades meant more contracts, and contracts meant more much-needed funds to send home.

Just a few minutes more.

She took a deep breath, filled her lungs with backstage air, and wrinkled her nose. It smelled like musty undergarments. But those kinds of thoughts didn't help. She rubbed her hands together, hoping the heat would miraculously travel to her frozen toes.

"What's the matter?" Miss Jones, her dresser, lady's maid and closest ally, fussed around, arranging her veil so the galaxy of diamantes sewn on it displayed to perfection.

"I'm getting too old for this," Sarah replied, feeling a familiar tremor start in her jaw. She stretched her neck to stop the jitters before they took hold.

Miss Jones continued to fuss. "Nonsense. You have at least five years left in you. Are your nerves affecting you?" She darted around like a wren, her tiny frame bursting with energy at odds with her somber black dress and tightly wound bun.

Sarah nodded. "They are trying, despite my repeated requests for them not to."

Miss Jones stood in front of her and rubbed Sarah's arms vigorously. "You're cold again. There's a hot brick in the dressing room warming your slippers, if that helps."

The tremor turned into a full-blown bout of shivering. "Can I wear them now?" It didn't matter what caused it, nerves or the cold November night—the result would be a disaster if she couldn't control it. A voice that warbled instead of soared. But she could control it—she had to control it. There were hundreds of people out there. She would not make a fool of herself.

"Never fear," Jones said, her brown-eyed gaze calm and steadying. "All will be better when you sing the first note. And somehow I don't think the Queen of the Night wears pink slippers."

Just the thought of sitting atop her crescent moon wearing

fluffy slippers made Sarah smile. She turned to Miss Jones. "Do you think anyone would notice if I did? It would be a wonderful joke."

"Let me assure you, they notice everything." Jones laughed quietly, finished her veil fluffing, and began prodding the star-topped tiara to make sure it was secure. It was, with the force of a hundred pins stabbing into her scalp. Sarah winced and waved a hand at Jones, who stopped fussing immediately.

"Very well," Jones said with her usual efficiency. "I'm off. Now don't let Edwina upstage you or confuddle you, or I'll have to kill her, and it would be sad to see me end my days in Newgate."

Sarah straightened her shoulders and looked ahead. "She won't. We had words. I'm sure she'd like to sing abroad one day, and if she crosses me tonight, I'll make sure she never does." She'd once been that upstart soprano, eager to shine, not caring who she had to stand on to do it. But never would she have risked the success of the opera she was singing in to do so. Unfortunately, Edwina, who played her daughter Pamina, seemed more than willing to do anything if it meant her star shone brighter.

"Bah," said Jones. "She's too stupid to realize how far your influence extends. Be on guard."

All very well for her to say. But Mozart's jewel of an aria, exhilarating, vengeful, and masterful, demanded her entire attention. In another five minutes, she wouldn't be thinking of her toes or Edwina or anything but the barrage of celestial high notes that stretched her beyond natural and into the supernatural. Anything else led to failure.

The stagehands lowered her crescent moon on a series of pulleys until it was directly behind her, and then, one on each side, they lifted her gently onto the white wooden seat, attaching her to it with a hook around her silver corded belt. She often wondered whether the hook would save her if she fell and had long ago concluded that it probably wouldn't. They stepped away and she was hoisted into the air like a sack of grain onto a cargo ship.

Jerk. Jerk. The tiara didn't move an inch.

Her feet dangled, and she took a deep, calming breath. *Think of something happy.* An image of Antony rose in her mind. Yes, that worked. Antony, Viscount Morley, waiting in the audience, full of pride and admiration, dressed in some glorious Weston creation with his romantic windswept hair. Not quite a lover, but more than a friend.

The man who had left a small but expensive present in the form of a diamond pendant for her before this last performance of the season.

Closing her eyes, she wrapped her fingers around the cold stone that now hung around her neck on a black velvet ribbon. She loathed to wear it in public like this—but loathed even more leaving it in her dressing room for anyone to take. Which was probably why he'd had it delivered just before her performance. He would want to see it on her.

But what did it mean?

Was it an 'I-want-to-marry-you' diamond or a 'would-you-like-to-be-my-mistress' diamond? If it was the former, it would be accepted with grace; if it was the latter… things were about to get complicated. Again.

Clinging to the rail at the back of the giant moon, she took another deep breath, and the nerves subsided somewhat. She continued the internal monologue to calm them even further. Listen to them, still chanting her name. Yet another breath and the nerves retreated, replaced with excitement. This was it—the final performance of *The Magic Flute*. Tonight, her contract would be complete and she would receive a draft for five hundred pounds to pay all the people that wanted a piece of her. Then life would be beautiful! She had no reason to be nervous. She smiled, and, as if in answer, the curtains drew open, the boys side stage pulling with all their might. The audience cheered and then stilled to the hushed quiet she was accustomed to and would have been aghast not to receive.

All gave La Luminosa her due.

The moon lowered slowly and Sarah, the Queen of the Night, floated ethereally. She looked around her in mock disdain. It was time to give her daughter Pamina a dagger and order her to kill the enemy.

In the nicest way possible, of course.

EVANDER AMBROSE, second son of the Earl of Wrotham, tipped his head back into the plush velvet of the seat and closed his eyes, letting the music flow over him. The opera, he supposed, was as good a place as any to question his existence. After all, there was sublime music to accompany the soul's descent, and nobody expected him to talk, least of all his father. He felt like he was floating on a river of sound, ebbing and flowing to Mozart's tricksy beat. *Feel it, damn you.*

It should have soothed and uplifted him, made him feel alive, and set his soul alight. Instead—nothing. Just the feel of his too-tight neckcloth and the aching throb of yet another headache.

Forget it, his soul said. *Nothing to see here.*

Indeed, there was nothing to see since Eleanor died, even though those dear scruffs he called sons needed him now more than ever. He had felt so good in the past days, finally through the worst of the grief, finally feeling like himself again. Then he'd seen someone on Bond Street that looked just like Eleanor from behind that had left him bereft for the rest of the day. He only hoped he climbed out of it faster this time. Heaven knew *she* would not have wanted him to grieve. She was far too practical for that.

He cracked one eye open in response to the unnatural quiet that had descended on the opera house. They'd finally stopped their rude chanting. He was alone in his thinking, but he could never understand why society came to the opera only to spend most of the time ignoring the music and the stage. Or jeering or heckling. They were ill-bred, the lot of them. Nothing could make him join that debacle.

"Evander, are you falling asleep? Wake up. She's about to come on." Father poked him in the ribs with a sharp, bony elbow.

The scenery of mountain ranges parted to reveal a lush garden complete with stone pillars and a fountain. The audience cheered as a glowing moon descended from the ceiling. Because there she sat, suspended in a sky painted with a thousand stars, her ridiculously long legs hanging from the side. Her gown was the color of midnight and tied with bands of silver, her hair billowing and dark. Her costume was low cut, revealing a glorious expanse of skin that glowed brighter than the moon beneath her as if made of stardust itself.

"By Jove," he breathed, not of his own volition.

"Indeed," Father replied reverently. "They call her La Luminosa. I can see why. Look at that bosom. Like two goose-down pillows. Oh, but I could sink into that." He lifted his opera monocle for closer inspection.

"Sink and then probably fall asleep, knowing you." Evander's eyes were good enough, and their box close enough that he didn't need the monocle. Although it wasn't the admittedly fine bosom that caught his attention. More like he didn't know where to look: her face, which was almost angelic despite that fact she was playing a devilish character, her hair, which was dark and glossy, or her long legs, which truly defied description of any kind.

His father sighed. "Ah, but what a fine sleep it would be."

Evander watched his father rather than the stage. Despite all the gadding about they'd done today, the old earl was still energized. They'd spent hours at Tattersalls alone, before settling on a beautiful mare called Midnight, then it was straight to White's in the afternoon for brandy and catching up with equally old and decrepit cronies, rolling straight into dinner at Boodle's. Evander had thought the day over until the earl announced he'd procured a box at the opera. Apparently, every ounce of fun was to be squeezed from this London trip the earl had assured his wife was "just to ensure my affairs are in order." It was all Evander could do to keep up.

"I want her so badly I can barely breathe."

Not *exactly* what he wanted to hear his seventy-year-old happily married father say, but Evander supposed the circumstances were extenuating. "It could just be your condition causing the breathlessness."

The earl quirked his white eyebrows, giving Evander the sardonic glare he deserved. "Must you remind me? Such a bore." He slapped his leg and turned to Evander. "Dammit, I'm going to have her."

A sentiment Evander could relate to and probably one every man in the theater had. Futilely, without doubt. "I'm sure Mother will be pleased."

Father shot him a wicked smile. "No, you dolt, for the musicale. My last Yuletide musicale."

Evander ignored the lump that formed in his throat at that statement. "More like you want her to sing to you in your sickbed. You know, I'm beginning to wonder if this illness isn't just a masquerade so you can do every bad thing you ever wanted to do in the knowledge no one will reprimand you." It wasn't true but was still worth saying, if only for the wicked grin it brought to his father's face.

"Well, the excuse 'I'm dying' tends to have the desired effect. Even your mother will welcome La Luminosa into the bosom of the family if I tell her it will make me happy."

"That's likely true." Mother was only ever happy when he was. Evander couldn't decide if it was ridiculously devoted or unhinged. Perhaps it was both.

There was a comfortable silence between them as the earl

gazed longingly at his newest goal and his son gazed at his father's beloved profile, the long, straight nose so like his own, silver hair caught at the back of his neck in an old-fashioned queue with a black velvet ribbon. This was a good day. Tomorrow might bring something entirely different.

The vision in question faced her onstage daughter, who sat on the edge of her bed and started talking. The room hushed further still, if that was possible.

Mrs. Hayworth uttered her lines, commanding her daughter to listen. Her gaze darted up to Morley's box, almost as if she couldn't help herself, and once she did, it seemed like she couldn't look away.

There Morley sat, looking like thunder. Next to him was what could only be a debutante in stark-white muslin and fresh-faced naivety.

Ah, he'd heard the wealthy viscount was recently betrothed.

He'd also heard that the famous La Luminosa was his light-o'-love. And if he was a wagering man, he'd wager his entire living that the opera singer was only just discovering Morley's tumble into the parson's trap. Evander smiled to himself. It was like watching an opera within an opera. And he wasn't the only one watching. Soon the entire theater was agog, the thousands of candles in those giant chandeliers illuminating the prima donna and Morley equally.

And if he looked like thunder, then she was the lightning, her countenance so electric that at any moment bolts would fling from her person straight to his heart. And that emotion, that darkness, it was riveting. Every word she spoke bristled with anger, and it was all directed at that bounder Morley. At least, he'd been a bounder at Eton, but perhaps he'd changed. Nothing else could explain him landing such a lovely. Unless it was his money. Ah yes, that always helped.

Then, in a moment that perhaps nobody else noticed, Sarah Hayworth's shoulders drooped briefly, and he'd swear he saw her blink rapidly, as though to hold back tears. It was gone in a trice, and she was the proud queen once again, but it was too late. His protective instinct was roused, and he knew that she wasn't as impervious as the newspapers and illustrators would like London to believe. He looked away, not able to watch her heartbreak. He willed her strength, strength to forget Morley and carry on as if he meant nothing to her. Strength to tackle one of the world's most difficult vocal performances, "Der Hölle Rache," which he knew was due to start any moment.

This song was what he thought he'd come to see until the sight of her dangling on a crescent moon had wiped all coherent thought from his mind. He closed his eyes again, knowing that it was disrespectful to watch her struggle even if he felt compelled to do so. He waited. The orchestra waited.

But no notes came. He cracked one eye open to see that she was blinking furiously again. And damn the crowd, they were lapping it up like cats with cream.

Evander sighed. Look how she loved him. Look how devastated she was by his betrayal. He couldn't fathom that kind of tempestuous love and would likely never experience it. The only love he'd experienced had been solid and quiet. It had left his heart in a cage of grief, whereas her disappointment soared around the theater for all to see.

What did Morley do to deserve such feeling? She was like a work of art, and Evander's heart was breaking with hers, damn the stupid pathetic organ.

He leaned forward in his seat, looking to his right, where Morley's box was. "You're too good for him anyway," he shouted, in the grand English tradition he abhorred of interrupting a stage performance. "Run for the hills, Mrs. Hayworth, and take that diamond with you." Evander's voice carried; after all, he'd trained it to do just that for ten years. The crowd cheered in delight. Evander sat back, half-horrified, half-elated.

"Well said." Father clapped him on the knee, warm approval in his eyes.

"It was the least I could do." Bounders like Morley had all the luck. A beautiful fiancée *and* London's most beautiful opera singer.

Vicars like him? Not so much.

CHAPTER 2

IN WHICH MORTIFICATION MAKES A
SURPRISE APPEARANCE

Sarah had always loved the way the boxes at the King's Theater were like miniature stages themselves. They were swathed in curtains with small chandeliers illuminating those who sat inside. It was nice not to be the only one on display.

After the well-timed outburst from the audience, the debutante stared at Morley's handsome face, her cheeks aflame with embarrassment while he glared at the stage. The young lady reached out her left hand, showing Sarah that rock-sized gem on her finger in case she'd missed it the first time.

Thank goodness she wasn't still suspended from that moon, or she would have fallen off it.

Morley was betrothed. But not to her.

She let that sink in.

Betrothed.

Which meant his whispers about marrying her were just that —whispers. She shouldn't be surprised. No matter what he said, no matter how virtuous she was, he would never marry an opera singer.

When would she realize they never did?

How many times would this happen before she understood?

This would be messy. Because all of London knew she didn't court married men.

If only she could look away. But it transfixed her. The young lady was a picture of indignation and outrage. Because Sarah's reaction had probably confirmed her suspicions. The audience was rapt, their necks craned around to watch the debutante battle with a world-famous soprano as though it were part of the evening's entertainment.

Her life tossed up for their amusement.

But Sarah wouldn't let them see her broken heart.

After all, they didn't think she had a heart to break.

Looking into the audience, a sea of raised monocular opera glasses met her, lapping up her bereft expression. She faltered; the next line had gone from her mind like a burst bubble.

Edwina turned to her. In her distraction, Sarah hadn't noticed that the sly thing had positioned herself to stand in front of Sarah, even though she had no dialogue and was supposed to cower before her mother in this scene.

The moment stretched out, and between Edwina and Morley, Sarah might never find her line again.

She stamped her foot, hoping Jones was watching from the side stage to help her. But before Jones could, Edwina took advantage of the situation, prompting her in a whisper that was more like a shout.

The coy expression on her face suggested Edwina knew exactly what had ruined Sarah's focus and was reveling in it.

Oh, for the love of puppies. Had this child no sense? Nobody made a fool of her, especially not an upstart soprano who wouldn't know a cavatina from a cabaletta.

Instead of repeating the line as it was so smugly offered, Sarah just raised one imperious eyebrow and let the moment slide a little further.

The orchestra stilled, waiting for their prompt to begin the introduction. It hushed the audience with what felt like a collective intake of breath. With a firm hand on Edwina's shoulder, she pushed her to her knees, lifted both hands to the sky, and said the magic words in German. *"You have heard your mother's last command."*

The strings began the introduction, and the crowd burst into applause. Maybe she could save this after all.

In my soul is the depth of hell's bitterness. A corner of her mind was amused at how closely her sentiments matched the character's.

All else fell away, Edwina and Morley relegated to the detritus they were as the music picked her up and carried her away like Perseus rescuing Andromeda. Note after note, she wove the beauty, the vengeance, and the strength of the queen into herself.

Fuelled by the sheepish look on Morley's face and Edwina's insolent behavior, the melody effortlessly sprang forth, saying everything she couldn't.

She *was* the Queen of the Night, her skirts swirling, the fury in her heart too much to be contained, thrown out into the night air in a cascade of sound. The notes lingered, suspended, then fell, her liquid voice chasing them higher and higher until, in a crescendo of sound, they hit high F—as far as any soprano could go.

There, you see, I am not broken-hearted.

She finished, and there was a dumbstruck silence because, in all the months this opera had run, never had she sung Der Hölle Rache quite like that.

The silence was replaced by thunderous applause and the sound of eight hundred people jumping to their feet. The hair on her arms rose as their excitement and energy hit her in a wave.

The "brava" they shouted was a balm. For a beau now lost, for a cast member who thought she could dislodge the reigning queen. She didn't look across at Morley, didn't look down at

Edwina, just accepted her applause as it poured into the hidden holes in her heart, where it settled comfortably and took hold.

~

AFTER THE PERFORMANCE, all Sarah needed was those slippers and all the horrible paint off her face. But Jones wanted answers.

"I heard the news. You didn't know?" Her dresser paced the small room, kicking up dust and diamantes as she went.

It took all her control to keep calm and not burst into hopeless tears. "It didn't come up in conversation, no. But it is to be expected. He has his duty." If she could convince Jones she wasn't bothered, maybe she could persuade herself too.

Jones stopped and turned, looking at Sarah in the mirror. "You don't fool me. Cry if you want to, but let's be straight about why we're crying. It's not for Morley."

Sarah offered her a weak smile. "He does look dashing in buckskins."

"Sarah," Jones said sternly.

"Oh, very well. It's not for Morley. Although you must admit, he almost came up to scratch."

Jones stared at Sarah's reflection in the mirror, her gray eyes all concern. "But he didn't. They never do. Is it time, dearest?"

Sarah knew what Jones was asking. Was it time to stop aiming for marriage and accept the fact she should take one of those lucrative offers that came her way every other week to become a noble man's mistress?

It was not a question for tonight. "Time to leave for a quiet brandy at home?" She nodded. "Yes."

Jones saw through the subterfuge. "Very well. I won't push you. But if the aim is to ensure Rebecca is cared for, who cares where the money comes from?"

Sarah shrugged. "It matters to me. One day she will ask who her mother is, and I don't want the answer to be 'a jade.' I'm just glad those evil caricature artists never got wind of my pretensions." Because that *would* be embarrassing.

They weren't pretensions; they were more like dreams. A secret dream of finding a man to marry who was rich enough, powerful enough, that her sending regular money to her parents for Rebecca would be no problem. A man who loved her enough to overlook what happened in Italy all those years ago.

If she were being frank, her first reaction when she'd realized the woman sitting next to Morley was his fiancée was pure jealousy. She had what Sarah wanted. A man who would stay. When her beauty and youth were gone and her voice lost, a man who would love her for her.

"Fleet Street will be in an uproar if you continue to let him hang around you."

"Fleet Street can—" She was about to say something crass, so it was lucky there was a knock on the door.

Jones braced the back of her chair. "That's him," she whispered, her eyes reflected in the looking glass, bright with either fear or excitement.

"I know," Sarah whispered back. "I'll be fine. If you could fetch the carriage so we can leave, I would very much appreciate it."

Looking grateful, Jones opened the door and slipped under the arm of Morley, who braced himself against the doorjamb and looked at her in the mirror, his expression unreadable.

Sarah swiveled in her chair to face him. With her costume and stage paint still on, she felt somehow protected. She took a deep breath. The nerves were worse than before her performance, if that were possible. She clenched her jaw to stop her teeth from chattering.

Morley entered the room as if he owned it. Which he was rich enough to do. He had turned thirty a few weeks before, but had not started to lose any of his golden mass of hair and perhaps never would. Sarah was taller than him, so he had his boots raised an extra inch for his vanity. Was his new fiancée shorter? He would adore that.

"Brilliant, as usual, my love." He turned her around so she was looking at both of their reflections in the looking-glass, his gloved hands resting lightly on her shoulders. "But do you think it was wise to wear this? The gossips will be agog."

"If you didn't want me to wear it, you should not have sent it just before a performance when I had nowhere safe to put it." She fingered it lovingly. "In any case, I will give it back to you tonight." She said it with a pang of sadness. It was a beautiful stone, and the sale of it would keep her mother and father in coal and wax candles for years. But she couldn't in conscience keep it.

The grip on her shoulders tightened, and she winced. "Don't be silly. Why would you give it back?"

She smiled slightly, although nerves were churning in her stomach. "Then that wasn't your fiancée with you tonight?" Why had she let Jones go? Now she had no ally.

A vein popped out at the corner of his fine, square jaw. "Of course. I'm getting married. It's my duty. Obviously, I'm sorry it is not to you. Let's talk of something else. I won't let that ugliness come between us."

Sarah smiled broadly. "Oh, I thought she was quite pretty. You chose well."

He pouted. "I said I didn't want to talk about it. And she could never hold my heart as you do."

"And she never *will* if I loiter around your marriage like a Covent Garden pickpocket." Sarah reached up behind her neck and undid the knot of velvet. The large stone fell into her hand, cool and smooth. She wanted to stand, but he blocked her. "I do wish you happy, Antony, but the last remnants of my upbringing as a gentleman's daughter mean that I don't have affairs of the heart with married men."

She saw the shock register on his face, replaced quickly by urbane nonchalance. It was hard to believe, but in all the time they'd been together, her background had never been discussed. Only his. She knew about Eton and summer in the Lakes District and his boyhood retriever called Pogo. He knew…nothing. He'd never even asked her if she had a husband. She styled herself Mrs. Hayworth, but in fact, there had never been a Mr.

"I think you'll find you left your reputation behind some time ago." He smiled at her in the mirror, but there was an edge of hardness to it. "Needless to say, I can make it worth your while to put your scruples aside."

This was the moment Jones had been thinking of. The moment to jump ship on her pride into the cold sea of reality.

But it was a step she couldn't take. Not yet. She may have lost her life savings in a singularly bad investment, but she'd scraped by so far without resorting to what he was offering right now.

If she was lucky, her voice would last long enough to recoup the ten thousand she'd lost. And if it didn't, she could always teach others how to sing. She could always earn her keep. Men were not her only option.

"Ah, Antony. It's not about the money. You know that."

He pushed himself off the back of her chair and prowled around the room. "Women like you always need a protector. And better the devil you know, don't you think? You're not leaving me." He said it like it was a forgone conclusion, and she was making a fuss about nothing.

It would be too easy to lose her temper and give him the verbal dressing down he deserved for not thinking this was important. But a smart lady didn't do that. A smart lady knew she had to traverse the same world he did and couldn't afford his bad opinion or the newspapers getting wind of the drama.

A smart woman made her revenge on him sweet by finding a beau who was better, stronger—his superior in every way.

A man who would probably also want the same thing—a mistress.

I don't want that.

And there it was. That niggly little voice wanting something more substantial than glittering baubles. It wanted a husband, someone to keep her warm in the early hours of the morning when the bed bricks had gone cold. Someone who didn't care if she never sang again, or sang only lullabies, softly and sweetly to a flock of little ones.

Yet here she would go again, trying to find that elusive good man—it would end the same way. The only thing she could do was save and squirrel away as many of her pennies and pounds as possible. For a rainy day, for Rebecca.

She pushed back her chair and stood, closing the distance between them to press the diamond firmly into his hand. "Yes, yes, I am. Thank you for all we've shared, but if you could leave now, I'd very much appreciate it."

He looked down at the diamond in disbelief. "I am to be dismissed? Like your maid? My dear, you cannot dismiss a peer of the realm. He dismisses you."

"So dismiss me," she said, looking at him with expectation. *Just do it.*

If only he would leave. But he had that stubborn look on his face that she remembered from countless other times. Like when he wanted her to keep singing to him, but she was tired and only wanted to sit quietly together. He would get that look on his face until she gave in to his demands. In fact, now that she thought back, she had always given in to him.

"I will not dismiss you, Sarah. And you will not just dismiss me as you have all the others. I will not be laughed at."

She could feel the temperature of the room rising. "Perhaps we should talk about this at a later date; your fiancée must be waiting for you."

"I sent her home with her mother. She will soon understand the way things work. And so will you." He took her by her elbow. "Come, we are going."

She pulled back. "Morley! I am not dressed."

He tugged more forcefully. "*I* want to leave. Now. I always hated this place. Maybe I should plant some children in you so you can't sing anymore."

Sarah gasped, the vehemence in his voice taking her by surprise. Nobody wanted a family under those circumstances. "You cannot mean that."

He grabbed her arm and pulled her to him, pushing his mouth on hers. Their teeth clashed when she kept her mouth closed. But he was insistent. She tasted blood, sharp and metallic, and didn't know if it was hers or his. She lifted her knee, aiming for his groin, and broke off to scream for help.

Her voice, always so dependable, refused to come to her aid.

CHAPTER 3

IN WHICH RIGHTEOUS WRATH PLANTS
MORLEY A FACER

Being the son of one of England's wealthiest earls had its advantages, such as the way they beat a path through the young bloods waiting at the stage door for La Luminosa to depart. A few well-placed words to the manager of the theater had him and his father standing outside her dressing room.

The door was shut.

"Knock, perhaps," his father offered, pushing him forward. "Off you go, there's a good lad."

Evander turned. "Not scared, are you, Father? I thought you were braver than that." But even the bravest of men, and his father was certainly that, could cower before a beautiful woman.

He never got to find out precisely what the issue was because an almighty crash made the door and floor shake. Manners gone, Evander pushed the door wide, his father peering over his shoulder as they took in the scene.

As dramatic as any opera, the diva was backed up to her dresser, with Morley accosting her.

Or was he?

Evander looked closer. Yes, she was definitely horrified.

She squawked, a sound that was rough and raw, without any of the power she'd displayed not a half-hour earlier.

"Why don't you try someone your own size?" Evander lunged forward, aided by a push in the back from his father, grabbed Morley by the shoulder, and pulled him into a headlock as he'd done a hundred times to his brother.

It didn't hurt that Evander was a foot taller and probably had twenty pounds on him. Morley twisted, trying to free himself, but Evander just tightened the hold, increasing the pressure around his neck.

He felt Morley submit, so immediately slackened his grip. "If I let you go, Morley, can you refrain from assaulting a defenseless lady?"

Morley slumped. "Yes."

Evander released him, and Morley straightened and faced him, his cheeks mottled red and his long blond hair in more disarray than usual. He straightened his golden waistcoat. Then he wound back his arm in preparation for a punch.

Evander put up a hand. "Come now, no need for that. Just leave the room and find your fiancée."

Finally, the blow arrived, hitting Evander on the jaw. It hurt. A little. "I asked you to leave."

Morley had a smug smile on his face. "It's against your moral code to retaliate, isn't it?" he said with a sneer. "Honorable man of God that you are. Turn the other cheek, and all that?" He turned to the singer, grabbed her by the arm and pulled hard. "Come."

Evander rubbed his jaw. "A misguided notion." Certainly it took a lot for him to retaliate, but the way he was treating the lady was more than enough.

There was no theatrical wind-back for Evander. He balled his hand into a fist and planted it on Morley's face with a thud. "You will leave the lady alone."

Ah, that felt good. A balm for the soul.

Morley reeled back, blood dripping over his snowy white cravat. "You dolt, you broke my nose!"

Ah, the shock of discovering vicars were real men too. Evander tilted his head to one side. "I must be out of practice. I was aiming to break your jaw. I hope it doesn't affect your good looks."

"I'll be back for you later," the viscount said to Mrs. Hayworth. Then he turned to Evander. "And you, you are a disgrace to your calling."

"I've thought that for some time," Evander answered easily.

Mrs. Hayworth stepped forward, holding her throat. She had red marks the size and shape of Morley's fingers that made Evander feel sick. He only hoped this was the first instance of violence rather than the last of many. "Take the diamond," she said to Morley. "I don't want it."

He shook his head. "Of course you do."

So nobody wanted the enormous glittering bauble that could feed a village for a year. Typical.

Evander reached forward to take it from between them. "I can find charitable uses for it if neither of you wants it. My thanks, Morley. Perhaps it's time for you to leave now. You seem to have outstayed your welcome."

Morley backed toward the door, pulling a large handkerchief from his pocket and clutching it to his face. "This could have been so different, Sarah. I could have given you everything you ever wanted. Nothing needed to change." His grand exit was somewhat marred by the door sticking on the uneven floor and not slamming.

"Still a bounder, then," Evander said under his breath. He looked over at Mrs. Hayworth, expecting to catch her falling into a faint, or at the very least beginning some well-earned hysterics. But she was standing very still, looking at her shoes. They were slippers, actually. Woolen and pink, with a little satin bow on the front of each. Then she looked up at him, her eyes large pools of the most amazing blue, so deep and lush they were like a pansy petal, and filled with tears. His dratted protective instinct kicked him so hard he almost lurched forward.

Her hands were shaking, and all he wanted to do was scoop her up and tell her that everything would improve from this moment on.

But of course, he was English, so instead, he bowed and apologized. "We are so terribly sorry for intruding."

"No, we're not!" his father announced from behind him. "Deuced shame we didn't come a few minutes earlier."

"And happily not a few minutes later," Mrs. Hayworth said, her voice low, but not shaky, thank goodness.

The earl clapped Evander on the shoulder. "He always did have a bruising right hook. I did you a disservice gifting you the living at Six Oaks. You would've made an excellent pugilist."

"A minor talent, Father," Evander said, adjusting his neckcloth. "And only to be used in times of dire need."

"I am grateful for your intervention." She curtsied as gracefully as any noble lady. "Even if we have never been introduced."

"Ha!" Father said, for once happily ignoring the etiquette of introduction he normally lived by. "I'm Wrotham, and this is my son, Mr. Ambrose."

"I am forever in your debt," she said simply. "Not that there is any way I can repay you, my lord."

"Actually, Mrs. Hayworth," Evander said, "my father is here to invite you to his Yuletide musicale in two weeks." It was blunt, but it was all he could manage under the circumstances. Once, he'd had a way with words. It felt like years ago. "The cream of society attends, and this year, the Arch Bishop of Canterbury will be in attendance." Why on earth did he think talking about the head of the church would be a lure for her? He was crazy.

"I see," she said, a small smile playing across her lips. "Shall I be a guest or a performer?"

"Both," his father said. "You would be our special guest with a suite in the west wing, but also receive a generous stipend for singing at our musicale."

She smiled at them both. "While I am most honored by the invitation, I truly am, I'm sure you can appreciate that I would prefer to leave England altogether. There is a season at the Venice Opera House that I should be preparing for."

It had the ring of untruth to it, and Evander wondered if she would be leaving England if Morley hadn't become betrothed. Somehow, he thought not.

She smiled again, perhaps trying to lessen the blow, but beside him, Father crumpled at her rejection, and Evander knew he was to blame. Dazzled by her to the point of witlessness, he hadn't asked her in such a way that she couldn't say no. And considering that was his particular speciality, he was disappointed with himself. He was always asking people to do things they would prefer not to. "*Mrs. Carson, could you please take the village school classes today as Miss Wren is ill? The children all have snotty noses, and you might catch it too.*" That would never work. But, "*Mrs. Carson, it was suggested to me by the countess that you would be the perfect person to fill in for Miss Wren,*" worked every time.

He gathered his wits. It was time to use them. "Ah well, Father. It was a long shot. But how could we not ask after seeing that performance? We're only human, and your musicale has never hosted such talent. But I'm sure the other soprano will be most grateful for the opportunity, so perhaps it is for the best."

"Oh," she said sweetly. "Who is that?"

He shrugged. "The lady that played Pamina tonight."

"Really?" Her eyes widened.

"Thank you for your time," Evander said, eyeing the door. "We'll leave you to your adoring fans."

He turned, ignoring the alarm in his father's eyes. It was obvious he'd just roused her fighting instincts against the woman who'd tried so hard to upstage her all evening.

"I will come," she said quickly.

Evander turned, hiding a smile of triumph. "Oh?"

"On one condition."

"Name it," his father said, his voice suddenly jubilant. He would meet whatever her demand was. Evander would have to stop his father from giving away the family silver if that was the price she asked.

"That Edwina does not come. She tried so very hard to upstage me tonight, and I am not in the mood for a repeat performance. Oh, and also Morley. I cannot attend if Lord Morley will be there."

"Done!" the earl said with glee. "Excellent. We'll take good care of you, my dear, you can be sure of it."

She curtsied gracefully. "I'm sure you will. I've already seen what good men you are. I cannot wait to tell dear Edwina what she is missing out on."

He was surprised at the small well of disappointment her behavior caused him. She was so quick to stomp on her rival when she was so obviously superior. Was the opera so harsh?

The earl kissed her hand in the old style. "We can have a carriage pick you up on Thursday, if it pleases you."

"Thank you, I am most grateful and already looking forward to it." There was a sparkle to her eye that suggested she really was. He was only surprised she hadn't asked for her diamond. It sat in his pocket like a rock one might save for skimming across the water.

As they turned to leave, he felt a light touch on his shoulder. He swung to find her looking at him with one perfectly arched eyebrow and a smirk. "I believe I will have my diamond back now, Mr. Ambrose."

He dropped it into her hand. "Charity, as they say..."

"...does begin at home," she finished, closing the door in his face.

CHAPTER 4

IN WHICH DISAPPOINTMENT IS A
BITTER PILL

Sarah waited at the front window for the earl's carriage to arrive, her valise in the hall. Forty-four Curzon Street was quiet as a grave around her, the servants gone, and the furniture, which came with the house, hidden beneath Holland covers.

Her meager possessions were packed into tea chests and bound for a warehouse in Spitalfields. Now that her opera season was over, the rent on the townhouse was unaffordable. She was, at that moment, literally homeless and fully dependent on the kindness of others. It was a sobering thought. But for the next week, at least, and more if she could wrangle it, she was to be ensconced in luxury at the Earl of Wrotham's country seat.

Much better than the previous plan to visit friends from week to week.

She looked around. Everything was neat as a pin, except for the red ribbon that hung from the chandelier in the hallway, a remnant of a particularly boisterous party. Neither she nor Jones could reach it. It was just going to have to stay there.

"I have packed some ginger biscuits in the pocket of your cloak in case you feel queasy on the trip. Try not to crush them."

Jones brushed down her velvet cloak. "I could still come with you."

Sarah put a hand on her arm and smiled. "No. Please visit your sister. She will never forgive me if she has her baby without you. There will be someone to help me at the Lord Wrotham's estate."

"A scullery maid or someone with no idea how to dress you correctly." Jones frowned. "But you are right, I do need to go to Verity. I just wish I could be in both places at once."

Sarah looked down at her trunk, which sadly contained her entire wardrobe. "I do not have much clothing to care for now. Did they take all of them?" Jones had spent the morning visiting shops that accepted second-hand clothing.

"Every last one. With glee and relish."

Sarah nodded. "Good." There had been a letter from her parents in the week after her final performance. They needed new bedding and carpets after a major roof leak, and with little money left after paying the creditors, Sarah had sold her wardrobe to replenish her funds. "In the meantime, I can blame my lack of wardrobe on my clothing going into storage for my move to Italy."

"Excellent thinking. I hope your parents appreciate your sacrifice. I almost cried when I handed over the green silk."

"They do, Jones. I am almost certain of it." And the thought of them living more comfortably because of her was one that kept her warm at night when the fire was all but gone. They would never want for anything. Not while she had a voice to sing.

"Not that you'd know," Jones said darkly. "Do you think one day they'll repay all your kindness and allow you to come home?"

Sarah peeked out the window, ignoring the bloom of sadness this kind of conversation always created. "Unlikely. Not unless I can completely redeem myself. And I have no idea what that would take. You didn't know me when I was young and wild. They are justified in their position."

She looked back at Jones, who was busy rolling her eyes. "Yes, yes. I know. You ran away from home and sent them mountains of money. I remain underwhelmed."

"I ran away to sing at Vauxhall, then continued to run to Italy where I conducted a relationship so scandalous—"

"To a prince no less!"

"—that it made the papers in London."

Jones shrugged. "If your own mother can't forgive a body, I'm not sure who will."

Least of all Sarah herself. But the opera was a siren call she could never have resisted. And as for Enzo, well, he could not be resisted either, and even though it ended in disaster, she would never take that time back.

"In fact, the only thing they think I did right was keep my illegitimate child so secret that it was easy for them to raise her as their own. Well done, on my part, apparently."

"But to say you were to have nothing to do with the raising of your own daughter. It is just cruel. You could at least be a treasured aunt or cousin."

"That is what I hope for. If I can find marriage, not a lover, there is a chance that over time…" She left the sentence unfinished, but the point was clear.

"Very well. There will be no more talk of taking a lover. We shall find a man, there has to be one in all of England, who will take you on. Bad bargain that you are."

"I am indeed." Nobody knew her better than Jones, and she was certain she drove her dresser mad with the cosseting of her health and peculiar ways to keep her voice strong.

"I was joking. You would make a splendid wife. You only have to give up your current love."

"I have, last week, remember?"

"No, I mean the singing. You will find it hard to find a husband who will share you with the opera."

"Then I will give up my music. If that is what it takes. Not for him, for her."

"Goodness," was all Jones replied, but there was a world of feeling in it. She shook her head in disapproval, but let the conversation go, thankfully. "Who do you think they will send to pick you up? The elder son or the younger one you met?"

The earl's note said he was sending his son to accompany her, but not which son in particular. The earl would definitely assume she'd have a maid accompanying her to take care of the proprietaries. She smiled to herself.

He would be wrong. "Hopefully, the elder. I would dearly like to make a good first impression." Could her parents refuse her if she had a future earl on her arm? Or was that just another road that would end in heartache?

Amazingly, her path had never crossed that of the earl's eldest son, who was known for his taste for tight races and fast women. But she herself was not what the newspapers said she was, so perhaps neither was he. Who was she to judge? The word around town was that he was in the market for a wife, and she at least needed to be at that market with a basket in her hand if she was to have a chance.

Jones's eyes widened. "He has quite the reputation. I fear he will assume you are looking for a lover and not a husband."

"Then I will disabuse him of that notion. I am a gentleman's daughter. I *can* be circumspect and modest, you know."

Jones turned to look at the red ribbon hanging forlornly from the chandelier behind them and rolled her eyes. "When I look at you, circumspect and modest are not what comes to mind."

"Then what does?"

"A jolly good time." Jones snickered, then frowned. "Perhaps we should get you some dowdy gowns and braid that hair into submission."

"A good man will accept me as I am." It was a thought she'd

held on to for an age. A belief that suffered pieces chipped off of it with every failed romance.

"A good man. For all their talk of manners and honor, I'm not sure how good any of them actually are."

Sarah's shoulders fell. That was a depressing thought. And if you added to it the fact that a good man probably wouldn't be interested in *her*, it was lowering further still. Perhaps she should just overcome her scruples and take a lover. Do what everyone thought she already did. It wasn't as if it would surprise the world. But *she* would know it was the end of the road, that she had exhausted all other options and held no hope for a future with a family.

No.

"I must marry and marry well." The thought, as always, overwhelmed her. She couldn't *make* someone marry her. The most she could hope for was weaving such a seductive cloud around the poor man in question that he married her through sheer inability to think straight. Then do her best to make sure he didn't regret it.

A carriage pulled up outside the house, shiny and black. It had a coat of arms painted on the door with six trees in one corner and a griffin in the other.

"Here we are," Jones said briskly. "And it looks as though some reporters have come to see you off." She smoothed the front of her dress in satisfaction. "I'm pleased that worked."

As usual, Jones had left word with the newspapers so that when Sarah emerged, dressed in her traveling ensemble wrapped in the prettiest red cape trimmed with fur, an illustration likely drawn by the modiste and supplied by Jones herself.

They would note her departure to the noble house and speculate on what she might sing at the earl's musicale. Normally she would be thrilled, but today she just hoped they would keep their distance and not ask any awkward questions, like 'why does Lord Morley have a broken nose?'

Someone tall and broad alighted the carriage, taking a moment to stretch his legs. The sunlight hit his thick dark hair bringing out reddish highlights.

Her heart sank.

Mr. Ambrose.

A safe and respectable choice.

She had an inkling he was anything *but* safe. She knew a man seething with inner turmoil when she saw one. But he was definitely in the category of good men, and if she were being honest, good-*looking* men, who would never be interested in her. She could tell by the way he'd looked at her when she took the diamond back.

She opened the front door, leaving her baggage on the top step so that Mr. Ambrose might not notice she had no staff to take it to the carriage.

A liveried servant jumped down from his seat next to the driver, ferried her luggage, and stowed it without question. When he picked up the medium size square case, she stopped him.

"Please be careful with that. It has glass inside." The last thing she needed was a case of broken medicine bottles. Then nothing surer she'd be struck by illness in the country with no medicine, and a doctor who would order the leeches. Her worst nightmare.

The footman nodded. "Yes, Madam."

Mr. Ambrose inclined his head and held out his hand to help her into the carriage. "Good morning, Mrs. Hayworth. Lovely, as always, to see you." His gloved hand touched hers, and the very strength she felt there supporting her gave her a thrill it ought not to have.

"Sarah!" A masculine voice rang out.

She turned with one foot on the step. It was the same reporter who often waylaid her at the stage door.

"Yes, Mr. Hitchcock?" There was no need for both of them to be on a first name basis, after all.

"Is it true you and Lord Morley are finished due to his

betrothal?" He had a pencil at the ready, his seedy little notebook clutched in his hand.

"Of course, Mr. Hitchcock. I do not need someone else's husband hanging off me. So tiresome." She laughed, and the small crowd around the carriage laughed with her.

Let them laugh. Hopefully, they would print that she still had *some* scruples, despite what those horrible caricatures said.

Sarah stepped into the carriage. The interior was navy velvet, as plush as any sofa she'd ever seen. There were tapestries in the interior door panels and a carpet on the floor. Traveling in style, then. She took the forward-facing seat, settling her skirts and wrapping her cloak around her. "How nice of you to fetch me, Mr. Ambrose." *How disappointed I am that you are not your brother.*

He sat opposite her and smiled like he knew what she was thinking and what's more, it amused him. "Yes. Father thought you might like a familiar face. And a non-threatening one, after what you endured at the hands of Morley."

He knocked on the roof of the carriage with a walking stick and they took off onto Curzon Street. Sarah waved at the collection of people watching their departure.

She feigned surprise. "And he sent you? The man who was upset he broke Morley's nose only because he actually meant to break his jaw?"

"Deservedly," he muttered under his breath, straightening his black waistcoat. In fact, he was dressed almost entirely in black. It suited him well with his dark hair and strong, well-drawn eyebrows. He could definitely carry it off by the sheer beauty of his bone structure. It boded well for the brother. He would likely be just as handsome, and hopefully, with none of the quick intellect she saw lurking behind Mr. Ambrose's gaze. Dumb as an ox was always to be preferred.

They went at a slow pace, the horses clattering down the street. "You look like a vicar in all that black, Mr. Ambrose," she smiled, naughtily, happy to needle him a little.

"That makes sense, as I am the vicar of my local parish, Mrs. Hayworth," he said levelly. He was looking at her seriously too, his eyes the most remarkable shade of green, flecked with gold. They made her breath catch in her chest for a moment. She recovered herself quickly from such folly.

"And I am the Abbess of the local convent," Sarah replied saucily. Then she blushed, realizing that in modern parlance, she just called herself the head of a brothel. But he didn't seem to notice, thankfully.

He blinked rapidly and tilted his head to one side. "No, truly. I *am* a vicar."

She kept a straight face this time, but only just. "Yes, of course you are. A man of your peaceful and placid nature would make the perfect vicar."

His mouth tightened into a straight line. "I am generally seen as a *positive* influence."

"Positive influence?" She smiled even more broadly. "Obviously, they have not seen you at your best."

He looked down at his hands, inspecting his knuckles. "Or some would say my worst."

She stilled, the truth dawning on her like a fabulous joke. "Good Lord, you really *are* a vicar. What a strange thing."

Sarah spent a moment rearranging everything she knew about him, trying to make it fit into the neat and circumspect hole a vicar would fit in. It didn't work. Although the comment Morley made about Mr. Ambrose not wanting to hit him back suddenly made much more sense. And, if she thought back a little further, the fact his father had mentioned gifting him the living instead of making him a pugilist.

He changed the subject abruptly. "How much did you pawn that diamond for?"

"Oh, no you don't. I'm intrigued. Did you think you could curb your violent streak with services to God? I assure you, it seldom works." She'd tried that often enough, curbing her own hedonistic tendencies.

"I don't have a violent streak, Mrs. Hayworth." He looked out the window in a fine show of boredom. She wasn't fooled for an instant.

"Apologies. Of course you don't. What you have, rather, is an overdeveloped sense of delivering divine retribution."

He glared at her.

"Oh, pray don't take offense. We have a wonderful opportunity at this early point in our acquaintance to be *completely* honest with one another without rancor. For example, I think you are prone to violence and snap judgments, and you're quite sure I'm a mercenary trollop who thinks nothing of standing on anyone who gets in her way." She tilted her head to the side. "No?"

"Brutal honesty. It sounds like a good basis for a friendship," he said, his mouth set in an unimpressed straight line.

"But it is!" she exclaimed, warming to her idea. "After all, I am the last woman on earth you would try to impress, and you are the last man on earth I would try to seduce. That leaves us with blunt honesty and a smidgen of respect between us. I tell you, it is a great relief!"

He nodded. "I suppose there is something to be said for a friendship based on total honesty. At least we each know the other has no reason to ever tell a falsehood."

Sarah liked that. "Precisely!"

"You are quite unusual, Mrs. Hayworth." She saw a sparkle of interest in his gaze and relished it.

She nodded. "The sooner you realize I am not like the ladies in your social sphere, the better we will rub along. I will never simper or remember my manners in time not to offend. I am what I am. I am successful because I am what I am. If you don't like what I am, I assure you, I care not a jot."

He shook his head. "It is not that I don't like you, you know.

It's more that I feel your behavior is beneath you." He said it gently, like the kind rebuke it was.

She sniffed. "How so?" It was all very well to be honest until someone put a mirror up in front of one. Then it was not so much fun.

They were stuck behind a wagon on Pall Mall, so it wasn't like she could escape his answer.

"You are far and away the best soprano in England, possibly the world, and yet you felt the need to crush your rival. No matter what she's done, you should be above that." He sat back, eyes bright, waiting for her answer.

She should be above it, should she? "Little do you know of the cut-throat world I live in. I have been on my own since sixteen, singing to support my family, enduring their great disapproval. I have had to fight my way across countries and continents, fend off a Russian tsar and a royal duke. Your naivety is endearing but misplaced."

"Good behavior is never misplaced. It just takes strength of character."

Sarah rolled her eyes and made sure he saw it. "I think I may hate you after all." She looked out the window, at the buildings of St. James. The cold radiated from the rain-streaked glass. She should let down the thick velvet curtain, but she didn't want to feel any more enclosed with him than she already did.

Most men were in awe of her from the first moment of their acquaintance. She'd seen that in him briefly, just before she'd refused his father's offer. But it was well and truly gone now.

"Already? It generally takes people a few more days of my acquaintance to come to that conclusion."

She caught the twinkle in his eye and realized that he was having fun and possibly even teasing her. "I am obviously quicker than most people and have come to the conclusion that you are a judgmental ogre in a more timely fashion."

"And I have come to the conclusion that you have been

allowed to have your own way in all things for much too long and have become exceedingly spoiled when your plans are thwarted. Take now, for example. All it took to put you in a high pet is the fact that Father sent me instead of my brother."

"Bunkum," she said, with less hostility because, well, it was true. He raised an eyebrow in acknowledgment and they sat in companionable silence for the next ten minutes until her curiosity got the better of her.

"What makes you think I sold it?"

He folded his arms across his chest. "My superior understanding of human nature. Well?"

She stared back into that ugly mirror he held that showed her all the things she didn't like about herself. "It was a superior Austrian crystal and therefore close to worthless."

He whistled. "Dastardly."

"Now that I look back, he never actually said it was a diamond. He just let me assume. I am only glad the gift did not do what he wanted it to do." It explained why Morley had left it to her without an argument.

"I suppose I can guess what that was."

"If your guess is me, installed in Morley's bed, you would be correct."

"I was trying to be diplomatic," he said gruffly.

"A waste of your effort," Sarah replied. "But imagine if I had been the kind of woman who would fall into a man's bed for a pretty bauble! I would've been duped in the worst way."

"I'm sure a woman like that would have the jewel appraised first."

"Oh. I suppose you're right. But it doesn't matter. I'm free of him, and I have plenty of funds," she said airily. She couldn't let it get around that she was penniless. That would be a death knell to her aspirations to find a husband—desperation bred contempt.

He raised one eyebrow in obvious doubt. "No, I don't think you do."

She gave him the look one would give a fly in a good glass of Madeira. "That may have been the time for your vaunted diplomacy."

He shrugged. "I thought you found honesty refreshing. I'm beginning to warm to it myself. But if frippery is what you prefer—"

"I would prefer to read my book, I think. Thankfully, I brought it with me." She reached into her traveling bag and pulled out her novel.

He smiled as if he had won the encounter. "And thankfully, so did I."

"I suggest we read until we reach — where is it we are traveling to again?"

"Six Oaks. In Kent." He reached into a side pocket on the door and fished out a well-worn copy of Paterson's Itinerary. He opened the page to Kent. "See there where it says E. of Wrotham?"

She nodded.

"That's us." He handed her the book. "You can follow along if you like and count down the number of miles you have to spend with me. It's twenty-seven. But the roads will be muddy, so it will feel like fifty."

"I would rather read my book." And hope to Hades she didn't succumb to travel sickness.

"As you wish."

He looked down at his itinerary and smiled again, drat him, like she was amusing him no end.

CHAPTER 5

IN WHICH THE VICAR CROSSES SWORDS
WITH MRS. HAYWORTH

Evander tried to move his legs without brushing up against Mrs. Hayworth.

It *did* feel like fifty miles instead of twenty-seven because being in a small enclosed space with Sarah Hayworth was like an exquisite form of torture. Thankfully, she seemed to have taken him into great dislike, making the task of inhaling her scent, breath after breath, somewhat more bearable. In seriousness, what was it? She smelled like all the best things of winter. Hot chocolate with cream and ginger biscuit. If he didn't know better, he would think she had all three stashed in the side pocket of that lush cloak she was wearing.

As she read, he felt his glance slide her way, seeking her face, or her shoe, or the delicate arch of her neck. Every piece of her was of divine interest, every new thing he discovered, squirreled away to enjoy at a later time. Like her hands, not small and delicate, but long-fingered and strong. Able. That was it. Her body was as dexterous as her voice, curvaceous and yet lithe.

This was wrong. He should not long for her like this. But he was no longer anyone's husband, and he guessed she wasn't anyone's wife, so where was the harm? He was heartened by this surge of attraction he felt, as it suggested he might finally have a heart that beat again.

"You're not actually married, are you, even though you call yourself Mrs.?" Best to be sure. He would hate to break a commandment inadvertently.

She tried to look at him sternly, which unfortunately, only made her look more enchanting. "I fail to see how that is your concern."

Just trying to stay on the right side of God. "Just wondering."

There was a long silence, during which he took up staring out the window and thinking about her ankles.

"No," she said abruptly. "I have never been married."

Excellent.

"It would be a special man who could lure me away from my singing and into marriage." Was that really true? Did she love her opera so much that it surpassed all thoughts of love and a family? He'd never had a creative passion like hers though, it was entirely possible.

"Define special. After all, you thought Morley was a worthy recipient of your affection."

She glared at him, then pursed her mouth together in thought. "Highly intelligent, of course."

Yes, that's me.

"And well to do."

Definitely me. Although perhaps not to the standard she would like.

"Amiable."

He smirked. "You mean easily bent to your will." *We may have a problem.*

Her eyes snapped to his with a sparkle in them. "But of course."

It was fun to play along with her. "Very well. I may have some ideas for you. What other qualities must this paragon boast? Handsome, no doubt, with a finely chiseled physique?"

She nodded. "Of course, that would be nice. Know of anyone, Mr. Ambrose?"

He looked out the window as if thinking heavily on the issue. "Indeed. I believe I have just the man."

"Do tell." She leaned forward, her velvet blue eyes bright and alert.

"I saw a lovely man at the British Museum the other week with my father. Handsome brute he was, very noble, one might even say, Roman features. What's more, he will never gainsay you, and is said to be worth a fortune."

She rolled her eyes. "And also made of marble, I presume."

He laughed, delighted that she'd caught on so fast. "Well, yes. But he meets all the other requirements. You should look into it."

"You're an idiot." She said it without rancor, and with the small smile that accompanied it, it sounded like a compliment.

"Just trying to make you a good match," he replied.

Would she consider *him* a good match?

His blood started humming around his body at twice its usual speed. She was available; therefore, he had as much chance as any man. He shook his head, although nothing was likely to clear it now.

Her eyes narrowed. "You shake your head," she said. "Do you think me unmarriageable?"

He laughed at how off track she was. "Completely," he lied, breaking the honesty rule of their friendship without thought. "You are fire and brimstone and the kind of trouble that good men court at their peril."

"Fire and brimstone? I am not Satan, Mr. Ambrose."

"Very well. But you are, at the very least, his favorite firecracker," he replied. "Look at me, for instance. A perfectly peaceful and law-abiding vicar who, within two minutes of your acquaintance, has flattened a peer of the realm and taken what might have been a thousand-pound diamond for his own ends. That is the strength of your power."

She scoffed, but at least she didn't see the truth in it. "Mr. Ambrose, you, I believe, would be prone to violence in any situation. It is always lurking, just beneath your surface. You quite intrigue me."

"Do I?" he said. "Trust me, you will never see that kind of violence from me again."

"Oh, what a shame. I do like seeing a man give in to his baser nature."

"We cannot all be so hedonistic, Mrs. Hayworth."

They carried on in silence for the next while, Mrs. Hayworth reading her book, and Evander going over each thing she'd said, but most especially the thought she might, just might, be looking for a husband.

Every now and then, she would forget herself and start humming, her voice playing with a sweet melody she seemed to be stuck on. It was nothing he recognized.

Finally, they reached Dartford and the place he planned to stop for lunch, which was just as well considering his stomach had been rudely rumbling for over an hour.

"Here we are then," he said, as the carriage pulled into the courtyard of the Owl's Nest Tavern.

She looked up from her book, a flicker of surprise in her deep blue eyes. "Already?"

They went inside, whereupon inquiry, he found that the private dining room was reserved, and the only space available was a tiny table in the corner of the room.

"I'm sorry," he said to her as she waited just inside the door. "But we won't be here long."

She turned a bright smile on him. "Allow me to fix it." And with that, she brushed past him and into the main dining room.

What he saw next was nothing short of a revelation. As a vicar, even one well-born, he was used to walking the world in relative anonymity. He would never have expected people to recognize her outside the confines of London. However, when she entered the taproom and lowered her hood, it was like someone had lit one hundred candles. Heads turned, people stared, and the roar of the taproom coalesced into a running repeat of her name.

The owner of the inn rubbed his hands down his apron, showing much more deference and interest than he had moments before.

"Apologies, Madam. Allow me to show you to our private dining room."

"Unbelievable," Evander said under his breath.

She shrugged in response. "I generally get what I want."

"I'm beginning to see that," he said, following her into the room.

They didn't even have to order. Within one minute of being seated, ale was poured by the owner himself, and within ten, there was crusty bread with freshly churned butter, roast beef with gravy, and a lush cheese and dried fruit plate that was likely meant for the other party.

Sarah ate with just as much appetite as he did. Was that another sign of the 'honesty' between them? That she didn't bother to hide her appetite under ladylike bites?

He concentrated on the food but should have known he wouldn't get away with it for long.

"Well?" she said between mouthfuls. "Aren't you at least going to try to make polite conversation with me?"

"I thought it was a companionable silence." He'd certainly felt comfortable with it.

"It was a boring silence. I am used to my companions entertaining me on long road trips, Mr. Ambrose."

"Would you like me to dance? Perhaps a jig?"

"Perfect. When you're ready." She motioned to the floor and arched an eyebrow.

"Straight after you finish yours." He shook his head and slowly picked up a piece of bread, watching her over the top of it, keeping eye contact until he popped it in his mouth. It was invigorating, this sparring with her. It had been so long since a lady dealt with him with anything but respect. He quite liked the complete lack of deference she had.

"Even that's an improvement," she said, nodding her approval. "Flirting is always welcome."

"I wasn't flirting, I was glaring." But he was flirting, and they both knew it.

CHAPTER 6

IN WHICH MRS. HAYWORTH SNAGS THE
BLUE ROOM

They arrived at Six Oaks Manor later in the afternoon than Mr. Ambrose had foretold, chiefly because the vicar had squandered their afternoon. Firstly, finding the local magistrate whose lunch they usurped, and then, inviting him into the private parlor and sharing ale over legal anecdotes and strange cases.

Because on top of everything else that was upstanding and fine about Mr. Ambrose—he was also aiming to be the next local magistrate of his parish. Judgmental *and* law-abiding. Her favorite kind of gentleman.

Unlikely.

Their journey down the long, tree-lined drive was accompanied by his happy commentary of the place he grew up.

"That lake to your right is always full of trout. Do you fish?" There was an eager light in his eyes.

She rolled her eyes. "Of course not. Cold water, dead fish, standing around outside for hours on end." She gave a pretend shiver. "Riveting."

"Of course," he mused, looking out the window wistfully. "I do. In any case, it is a lovely walk."

"It looks to be three miles from the house. Perhaps it is a lovely *ride*, rather than walk?"

He shrugged and met her gaze with a challenge in his own. "If you like. Some ladies do have feeble constitutions."

She almost trod on his foot with her heel after that comment, and may have, if the manor itself had not come into view, making her gasp with delight.

Surrounded by lush rolling hills planted with centuries-old trees, the manor sat as though it had woven itself into the landscape. Although that was a silly thought, for it was far too large and imposing for that. So many banks of windows, turrets, and balconies. It was hard to know where to look.

"Why, it's beautiful," she said.

"Isn't it? It was a magical place to grow up. But you know, even the most stunning house would be a prison with a horrible family. It was only magical because my parents and the staff made it so."

"You had a blessed childhood. I envy you. And I look forward to meeting Lady Wrotham. I hope she is not upset by your father inviting me at the last minute."

His gaze swung from the window to her sharply, and she knew she had somehow hit on the truth in her meaningless prattle.

"Of course not," he said dutifully. "She plans things to within an inch of their lives, but always welcomes a chance improvement. I'm sure she will be there to meet you if she is able."

She was not.

When they arrived, Sarah climbed the stairs she'd seen from the carriage with her arm resting lightly on Mr. Ambrose's. She was quickly shown to her room and instructed to spend the rest of the afternoon recuperating from the journey.

A tea tray, accompanied by a young maid who introduced herself with a sweet curtsy, followed with a note on it from the countess.

"Welcome, my dear Mrs. Hayworth. I hope you will be comfortable in this suite, please ring for any requirements you may have. We shall see you at dinner."

Before long, another maid appeared to unpack her belongings. As she set to unpacking the trunk, Sarah stared out the huge windows. They were framed with ice, and the view through that frame was magnificent. Wintergreen lawns that stretched for miles, magnificent bare oak trees, and a poetic temple placed on a hill in the distance. What a place to live. Her mind was already trying to maneuver a way to stay. Could she feign illness for a while? It would be worth it.

There was a tap on her elbow. "I've finished, Ma'am. Where is your maid? I should like to help her settle in."

"She is not here. Her sister is in the final stages of her confinement. I'm sure I shall be fine without her."

"Oh," the maid said, obviously shocked. "Then who will dress you? Shall I ask Mrs. Kennedy if I can be assigned?" The maid finished the question a little breathlessly. It was probably a promotion for her to act as a lady's maid, even if only for a few days.

"That would be lovely," Sarah said, assuming Mrs. Kennedy was the housekeeper. "Although I don't want to be any trouble."

"Oh, no trouble, madam! It would be an honor."

The maid left with a smile on her face. Good, that was one dilemma solved. The next was, of course, her plan of action. It felt wrong, oh so wrong, to be taking advantage of people who appeared to be lovely. But if their eldest son truly fell in love with her, where was the harm if her own heart wasn't completely engaged?

She sighed. No, it was still wrong to take advantage of their hospitality in this way. But she was going to do it. If it was a choice between being part of Rebecca's life and her scruples, there really was no choice.

~

AFTER CHANGING out of his travel clothes, Evander went in search of his parents. As usual, he found his mother in the study helping his father with the paperwork. Or rather, his father was sitting in a snug wing-backed chair by the window with a blanket on his lap while she sat at the desk, writing letters that they both composed.

As the door swung open, they stopped what they were doing, looked up, and tilted their heads identically. They had been married a very long time, and with each passing year, they only got closer. This made him both happy and also sad with longing for the kind of union they shared. He and Eleanor had a comradery, but theirs had never been a marriage of high passion.

Mother placed her quill carefully on the stand and came around the barge of a desk to kiss him on both cheeks. "You're back. Welcome home, my dear. I trust you had no problems with our special guest?"

When she said 'special' it sounded more like 'troublesome'. Which wasn't far from the truth.

Evander sat on the matching wingback chair across from his father. "Only a small amount when we partook luncheon in Dartford. Suffice to say, she creates quite a stir just by lowering the hood of her cloak. There are gasps and whispering and then the men start betting on who will speak to her."

"That I can well believe," Father said. "But we're very happy to have her here, aren't we dearest?" He looked refreshed today, with color in his cheeks and an almost healthy glow. But Six Oaks was his country, his land. There was no place on earth where any Ambrose felt stronger, and his father had always felt the call of his own land keenly.

His mother nodded, but when she turned to Evander, she rolled her eyes slightly. "And at your father's request, we have placed her in the blue suite. After all, she's only here to make him happy. That is her one occupation. And she can't do it properly if her nose is out of joint because she is in an inferior room."

It was one of the best rooms in the best wing of the house, overlooking the currently frozen ornamental lake. "She would probably end up in the blue suite through her own machinations in any case," Evander said with a laugh.

"Is she really such a sublime being?" There was a note of incredulity in his mother's voice. "Do I have to watch that Marcus doesn't fall into her trap?"

Evander rested his head back into the plush chair. "The problem, Mother, is that she doesn't have just one trap, she has two, and if you manage to evade those, there is a third, and then a fourth. The first is her looks, which you will see soon enough but can be adequately described as a melding of Venus with Aphrodite. Then, if you avoid that trap, she'll start to sing, and you'll be lost forever. But if you somehow escape, she'll catch you with a mind as sharp as a fishhook."

"Oh dear," said his mother faintly. "I am beginning to wish I had not agreed to this. What, pray tell, is her fourth trap?"

"It's the most devious of all. Despite being the second strongest woman of my acquaintance, you being the first, she has an air of vulnerability about her that would make even the most hard-hearted man rush to her aid. It's quite disarming." He said it blithely, but noticed his father's gaze sharpen.

"You were untouched, obviously," his father remarked dryly. But then he probably remembered Evander's reaction to her at the opera.

Evander shook his head. "Not true. I'm just as susceptible as the next man. But fortunately, I am a lowly vicar and far below her notice. I find it provides a degree of immunity." Well, that was *almost* true.

Mother sighed deeply. "While it heartens me to see you even noticing another lady is pretty, I only hope she won't catch the eye of your brother, making him forget to court Lady Beatrix. Then blue suite or not, she'll be shown the door."

"I doubt he will forget." Heaven knew that Lady Beatrix's bountiful dowry, full to the brim with the profits of her family's mining, was all his father could talk about. It would set the Earls of Wrotham in prosperity for generations to come.

His mother looked mollified. "Good. I had a monstrous time convincing them to come here. They seem to think they are quite above us, despite the newness of their title." She stared off into the distance, probably thinking about future grandchildren.

She turned to him. "And I haven't forgotten you, dearest boy. Mrs. Armstrong is attending with her eldest daughter, Miss Lily Armstrong, whose looks are very becoming. And also Miss Tilly Davenport and Miss Georgiana Ascot."

Evander sighed inwardly. All those 'misses'. It would be like having another child rather than a helpmeet. "Thank you, Mother, for thinking of me. But I am nowhere near ready to be married again." *Although I would consider continuing my flirtation with a certain opera singer.*

Father nodded, but Mother had no such sympathies. "But Evander! You have grieved long enough. It doesn't have to be a love match. You just need a wife. And it would help *me* not to worry about you."

"Perhaps. But I can't help thinking that a *young* wife would be more harm than help. Any young woman on the marriage mart today would take one look at my household and run screaming into the night, never to be seen again."

"You're very pessimistic. It's not like you." His father shook his head. "When I found your mother, she was a fluffy piece of work with nothing more in her head than what color ribbons she liked most. Now look at her! Runs the estate better than I can!"

His mother smiled at him indulgently. "And when I met your father, he was a young fribble with nothing more in his head than the next auction at Tattersall's." She looked into the space above

Evander's head and frowned. "Actually...not a great deal has changed."

Father laughed. "You may have the right of it, countess of mine."

"Just promise me you will meet with them," she said.

He could no more deny the pleading in her eyes than swim across the channel toward France. "I will meet them," Evander replied. He normally met with every guest at the musicale event in any case. "But I make no promises."

His mother smiled, straightening. "Excellent. If I could see both my boys settled by Yuletide, it would make me happy beyond compare."

He softened immediately. It was amazing that she could still be happy with Father's illness hanging over all of them like a miasma. Having a long time to get used to the idea of losing him only seemed to draw out the pain. He had to commend her for looking to give Father even more reassurance that his line would continue. "I'm sure both Marcus and I will settle down very soon. We're too old not to."

Up until this moment, he'd thought of marrying again as something he would do later, rather than sooner. It was inevitable. A man in his position was just better off with a wife. And if it meant his mother and father would sleep better at night? Then who was he to deny them that? His carriage ride home with Mrs. Hayworth and complete inability to think of anything beyond her for the entire trip probably suggested it was nigh time too. A man needed a wife. Some more than others. He didn't have to try to recapture that special comradery he had shared with Eleanor. It would be impossible to do so. It just had to be good enough.

But it was more than likely nothing would come of it, in any case. Evander and everything that went with Evander was not for the faint of heart. Speaking of which, where were those monsters he called sons?

He left his parents and made his way up to the back of the east wing where the nursery that he'd been raised and schooled in resided. At the top of the stairs, one only had to follow the noise to figure out where the boys were. He could hear Bess's voice too, playful and excited, and knew the young maid was having as much fun as they were. It took so many people to raise his sons, so many generous and kind people in the wake of Eleanor's death. Often the help was accompanied by sympathetic and sad expressions, but that couldn't be helped. He was just glad they were there.

He opened the door to see a blanket fort in the middle of the room, Bess running around with a copper pot on her head and a wooden spoon in her hand. When she saw him, she blushed, but he motioned for her to continue. He could watch them play all day. Each of them was perfect. At least whilst they slept. But the minute they woke, it took two or three nursemaids to keep them in order if Evander wasn't there.

They were what he lived for. He leaned against the wall and drew a deep breath. *I'm home now.* There was riotous giggling coming from inside the fort as she circled it.

He pushed himself off the wall. "Who wants to take the ponies for a ride?"

Three faces, suspiciously smeared with raspberry jam, popped up from the middle of the blanket fort. "Papa!"

"Little monsters, how are you? Did you miss me?"

They were out of there in a trice, hanging on his legs in the second trice. "Is the weather well enough?" Alexander said. Being eight going on eighty, he was always worried about the weather, or the roads, or any other number of things that might not be safe. His mother had died falling from her cart in bad weather. It was a fair conclusion for him to base everything in their lives on safety. Benjamin was the bane of his efforts.

"It is, for the moment. But we'll have to be fast."

Bess looked at him with her usual mixture of relief and

concern. "You be careful out there. There was snow last night, there might be ice."

"Let's keep to the training ring," Evander replied. "But it will be better than nothing, eh boys?"

The jumping up and down could be interpreted as definite agreement. "I hope they've been good for you, Bess?"

"Well now, I'm sure they've been as good as they're able," she said diplomatically. She wasn't fooling anyone in the room.

He looked at them suspiciously. "What did you do?"

They shuffled from foot to foot, not wanting to lie and not wanting to tell him the truth either.

"Bess will just tell me anyway," he said. "You might as well beat her to it."

"Well, it wasn't my fault, really," Benjamin said. Which was, of course, the kind of fabrication of the truth he had a talent for, as did most five-year-old boys. Sometimes he could even see how Benjamin believed it, too. Things tended to happen one after the other, almost beyond his control.

Sometimes a day went by with no mishap, but that was unusual. It wasn't that the boys weren't supervised; they always were, whether it be by him or the nurse, or Bess. It was more that these things happened at times when nobody could be expected to have total control. Like the time Isaac got his tiny bottom stuck in a bedpan as he tried to ride it down the staircase like a sled. One could be forgiven for giving him privacy to use the bedpan. Who could foresee using it for that purpose?

"Just tell me what happened."

"Benjamin cut my hair!" Isaac said in outrage. "I didn't want it cut, but he cut it."

Benjamin leaped to his own defense. "There was glue in it. I had no choice. Bess was already mad at us because we got it on the curtains."

So, reasonably tame, on the scale of things the Ambrose boys usually achieved. "Turn around, Isaac."

Being only four, Isaac's hair was the blond and fluffy kind that wouldn't have been out of place on a duckling. "Oh dear." He now had a bald patch. "I suppose you shall have a cold head for some time."

"What have I told you about using scissors?" Alexander said. "I tell you over and over, but you still don't listen!"

Benjamin looked at his toes, just wearing a pair of gray socks knitted by his grandmother on Eleanor's side. "You're not Papa," he said darkly. "I don't *have* to listen to you."

"But in this case, I would've said the same thing. Which means you should not have used them. Now your brother looks like a shorn sheep." Evander contemplated Benjamin, who had dropped to his knees to beg, knowing that Evander was thinking about what the punishment would be.

"You can stay here while I take your brothers out riding. You will get your exercise book and practice your arithmetic by writing all the numbers counting by three to one hundred. If you finish that, do the fours and then the fives. I will return to see the results."

"Oh Papa. No!" Benjamin was outraged. He loved his horse more than anything, but Evander knew that five minutes into the mathematics, his mind would be fully engrossed, and they would come back to discover he'd counted in threes to six hundred. He might prefer riding and tree climbing, but he had the makings of a scholar.

Evander raised an eyebrow, which was enough to quell the protests.

"Yes, Papa." He turned to his little brother. "My apologies Isaac. You can wear my red cap until your hair grows back if you like."

"There, that was nicely done. Very well, boys, let's go riding." He swung to the maid. "Bess, would you mind sitting quietly with Benjamin while he practices his arithmetic? Do you need some time to organize yourself?"

"That's fine, Sir. I have some mending I can do in the other room." She bobbed a small curtsy. "How long will you be, Sir? I will order a tray for the boys' afternoon tea if I know when to expect your return."

"Just over an hour hence," he said. "Let me go and run some of this energy of theirs down."

And his, if truth be told. He felt like a coiled snake and had a very good idea why.

CHAPTER 7

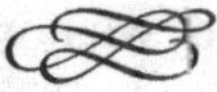

IN WHICH DINNER IS HELD IN A DEN OF VIPERS

This was not Sarah's first noble appointment, and since she had sung at for the Prince of Wales on many occasions, it wasn't even the loftiest. But it felt like the most important, as if the course of her life hinged on what would or wouldn't happen here. In one direction, she left bound for Venice, leaving England's shores yet again and the chance to live her life in the country she had never felt quite at home in. In the other direction, she became someone's wife and had to give up her singing altogether for the chance of security.

Why did both options scare her?

In any case, it was still important to make a good impression. She readied herself for dinner with the help of a maid, taking extra care with her hair and only applying the barest amount of face paint that even the highest stickler would not notice.

It was only when the group assembled for dinner in the vast salon that Sarah realized she may have an unforeseen problem. And the problem wasn't that she had *no* acquaintance to while away the time with, but that she had rather too many.

Of the male variety, that was.

Lords Fenwick and Pemberton, Lidcombe and Wentworth.

Married one and all. When Lady Wrotham brought her around for introductions, she curtsied to each like they'd never met, but the truth was that in the very recent past, they had each pursued her with vigor and, more often than not, they had been angry when they failed.

When introduced, each of them either nodded or gave her a shallow bow, the minimum of what was expected–and Lidcombe actually had an 'I'm bored by you' expression on his face when he'd spent at least five months creating more bad sonnets about her than she'd had cups of tea. Fenwick looked like he'd like to talk to her but dared not.

But the problem was not really the men; it was their wives. Whether they knew of their husbands' involvement or not, they each gave her the coolest reception they possibly could without giving offense.

Lady Wrotham frowned and became more animated and friendly with each slight rebuff. "It seems I have invited a stuffy bunch. Indeed, I am sorry, Mrs. Hayworth. I hope you won't take offense."

How could she, when it was said with such sincerity? But Sarah sighed inwardly. It was going to be a long evening if formal manners were adhered to and she was placed with the ladies. Lady Wrotham left her to continue her hosting duties.

Languidly, like she hadn't a care in the world, Sarah searched the room for a friendly face. Where was Mr. Ambrose? He could be counted on to talk to her, even if it was only to insult her. Surely someone had been tasked with escorting her into dinner? Or had her last-minute inclusion meant she'd slipped from her hostess's mind? The minutes started to feel like hours. It was going to be a tedious night. And, more importantly, a quick scan of the room revealed nary a bachelor. She knew all of these faces and they were all married. Hopefully, the musicale would offer more selection. It was difficult to find a prospective husband with no bachelors in the room.

"Mrs. Hayworth!" came a deep, rich voice.

All female eyes in the room turned to the voice, and she turned too, to see Mr. Ambrose coming toward her, dressed in his evening attire, which was a sight to behold. He was all broad-shouldered in his black tailcoat, every inch the earl's son and precious little of the judgmental vicar on show this evening. His elder brother, Lord Huntley, walked behind him. He was shorter than Mr. Ambrose, with light brown hair and a genial expression. Sarah nodded to herself. He looked kind.

The illustrious crowd parted for them, his brother going toward his father, while Mr. Ambrose strode toward her with a quirked eyebrow that addressed the pickle she found herself in.

"Why," he said, loud enough for all to hear, a skill probably honed through a hundred sermons, "is London's brightest jewel standing in a dark corner on her own?"

He took her hand and lifted it to his lips, placing a light kiss on her gloved fingers. "Perhaps to shine all the brighter?" Then under his breath, "Are they mistreating you, Mrs. Hayworth?"

She smiled. "Of course, it is their reason for being. Who am I to deny them their fun?"

"And you shan't deny me mine. I believe I shall sit with you at dinner."

She shook her head and withdrew her hand before it seemed improper. "Mr. Ambrose, these decisions are not yours to make."

It would be ill-bred to try to move up the table. This wasn't Carlton House, where just last month Prinny had asked her to feed him by hand the entire meal. There she sat next to the Regent. Tonight, she would be in the middle of the table, where she belonged.

He bent down to whisper in her ear. "Mrs. Hayworth, for the love of God, save me. My mother has three ladies here to bid for my hand. You must agree to sit next to me if I can arrange it."

Sarah rolled her eyes. "Ah, and here I was thinking you were acting my knight in shining armor, but instead, I am to be yours!"

"Yes, if you please. I will go and ensure we are seated together. To Hades with protocol." He kissed her glove again and disappeared, looking more anxious than she had ever seen him look. What a delightful twist. To think that he was just as much at the mercy of his mother as a matchmaker, as any young man was.

Lady Wrotham led the ladies from the salon through to the dining room, followed by the gentlemen. Lady Wrotham was of the older generation and the place settings were, as Sarah had expected, traditional. The men were seated on one end of the table with the earl and the ladies at the other with the countess. Sarah was right in the middle of the viper's den, but at least away from all the glaring men. Mr. Ambrose's elder brother, Lord Huntley, was seated way beyond her reach and far closer to his father.

And somehow, perhaps because she was in the middle of the table, or perhaps because he changed things, Mr. Ambrose was seated next to her.

"Good evening, Mrs. Hayworth," he said, as though they hadn't already spoken. "I trust you are happily settled?"

She nodded. "Indeed. Thank you for your kind assistance on the journey." She leaned toward him. "And I am glad you didn't have to resort to fisticuffs on my behalf again."

Nobody turned to look at her, but there was a long beat of silence as conversations stilled around her to listen better.

Other than Lady Wrotham, they wouldn't deign to acknowledge her—but were happy to listen in case she provided a juicy on-dit.

Sarah inwardly rolled her eyes. Society.

The lady on her left, Lady Highton, with golden hair that was woven into what looked like a basket on her head, gave a gasp. "You came to fisticuffs over Mrs. Hayworth?"

Mr. Ambrose closed his eyes. Perhaps he was hoping that if he didn't open them that the question would go away.

It did not. The lady waited patiently for his answer. Would he tell the truth? She couldn't wait to see.

"I have, and would do it again in a heartbeat under the same circumstances. Mrs. Hayworth definitely has the ability to make a man do things against his better judgment."

There was some masculine laughter from further down the table. Lord Fenwick laughed a little harder than the rest. "As many before you have discovered, Mr. Ambrose, Mrs. Hayworth, has us all on a string dancing merrily along behind her. Sarah, remember how Ludley stole that necklace from the Egyptian Hall when you absently said you liked it?"

"He put it back," she said defensively. But the damage was done. Fenwick had called her by her first name, letting slip their previous friendship.

She looked around to see all her ex-flirts studying their soup as though it was the most fascinating thing they had ever seen. The wives were much bolder, staring at her with a mix of interest, disgust, or bored disdain. She gazed over at Lord Huntley to find he was already looking at *her*–and he definitely seemed intrigued.

"Or when Savage bought out the entire stock of violet-flavored ices from Gunter's when you said it was your favorite?"

Sarah felt a blush rise up her cheeks as most of the table focused their attention on her. "I ate so much lavender ice I was totally cured of my love for it," she replied blithely.

"And isn't that always the case, my dear?" said Pemberton, from so far down the table it was a miracle he'd heard her. "That you often tire of things after a short while.'

There was a general intake of breath, not that she could really hear it what with her face flaming and the dull roar of blood in her ears. She glanced up the table at Lord Huntley, but he seemed involved in a conversation with his father, thankfully.

She had to brazen it out. These people would trample all over her if she showed the slightest weakness. Next to her, she noticed

Mr. Ambrose frown. Her makeshift defender was ready to pounce. She touched his leg softly without looking at him. *I can handle this.*

"Oh indeed, Lord Pemberton. Gunter's ices, bonnets-give me variety or I shall expire from boredom." Sarah rolled her eyes and smiled as if she found it all a grand joke.

"Variety is the very spice of life that gives it all its flavor," Mr. Ambrose finished, and there was a polite titter, acknowledging his clever quote from a poem that thankfully seemed to act as a bookend for the conversation. "Everyone at this table has likely spent a great deal of time and funds in the pursuit of variety in this dull old life. Thank goodness ladies like Mrs. Hayworth are here to provide both sublime entertainment and spice."

He inclined his head, a small smile playing on his lips, just for her. She relaxed back into her chair a little and shot him a grateful look. *Thank you.*

"What's the fuss?" the earl boomed from the foot of the table.

"He just wants to be down here where the action is," Mr. Ambrose said, for her ears only. "I don't blame him."

The earl pushed his soup bowl away. "Will you sing for us after dinner, Mrs. Hayworth? I'm not sure I can wait until the musicale, and I certainly didn't bring you here to entertain the riffraff surrounding you!"

The assembled nobility laughed in a good-natured way at being called riffraff by the earl.

"I promise to entertain you after dinner," Sarah replied.

It wasn't a bad idea to remind the table that she wasn't attempting to be a guest at their level, but was brought to Six Oaks for their entertainment. Then, perhaps, they would stop being outraged by her and start welcoming her.

"Good," said the earl. "I hope it's a song I like."

"It is a very special song I have never sung before, if you will all do me the honor of listening to it."

It was her own composition, not that she would ever tell a

soul. A sweet, soaring melody that had haunted her, brushing in and out of her consciousness mostly while she was in the nether-world between waking and sleeping. It was simple, like an old folk song, but so very close to her heart. And it was finally finished.

"I look forward to it," Mr. Ambrose said. "Is it perchance the one I heard snatches of in our carriage ride?"

She smiled a wicked little smile no lady should ever give a clergyman, putting a finger over her lips. "Oh no, that was just me trying to drown out the sound of your hungry stomach."

Next to her, Lady Highton bristled. "Mr. Ambrose is the best of men," she said, misinterpreting the conversation she was so desperately trying to hear. "He's near a saint."

"Hmmm," said Sarah, looking straight into his lush green eyes. "Questionable."

AFTER THAT OUTRAGEOUS COMMENT, Evander shouldn't have cared what happened to her, but despite her obvious ease in high society, Mrs. Hayworth didn't seem to notice the danger lurking at the table. She was merrily batting away the comments aimed at her as the ladies' gazes became sharper and sharper. No lady wanted her husband to spend his time dangling after a beautiful woman. And Mrs. Hayworth was certainly beautiful tonight.

She was dressed in simple white silk, but the puffed sleeves of her gown were seeded with pearls. The gaze of every man at the table was drawn to her.

He could only imagine her reception with the ladies after dinner. Oh, certainly, she'd tell him she was made of sterner stuff than to care about it, but he'd seen the look in her eyes when he'd first entered the salon before dinner. She was more vulnerable than she would admit.

CHAPTER 8

IN WHICH THE LADIES MAKE THEIR
POSITION CLEAR

Lady Wrotham smiled kindly at Sarah and motioned for her to sit next to her, near the large fireplace. Grateful for her kindness, Sarah perched on the edge of the sofa like a bird on a branch. She belonged here; she did. She was the daughter of a gentleman and had been taught ladylike manners from the crib. So what if her life had taken a different direction to all the ladies here? That didn't negate the training. She could do this.

Sarah looked around her. The walls of the parlor were pale blue with oil paintings of every size crammed on all available wall space. She looked up and gasped. The ceiling was a mural of angels cavorting around clouds with a very relaxed looking God watching on.

"How very pretty the ceiling is," Sarah said. All conversation stopped, and all eyes were on Sarah, with nobody even taking a glance at the ceiling. Then, without replying, they each went back to their conversations.

Lady Wrotham, seeing their rebuff, put her hand on Sarah's. "Yes, it is a masterpiece. The third earl had it done; he found the painter on a trip to Italy and brought him home. The painter then married the eldest daughter of the family in a great scandal." She waggled her eyebrows, and Sarah couldn't help smiling.

Thank goodness for Lady Wrotham. It was lucky there was a painting on every wall for her to inspect because, now that Lady Wrotham was pouring tea, it didn't look like any of the ladies were going to engage her in conversation. In fact, they were pretending, with a great deal of enthusiasm, that she wasn't really there.

What one quickly discovered was that being in high society with Prinny when he was throwing an outrageous party was quite different from the refined air of Lady Wrotham's withdrawing room.

Lady Wrotham served each cup of tea with grace, the epitome of a gentlewoman in her golden gown and silk shawl wrapped elegantly around her. She was nothing like Sarah's mother, who seemed to be made of hard edges and brittle laughs. Or at least she had been last time Sarah saw her. Perhaps that was what happened to a woman when she had to tell her eldest daughter never to return home. Sometimes Sarah regretted every moment from leaving the house at sixteen onward. Of leaving her brothers and sisters behind. Did her mother?

She closed her eyes and breathed deeply. With any luck, they would talk around her and let her quietly adapt to her surroundings.

"My dear Mrs. Hayworth. Come, regale us with your exploits," Lady Wrotham said.

Or perhaps not. "Oh I have a very boring life, truly. It is not at all as it seems. I would much rather hear about the construction of your new greenhouse, Lady Wrotham. It looks to be a magnificent structure."

There, attention successfully diverted.

There was a moment of silence and then a trill of laughter from the ladies that, for some reason, reminded Sarah of birds chattering in trees before dawn.

"We almost believe you, Mrs. Hayworth," said Lady Beatrix, a very pretty young lady. "Except that I heard Egerton threw himself in front of a carriage for you. Truth or falsehood?"

Sarah nodded, happy the lady had chosen a story that was fit for the younger ears in the room. And even happier that Egerton's wife was not a guest at the musicale.

Perhaps this young lady was friendlier than the others. It would be nice to have someone to talk to when Mr. Ambrose was not on hand.

"He threw himself in front of a cart, actually," Sarah replied. "It was filled to the brim with stale bread and on its way to feed the pigs. It was four in the afternoon, and I had just left the milliner with the most beautiful bonnet you ever saw. I suppose my attention was still on the bonnet because the next thing I knew, the cart was bearing down on me at high speed. I froze, unable to move, then suddenly felt strong arms clasp me around the waist in a most inappropriate fashion, and I was whisked to safety.

"'No bonnet is worth your life,' he said in that wonderfully deep voice of his, then gruffly told me to be more careful. Of course, he sent flowers that afternoon, a bunch of orchids from who knows where that lasted weeks and weeks." Sarah cocked her head to one side. "Much longer than his interest in me, truth be told."

One of the matrons with a black turban and beady brown eyes bristled. "There are young ladies with us, Mrs. Hayworth, I would beg you to remember."

"Oh, don't mind us, Lady Farrington, we've read far worse in the novels from the circulating library," one of the much younger misses said.

"Speaking of books," Lady Beatrix said. "Is it true that the heroine in Lady of Distinction is based on you?"

Where did they pick these things up? The gossip mill certainly had a lot to answer for. "Oh dear me, no. I hardly think I am the type to wander into the forest in the middle of winter, chasing a ghost only to expire in the snow. I cosset my health far too much for that kind of nonsense! I would much more likely be found by the fire with a cup of chocolate for company."

"So, you have read it?" Lady Beatrix asked, smiling, but the smile seemed to have a falseness behind it that had Sarah rethinking whether she was a friend or a decided foe.

Sarah laughed. "Of course. How could I not?"

"I still believe it is you. The heroine is a lady who becomes a world-famous singer, with dark hair, sparkling blue eyes, and a secret in her past that nobody can discover. That is you."

"I assure you, I have no deep dark secrets. Other than the cream I use on my face at night, which is more vanity than secret. But tell us, Lady Beatrix, I have heard on the wind that you have many accomplishments. Which do you love the most?"

Too late, she noticed ladies sharing sidelong glances and embarrassed expressions. Oh, dear. Perhaps Lady Beatrix was not accomplished in the way so many young ladies these days were. And now Sarah had embarrassed her.

The lady in question blushed deeply, and Sarah winced. "That is," she tried to amend. "What is it that you enjoy?"

Brilliant. She had just made an enemy of the one woman in the room she thought she might have been friends with.

"I'm sure I cannot sing or play well, but I do enjoy going on long walks."

Sarah threw a longing glance at her hostess, who had now finished pouring the tea and could give the conversation more attention. *Please help me.*

The older lady smiled. "There now. Lady Beatrix, I know my son, Lord Huntley, has been singing your praises. So, if the gentlemen do not care and I am quite certain they do not, who are we to spend precious time and effort on past times that gather dust in a corner? Indeed I remember none of the silly harp playing my mother made me learn. The household management was far more worthy of learning, and I hear you have a talent for that."

Lady Beatrix nodded and stared into her teacup. "You are too kind."

"I never did succeed with the languages," Lady Farrington added.

"And I was always a lost cause when it came to watercolor," said another.

Lady Beatrix smiled a little more.

Lady Wrotham, perhaps keen to put an end to the awkward conversation, called for the doors of the withdrawing room to be opened so the gentlemen could enter.

"And if you want any proof of my scant abilities, I will show you a sample of my needlework," Sarah finished. "Appalling. Not even fit for darning." Her eyes followed Lord Huntley as he entered the room, and his eyes met hers. *Definitely interested.*

Sarah looked back to see Lady Beatrix's narrowed eyes as she looked between them too. Then she looked back to Sarah and quirked an unamused eyebrow.

Oh, dear.

When the meal was over, and his mother led the ladies away into the withdrawing room, he went straight to his brother's side. It was time for port and the general talk of politics and horses that usually went on at this kind of dinner. Marcus hadn't sat yet, so Evander directed him over to the corner of the room, where his brother lit a cheroot and inhaled deeply.

"I see you brought London's finest to us today, my thanks." Marcus blew his cloud far from Evander, knowing how much his brother hated the smoke.

Evander shrugged. "Why do you thank me?"

"I like her singing," Marcus replied, but the glint in his eye suggested he liked more than Mrs. Hayworth's voice.

"Don't do it," Evander said, conversationally.

"Don't do what? I haven't done a thing." The more innocent Marcus pretended to be, the less innocent he actually was, in Evander's experience.

"Very well. Don't even *think* about doing it."

"Impossible not to think about, Ev," he replied with a smile. "She's dashed fine."

Evander tried the only angle he knew would work on Marcus—their mutual respect for the earl. "Father would kill you. You know he feels protective of women under his roof, and he particularly sought out Mrs. Hayworth. Spend your romantic thoughts on Lady Beatrix. Mother told me she's been invited so you could court her."

His brother looked pained. "Blast. I did wonder when I saw them at dinner. Mother and her machinations."

"Mother and her trying-to-settle the line-of-succession-so-that-Father-can-rest–peacefully-at-night."

That only made Marcus look more pained. "He can have your Alex for that. I cannot marry, Ev."

"Why ever not?" Evander searched his brother's face, looking for the answer. All he saw there was sadness, but whether it was at himself or at the thought of disappointing their parents, he had no clue.

"I…" Marcus looked off into the distance, just at the moment their father came up behind him.

"My boys," he said, looking happier than he had in an age. "What are you discussing?" He came in between them, putting one arm on each of their shoulders.

"Evander was just telling me how much he's looking forward to marrying this season," Marcus said. "And I was just agreeing to be his best man. Wasn't I, Ev?"

It was a double-edged lie. Firstly, he was asking Evander to cover his own reluctance to marry, and to top it off, he was asking him to take his place in actually *getting* married.

But why?

Father laughed. "An unlikely story. More likely is that you were asking your brother for inside information on our opera singer."

Evander gave Marcus a 'there you have it' look. Father had been able to divine their true intentions before they were out of leading strings.

"And I refused to give him the information. Unless he wants to marry Mrs. Hayworth, he needs to remember that she is a lady."

"Yes, precisely," his father agreed, nodding. "None of that under my roof, Marcus. I didn't bring Lady Beatrix here for you to spend your time dangling after Mrs. Hayworth. Your mother will never forgive you."

But really, how could the heir to the earldom have eyes for a simpering miss when Sarah Hayworth was in the room? And if he had any doubts about this forthcoming courtship, which it sounded like he did, they would only be enhanced the more time he spent around Mrs. Hayworth.

Evander would love to know how she was faring in the ladies' withdrawing room. Probably beating them off with her fan, but more likely being ignored by the matrons who would judge her for being on the stage. She was probably regretting her decision to come altogether.

"Jolly good to have La Luminosa here, old man," he heard someone say to his father. "However did you manage it?"

"Maybe he offered her Marcus to flirt with," another offered. "I hear she's free now. Morley couldn't manage to hold on to her after his betrothal."

"Nobody can hold on to her after a betrothal," Lidcombe said bitterly. "He should have seen it coming."

Father coughed, red creeping up his cheeks in what Evander

knew was outrage. He had always had a great dislike of speaking ill of people when they weren't in the room to defend themselves. More so if the object of conversation was a woman.

"Nothing of the sort," the earl said. "She is a lady, in case you haven't noticed. And is not deserving of those remarks."

He'd always loved his father's way of telling the truth, no matter who was in the room and what their station was. It was something he'd always tried to emulate.

"Not what Morley said," came the snide reply, but Evander couldn't figure out who said it. Because if he could, the man would find himself escorted from the room. Then he noticed Lidcombe looking far too happy with himself.

Evander placed his glass of port slowly and deliberately on the table. "Lidcombe, perhaps you could keep your scintillating thoughts to yourself." Once again, he found himself eager to defend her honor. Would he do this every time she was disparaged? Probably. Thank goodness she wouldn't be in his vicinity for long. It was getting tiring.

His father shot him a shrewd glance. "Sit down, Evander. I'm sure Lidcombe poses Mrs. Hayworth no threat. After all, it is well known she rejected him for many weeks before he got the message."

The men laughed, but Evander vowed to keep a close eye on Lidcombe and Marcus for the weekend. These weren't men Mrs. Hayworth could marry, but they were exactly the kind of man who could damage her reputation without thought.

And that wasn't going to happen while she was under his care.

CHAPTER 9

IN WHICH SARAH CASTS HER LURE

Evander noticed the doors to the withdrawing room open with a mixture of relief and foreboding. He scanned the room to find Mrs. Hayworth. She seemed... completely relaxed, talking to his mother as if they were old friends. So much for thinking she was a lamb to the slaughter in there. The sooner he learned that she didn't need his protection, or anyone else's, the better off he'd be.

While he watched her, he noticed she started looking around the room too–her gaze stopping on his brother.

A small smile played at the corners of her mouth. Marcus looked up, sensing her heated gaze and their eyes locked for a sickening heartbeat.

So that *was* her plan.

Replace Morley with his brother–a much bigger prize. A dark pit of anxiety opened up in his stomach and he knew not why. The entire thing made him feel ill.

Marcus's eyes flitted from Sarah to Lady Beatrix, the lady brought to the musicale solely to be courted by him. She was also watching the interlude. Her rapid blinking and the slow flush of red up her cheeks suggested she knew that Sarah had thrown a lure to the man who was supposed to be courting her.

The lady stepped forward, pulling her mother with her toward Marcus. "I think I should like to enjoy the entertainment with you, Lord Huntley," she said.

For a usually quiet and shy young lady, she was certainly staking her claim.

As Marcus talked with Lady Beatrix, Evander took that chance to address Mrs. Hayworth.

"Best look elsewhere," he said quietly. Then he remembered what the gentlemen had said about her not carrying on affairs of the heart with married men. "He is close to a betrothal, from what my mother says."

She turned, closing her fan, and tapping him on the wrist with it. "Ah, but he is not betrothed yet, is he?"

"The contracts have not been signed, no."

She smiled brilliantly and laughed as if he'd been witty–drawing the attention of every man in the room, his witless brother included.

"Stop it," he said, grinding out the words.

"Stop what, Mr. Ambrose? You are so droll." She tapped him with her fan again. "He is unmarried. I am unmarried. According to my strict moral code, he is fair game until a shiny gold ring sits on his finger."

She had the grace to look pained by the crassness of what she just uttered and he had the fleeting impression that she was just as horrified by what she was doing as he was.

"Find someone else."

She whirled away from him. "Because you said so? I think not."

And she was gone, over to the piano where she picked up a sheet of music waiting for her.

He strode to the piano, angry at her for refusing him, and another reason he didn't want to examine too closely–jealousy.

"No good can come of it. The lady he's courting is a sweet girl, but she already knows you're flirting with him."

She didn't look up from where she sat, examining the sheaves of music. "Then the sooner she becomes used to other women flirting with him, the better off she'll be. Thinking you can monopolize your husband from other ladies will only make you a laughingstock."

"She doesn't need to get used to it. Marcus will be faithful."

She snorted, but so softly he thought he had misheard. "Faithful?" she said in an angry under breath. "None of them are."

"I thought you said you left the married ones alone?"

She looked at him with the same derision he felt for her. "That doesn't stop them trying, Mr. Ambrose. The only one of Prinny's set that hasn't propositioned me is Lord Felton, and I think he has his reasons."

"Good Lord," Evander said, shocked despite himself. "I can't understand it. Perhaps your name was in the betting books at White's, to see if there was any married man who could win you? You are well known for your scruples, it appears."

She brightened slightly, throwing him a saucy smile. "Oh, it was. I know because I had a great sum of money put on me *not* succumbing."

He laughed now. "Minx! I hope you made a pretty penny."

She inclined her head. "Indeed, I did. Now, if you will excuse me."

It was clear she wanted a moment to prepare herself, and finding himself dismissed and suddenly in charity with her for some reason, he found a chair in the corner that would bear his height and bulk and settled into it.

EVANDER WATCHED as Sarah sat at the grand piano his father had purchased for his mother as a first-anniversary gift. The light in the room seemed golden from the many candelabra, and the room had never looked richer and more welcoming. Sarah's eyes were closed, but every other eye in the room was open and on her. As she opened them and began to play, he had the sense that they, the audience, were a school of cagey fish that she was going to gently and patiently reel in. Sure enough, stiff backs relaxed into chairs as she played her long introduction.

It was a curious piece, with a strong and almost folk-like melody that was both haunting and sweet. Listening, it felt like she was experimenting with the melody, trying to find her way to the heart of it. She had no sheet music in front of her, so perhaps he was right, and she *was* improvising everything about this performance.

Just when she had lulled them into thinking she would not sing at all, her voice drifted across the room, ethereal and so light it felt like it might float away.

There it was again, that magic she worked that stole its way into the very heart of him. And once there, it ripped away layers of the masks he wore for society and for his role in it, leaving him with a raw and dreadfully earnest longing with no way to fulfill it.

He didn't even need to hear the words to know she was singing of love. The lost kind. The kind that left a hole in a person's soul that nothing could fill. Of a life wasted, of the warnings that came and were ignored as the lover sacrificed herself to a wastrel she thought she could save.

It wasn't operatic. It was heartfelt and real, and it was impossible to believe it didn't come from her own experience. The thought made him sad because the woman in the song was lost and suffering. She needed protection and healing.

Which led his ridiculous mind to the ways he could help her and heal her. He looked around the room and—with the exception of General Fontaine, who likely didn't have a heart at all, every male in the room was looking at her softly, probably thinking exactly what he was–that all he wanted to do was scoop her ethereal figure into his arms and to safety.

Ah.

With that, Evander was suddenly alert and smiling the smile of a man who was finally a step ahead. This song was a lure! Every man in the room would want to be by her side, do anything to save her. She came here wanting a husband and was going about the process in a delicate and artistic way. Good for her.

She peeked a glance around, looking mournful, until she got to him, and noticed his smile.

Then she frowned.

He motioned for her to continue and smiled some more.

Her eyes narrowed, and she turned away from him, leading the song into its climax – her death.

It ended with a vision of her being found floating in the river, which was when he heard some muffled sobbing around the room.

He looked around to find every lady dabbing her eyes with a handkerchief, while Lady Farrington was actually red in the face and weeping. And damned if his own brother didn't wipe a hand over his eyes.

She'd hooked them, one and all.

SARAH WIPED a tear from the corner of her eye. How rewarding to sing something that allowed her to feel and express her senti-ments. She should write her own songs more often. Her usual coloratura soprano roles were so complex that it took all of her focus and concentration to achieve the required result. A surfeit of emotion spelled disaster. But not her own simple song. It seemed that the more feeling she poured into it, the more intense it became.

It put her in mind of when she was a girl and sang in church, her mother and father so proud, her voice so pure. She would finish her hymn and look up to see their eyes glistening with tears. But to make herself cry? A ridiculous thing to do. She couldn't afford to weaken or allow herself these indulgences. She needed to watch every reaction to see if the men were affected, and yes, by God, they had been affected, well, all except Mr. Ambrose, who had sat there with a self-satisfied smirk on his face. Curse him.

Like he knew it was all an act.

She shrugged inwardly. Of *course* he knew–he'd known everything about her from the moment he'd seen her screeching like a banshee at Morley.

But his brother, that was a different story. Lord Huntley had come straight to her side when the piece finished and didn't leave until the party broke up for the evening–Lady Beatrix or not. He straightened the sheet music for her next piece and spoke with deliberate casualness. "I do enjoy spending the late evenings in the library, don't you?" he'd whispered to her.

And, wouldn't you know, she found she had a hankering for a book.

CHAPTER 10

ASSIGNATIONS OF THE FOOLISH KIND

Sarah sat in front of the mirror with a dampened piece of linen in her hand and wiped off the face paint of the evening. The rouge used to heighten the color of her cheeks, the Kohl, used very sparingly at the corner of her eyes. All of it an elaborate ruse to make her look more exotic and younger than she was. Now it was off, and hopefully, nobody realized it was ever on, because if there was one thing the nobility looked down on, it was artifice. She stared at her freshly scrubbed face. Not as fresh as it had been at nineteen when she'd first traveled to Italy, but there was still some semblance of youth to be found.

The Sevres porcelain clock on the mantelpiece said it was five past midnight. The night would just be beginning in London, but here in the country, the house was quiet around her, her maid sent off to bed once she had changed Sarah into her nightgown.

She undid the top button the maid had been adamant needed to be done up on such a cold night. The gown may be long-sleeved and have a high neck, but the entire concoction was a lesson in subterfuge. She guessed that under the gentlest of light, the fabric would show an outline of her figure, leaving

76

modesty behind on the side of the road like an abandoned kitten.

Wrapping a shawl around the misleadingly demure nightgown, she picked up the branch of candles from the dresser and took herself off to the library for the assignation.

Marcus, Viscount Huntley.

Lady Huntley.

There was no flutter of nerves in her stomach, which was concerning. Had she become so used to these flirtations that her heart was hardened? Or perhaps her heart just wasn't in this at all. Either way, there was nothing to be done about it. She had a job to do, and there was no point backing out now when she'd worked so hard earlier. She'd almost convinced *herself* she needed rescuing with that song.

She tried to imagine him sitting in the library, alone, now that the house had settled down, nursing a brandy in his hand. Waiting for her so they could have a private conversation.

Slowly and quietly, she made her way down the stairs to the ground level, glad for the moonlight shining through the cracks in the curtains. The freezing December night had her pulling the shawl tighter with her one free hand. The library door was ajar, and soft candlelight spilled into the hall. She pushed the door open, careful not to catch her hair on the candles as she slipped through the door.

His chair sat facing the fire, a pair of long and very well constructed legs, still in evening dress, stretched out before him.

What would a viscount do to get a physique like that? Riding or striding through fields, she supposed. Something bucolic.

She tried to make herself imagine him riding across the fields romantically, but there was no response. Maybe she wasn't ready for this, but it was the only chance she was going to get.

Resolutely, she put one foot in front of the other, pretending not to see him as she made her way to the bookshelves. She placed the branch of candles high on the mantel above the fireplace and dropped the shawl. With luck, the light would work its magic on the fabric of her gown, even if she froze in the attempt. This was her chance to bamboozle him into that seductive haze that would hopefully lead to matrimony.

With a squinting attempt at reading the book titles, Sarah reached for one on a high shelf, knowing how it would outline her figure. She pulled the volume down, humming softly to herself in a variation of the song she'd sung after dinner.

"Modern methods of irrigation and farming method," said a deep and all too familiar voice. "I wouldn't have picked you for a dirt aficionado." Smug laughter followed the pronouncement.

She whirled around. "You!"

Evander uncrossed his legs and swirled his brandy around the crystal glass. The smug do-gooder had come to ruin her plans.

"Yes, me," he said idly. "What brings you to the library past the midnight hour, Mrs. Hayworth?"

For a moment, she was struck dumb by the way the candle-light threw shadows under those strong cheekbones. The hero and savior of Six Oaks suddenly looked like a world-weary trav-eler who'd done and seen too much. Even so, he was easily the most handsome man of her acquaintance. Her extensive acquaintance.

But then he spoke and ruined the illusion. "Insomnia? Bore-dom? An insatiable need to study modern agricultural methods?"

She shrugged. "I simply wanted to relax by reading a book. Not that it is any of your affair."

"Oh, but it is." He paused, looking at her with a direct gaze that made her feel more transparent than her nightgown.

Oh Lord, her nightgown. She hurriedly put the book down and picked up her shawl, wrapping it around herself. But the shawl couldn't cover everything, and she knew she was on display with no-one but herself to blame. The room suddenly felt very warm.

"What a lovely picture you make," he said. "Wholesome,

almost innocent, except for the fact that that nightgown is somewhat sheer. A fact of which I'm sure you are aware."

She held her head high. "I hope you enjoy looking at something you shall never see again."

He stood, still looking at the floor, and she took a step back, not knowing what his purpose was. Normally, she would brazen it out, but to her horror, she was truly mortified. But why? She didn't even like the man, much less respect him. Perhaps that was the answer. She didn't like him having her at a disadvantage. That must be it.

He shrugged himself out of that beautiful tailcoat she had admired earlier, and placed it gently over her shoulders, then stood back, leaning one arm on the mantel.

It was warm and enveloped her completely. She wrapped her arms around herself.

"One would almost think," he continued, "that you hoped to find someone here. Perhaps my brother?"

Her heart sank into her kid slippers. He knew everything. It was to be expected. But damn him. "He would be a lucky man if that were true. But no, I'm here only for a book."

Disbelief was etched on his face. "I'm glad to hear it, because as I said earlier, my brother is not in a position to indulge you." He swirled the brandy, looking into its amber depths. "Are you aware my father is dying?"

He didn't look up, but she felt, in the very hushed way he said it, that talking about it was difficult, almost impossible.

"No, I wasn't aware. I'm terribly sorry. He is a wonderful man." Suddenly many small things fell into place. Like how Lady Wrotham looked at the earl sadly, or the way Mr. Ambrose had put his hand under his father's elbow when walking with him, as though expecting him to stumble. "Please. There is no need to say more."

Because she understood. Lord Huntley had promised his father he would take a wife, to comfort the old man that at least the direct line of succession would be cared for. And that wife would not be an opera singer, no matter that she was a gentleman's daughter. It would be a woman of impeccable breeding and accomplishment. She was a fool, and this plan had been doomed from the moment she stepped into the carriage to find Mr. Ambrose sitting across from her.

"With luck, they will announce a betrothal by the end of her stay."

Sarah's heart fell. Another dead end. Why had she not just stayed in her room? It was warm there, with a nice fire and soft blankets. Instead, she had to contend once again with Mr. Ambrose and his superior understanding of everything in the world. "Please pass on my felicitations. And perhaps mention to him that if he is preparing to marry, perhaps he ought not make assignations with other women."

"Yes, well, he is an ass." He shrugged as if this was something he dealt with on a regular basis.

"And you're here to clean up his mess."

"You're not his mess, Mrs. Hayworth," he said, shaking his head. "It is hardly your fault he offered something he can't make good on. I'm sure he wanted to if that makes you feel better."

It did not. The whole plan was crumbling apart. She didn't even have the money she'd just earned, by the time she'd paid her debts. She rolled her eyes at her own stupidity. Who did she think she was, thinking someone else would solve her problems for her?

She had to save herself.

If only the contracts from Venice had arrived, she would know what she was doing next. But as it stood, from here, she had nothing. She needed time, time to think about her next move. She needed to get out of this library and back to her room.

"I'm obviously mortified," she said, unconsciously telling the truth. He had a habit of luring her into that.

"I know. But there is no need to be. I understand that you're alone in the world. A husband, rather than a lover, would make your position in the world…" He paused as if searching for the right words. "…less precarious." He went to the bookshelf on the other side of the room, taking a slim volume off the shelf.

"That is more difficult than it sounds. No man wants a wife who spends three months traveling around Europe singing or who can't give him children because she has a season booked at The Kings Opera House."

Once again, unconsciously, she'd told him her deepest fear. That she could want marriage as much as she liked, but nobody would see her as wifely.

He looked at her steadily. "Your music leaves no room for anything else? No family of your own? She is a hard mistress." It wasn't a question but an observation, and worse still, an accurate one. She couldn't think of how they would fit together. It must be all of one or all of the other. But if it meant seeing Rebecca, it was a sacrifice she would gladly make.

"Music has been my life since I was five. It has never let me down." She spread her hands out to him, imploring him to understand. "It is all I know."

"It's a shame. I can't help feeling you would make an excellent wife and mother while still managing to sing in some capacity. Other opera singers do it, I believe? Mrs. Billington, I'm sure I heard there actually *was* a husband involved there. I'm sure if you wanted it, there would be a hundred men who would understand that being a husband to La Luminosa would come with special circumstances."

She raised her eyes to him, surprised to find warmth and kindness there. "Do *not* be nice to me, Mr. Ambrose."

He smiled, and it was the most welcoming thing she'd seen in an age. "It sounds like you need a friend." He held out his hand to her. "I offer my friendship."

She put her hand in his. It was warm, as warm as his smile,

and that warmth spread up her arm until it reached her heart. "I like this better than when you judge and criticize me."

He winced and pulled his hand away. "I have never done that."

"Not in words, perhaps, but I have felt your displeasure." She smiled up at him. "If you are my friend, perhaps you will help me find a husband?"

He looked at her curiously. "I would be a poor matchmaker. But why must it be now? Are you so desperate?"

And that was the crux of the matter—the secret that even he couldn't ply from her. Apparently, she still had some pride, after all. She may have no home, precious little money, but she had a smidgen of pride. "Oh, I just wanted to show Morley that he'd lost me entirely. Ugly revenge, nothing more."

His eyes shuttered, and she could no longer tell what he was thinking. "I'm sure he's fully aware of what he has lost. And what's more, he never deserved you to start with." He handed her the book. "Here. Take this to your room. It will be much more entertaining than the farming methods or my brother."

She took the book and opened it to the title page. "Fanny Burney. Cecilia."

He bowed his head. "My favorite of hers. I hope you enjoy it."

"Thank you." He read novels. What a strange and unfathomable creature he was.

He picked up her branch of candles from the mantle. "Shall we?"

Sarah took her candelabra from him. "Do you think your mother would like to announce *your* engagement at the musicale too?"

He followed her out of the room. "She would die of happiness to see us both settled. But I think in my situation it would not be so easy to accomplish."

What did he mean by his 'situation'? Being a second son, or being a clergyman? She wouldn't ask. "But it would make *you* happy to have a wife too, would it not?"

The look on his face was all the answer she needed. His shrug was a mixture of hope and futility. Some men were just born to be husbands and fathers. He was likely one of them.

"I must admit," he said. "The thought of my future wife being at this gathering is becoming appealing. I need more order."

"Is your rectory in such a mess that you need a wife to clean it?"

He barked out a laugh. "Well, yes, but it would be best if she didn't know that was the case."

"Nobody wants to be courted for their ability to order a pantry." She smiled and made a beeline for the door. "In any case, I wish you luck in finding her." The hollow feeling inside she felt wasn't worth looking at too closely. Jealousy seemed to come easily to her these days. "It sounds like a nightmare to me." She'd wanted to sound witty and sophisticated, but instead, she heard the bitterness in her voice.

"What does?"

She shrugged, keeping in step with him as he strode forth. "Being the vicar's wife. Tending the sick, consoling the lost, feeding the hungry. I can't imagine I'd be any good at it."

"Well of course not," he said, slowing down to face her. He sounded amused rather than insulted. "Nobody would expect a woman like you to enjoy such a mundane existence. But for a different woman, it could be a satisfying enterprise."

Sarah picked up her speed. "I shall find my satisfactions in other ways."

He allowed her the last word, which was good of him, because that last comment begged a witty response. But he wasn't crude, so he stayed silent.

They walked in silence, only the sound of his heels hitting the wooden floor. When they reached the bottom of the staircase, he turned to her once more. "Now I won't escort you to your room, because if someone should come across us, it would not look good for either of us."

"I would hate to ruin your reputation, Mr. Ambrose. If someone finds us, *you* would be compromised beyond redemption, and *I* would be forced to offer for your hand."

He laughed, his eyes dancing, and in that moment, he was far more attractive than any man she'd met. "Heaven help us, we don't want that."

No, they certainly did not.

Married to the vicar. What an idiotic notion. It certainly hadn't suited *her* mother and would suit her even less. She would go straight up to her bedroom and find a solution before morning if she had to stay up all night.

She shrugged out of his coat and gave it to him, and immediately felt cold.

CHAPTER 11

IN WHICH A CRUMPET LEADS TO A GREAT DOWNFALL

It was past nine o'clock the next morning and Sarah entered the breakfast room looking for coffee with puffy eyes and a heavy heart. After a long night of list making, she accepted that, with the scant amount of bachelors on hand, she wasn't going to find a husband while at Six Oaks. And considering how bruised her heart felt from a single try, perhaps it was for the best. But at least she was earning well-needed guineas.

The only solution she found, after all those lists, was to write letters to the managers of both Drury Lane and the King's Theater, prostrate herself before them and see if she could, between them, have a solid season of opera to build her funds up once again. If she could find some cheap rooms in London on a month-to-month basis and lie low until her contracts began, she might buy herself the time she needed. It wasn't unheard of for opera singers of her stature to make considerable funds in a season. She would be frugal and stop sending her parents so much money. Surely they had enough by now. She would rely on herself and not on the slim chance of twisting a man's arm into marriage.

Mr. Ambrose would be happy to hear it. Which was why she had to make sure she sat *nowhere* near him at breakfast. Without a doubt, he would divine her decision just by looking at her face. It was his way.

She was helping herself from the sideboard, using the tongs to take a thick slice of fresh bread, when another lady joined her, far too close for anything but a private conversation. She turned slowly, knowing before she'd even caught a glimpse that it was Lady Beatrix. She was taller than Sarah, with blond hair styled so elaborately that she must have risen at the crack of dawn to have it arranged.

"Let me be perfectly clear," Lady Beatrix said, a militant gleam in her eyes. "I would prefer if you left Lord Huntley to me."

Sarah looked at the large diamond pendant around the young lady's neck, fixated. It reminded her of the false one Morley had given her. Which in turn, reminded her of Morley. She sighed. Being browbeaten by a twenty-year-old miss who thought diamonds at breakfast was a good sartorial decision was lowering.

"Would you?" Sarah asked politely. "How lovely. Are you afraid he'll slip the hook before you've landed him? I would be too if I were you. He has a roving eye, doesn't he?"

Delicately picking up a piece of crusty bread, Sarah moved down the sideboard toward the preserves. This small contretemps wasn't going to rob her of tasting the earl's raspberry jam.

Lady Beatrix followed her, putting jam and a crumpet on her plate. "You're so sure of yourself. So unbecomingly confident."

Sarah turned, feigning surprise. "Oh, my dear, there is nothing unbecoming about confidence." If only she knew how unbecomingly *terrified* Sarah was most of the time.

Nobody at the breakfast table would suspect they were having anything other than a friendly conversation, but from Lady Beatrix's point of view-this was war. Of course, she was wasting her time, but Sarah wasn't about to tell her.

"Unbecoming or not, you will not get him. Not before our marriage and certainly not after it." The rosebuds sewn to the neckline of her pretty muslin dress shook with rage.

"My, my, your looks are quite misleading, aren't they? Sweet as honey on the outside and as fiery as a curry house on the inside. I find I almost like you." What's worse, it was true. Ladies of the nobility generally simpered and fluttered too much to actually be effective. Their barbs were normally covered in layers of innuendo and civility. At least Lady Beatrix was blessedly straightforward.

Lady Beatrix bristled. "Well I find I *do not* like you at all! And neither does anyone else! You might as well pack your bags after breakfast because you won't be staying any longer. I think you'll find that the earl wants me to marry his son more than he wants to listen to a five-minute song, no matter how pretty it might be." She turned to leave. "Trollop," she said under her breath.

Sarah raised her eyebrows. That was *more* than enough mortification for one day.

But before she could deliver the set down Lady Beatrix deserved, the lady in question caught her foot on the plush Turkish rug. She tripped magnificently, her head flung back, her beautifully proportioned breakfast plate flying high above their heads and landing on the carpet with a satisfying thud.

The crumpet rolled like a lonely carriage wheel until it hit the sideboard.

Lady Beatrix also landed on the carpet, her skirts about her knees and jam on her cheek.

Sarah laughed, first a small chuckle and then a belly laugh that made heads turn. "Oh dear," Sarah said. "What a sad end for a lovely breakfast."

I am not a good person. A nice person wouldn't laugh at something like this, no matter the provocation. The giggles bubbled up again because she didn't seem to be able to stop them.

Think of something sad.

It was unfortunate that the countess chose that moment to come into breakfast with her husband. She took in the sight of Lady Beatrix sprawled uncomfortably on the floor and immediately came to her aid, motioning for the footmen to help her.

Upon seeing the countess, Lady Beatrix stopped glaring at Sarah and instead whimpered and started to cry in a most affected manner. "She tripped me! You must have seen it."

"I'm sure she would never do that," the countess said, soothingly. "It's very easy to trip on the carpet edge. I do it daily."

Sarah smiled brightly at the countess. "Of course I did not trip her." *Although if I had thought of it ...*

Lady Beatrix sat up, then was helped to her feet by a footman. "She tripped me and then laughed."

Sarah shrugged. "You must admit, it was a little funny. The way that crumpet just rolled across the floor."

It was only when she realized that the room was hushed, with the only sound being Lady Beatrix sobbing that Sarah realized she had grossly miscalculated her audience. They were not amused. They did not think Lady Beatrix had needed a dressing down. They saw an older woman laughing at a younger woman's misfortune and pronounced her well beyond the pale.

They were right.

She'd spent too much time with a fast crowd and forgotten the gentle art of being a lady.

The countess actually *turned* pale, her eyes wide with shock. "Mrs. Hayworth, you forget yourself," she said it quietly, which somehow made it all the worse. "I'll show Lady Beatrix to her seat, then I wonder if you would join me for a turn around the terrace?"

Sarah frowned. Not the terrace. No good ever came from a turn around the terrace.

Mr. Ambrose rose from the table and waited by the door. A faint hope rose in her breast that he was there to help her, knowing, as he did, her tendency for doing rash things.

More likely, he was there to help her pack her bags.

CHAPTER 12

IN WHICH MRS. HAYWORTH IS SENT TO THE NAUGHTY CORNER

Evander followed his mother and Mrs. Hayworth out on to the terrace. He'd seen the whole episode, from the terse tete a tete to the awkward tumble. It hadn't made him want to laugh, but then, he had not heard exactly what was said. Lady Beatrix might be overbearing, but that didn't mean she deserved to start her day wearing crumpets and jam.

They exited the breakfast room onto the terrace, his mother leading with her head held high and a glacial expression on her face that did not bode well. Nothing would get in the way of her making a match between Marcus and Lady Beatrix, and especially not a lady who had attempted an assignation with him the night before. His mother wasn't blind.

This would be a punishment for that, rather than what had just occurred.

Sarah followed behind, her chin also held high, as though ready for battle. She caught his eye and her look of relief could mean a few things. Either she feared his mother, or she didn't want to leave and was happy to have a defender. Or maybe both. In truth, *he* was scared of his mother when she wore that expression. Last time he'd seen it directed at him was when he'd been sent down from Cambridge midterm. He smiled to himself. A time best forgotten.

Mother raised an eyebrow at his smile, followed them out, then motioned for Sarah to take her arm. Evander was left to follow. "Please walk with me, Mrs. Hayworth, while we decide what is to be done."

It was a chilly morning. The rolling grasses of Wrotham House were icy, looking like they had been dusted by confectioner's sugar. Nobody should be out in this cold air, but once his mother got an idea in her mind, it was impossible to budge her.

Sarah shot him a glance. "It was badly done, and I apologize." She shuffled from foot to foot as if to ask, 'now can we go back inside?'

The countess's eyebrows raised ever so slightly. "Perhaps you would have been better to apologize to Lady Beatrix, rather than me."

Sarah looked at the toes of her slippers and he would have assumed her regret was an act too, but he could see the blush rising on her cheeks. She was embarrassed. Or angry? It could be either.

It was probably time to enter the fray before the countess had Mrs. Hayworth packing her bags and his father crying into his tea. "What happened?"

The countess turned the arctic glare in his direction. "Don't be disingenuous, Evander. You were there, I saw you. I also saw you follow us when your father made a face at you. But neither of you can stop this chain of events."

"True, but she was too far away to trip her. Physically impossible. You'll upset Father if you send Mrs. Hayworth back to London before she has had the chance to sing at his musicale."

"I had a very difficult time getting Lady Beatrix here, and now she is mortally offended. I have no choice. If I am to keep the hopes of the betrothal alive, I must send Mrs. Hayworth on her way. Marcus will make her an offer this week, I'm sure of it. I cannot have anything stand in the way of the future of the earldom." She turned to Sarah, her expression slightly softened. "You must leave, don't you see?"

Sarah's eyes widened in horror. "But then *I* will be mortified and made to look a fool. I have a reputation to uphold too. By tomorrow morning, London papers will shout how I was chased from Six Oaks by a chit barely out of the nursery with my tail between my legs. Please don't do that to me. I did not trip her, although I admit to laughing at her. But she had just insulted me quite vilely, and I must admit I thought it was divine retribution when she tripped."

His mother shook her head, her mouth pursed. "Did she? That does complicate things. I do wish you had been polite enough to hold your laughter. I would hope you were above such pettiness being a gentleman's daughter. If the rumors are true?"

Mother had already looked into her background. Of course she had.

Sarah shrugged, neither confirming nor denying his mother's question. "I could not do anything but laugh after the insults she had just thrown at me," Sarah said. "I cannot dissemble to that degree."

"I find Mrs. Hayworth's honesty refreshing," Evander said. "We spoke at length about it on the trip here."

She looked at Evander thoughtfully, then to Sarah as if sizing her up. "Society would implode if we all had her honesty. But perhaps there is a way around this, because your father sorely needs his spirits raised, and I know Mrs. Hayworth is the one to do it. Any ideas?"

Evander looked out over the formal gardens, knowing what his mother was thinking, and appreciating that she was allowing him to suggest it rather than dictating.

His small estate, the one that had belonged to his mother's mother, had not only the large house he lived in but also the very quaint original cottage close by it. It was a favorite spot of the whole family, with many beautiful memories of his grandmother.

"Is the idea of removing Mrs. Hayworth from the immediate vicinity? Perhaps to Grandmother's cottage? Then Lady Beatrix gets her clean shot at Marcus."

He looked to Sarah, who had her head tilted to one side. "Where is the cottage?" she asked.

"I was gifted an estate by my maternal grandmother. I live in the main house, rather than the rectory. There is also a small cottage on it that I often use for visiting clergy. It will serve the purpose. Stay for a few days, then you can still sing at the musicale."

The countess smiled. "Clever boy. The perfect solution."

"I accept," Sarah said quickly.

"Very well," the countess replied. "You have been saved from an annoying trip back to London in this horrid weather."

"Thank you again, Lady Wrotham." Sarah curtsied most elegantly and smiled at his mother. It was all dimples and sparkle.

His mother smiled back, proving that even women were not immune to her charms. "Yes, well, I daresay she must have said something frightful to you to make you laugh like that at her misfortune. And I suppose you have had to be your own protector for some time now."

They turned and walked back toward the house, entering the parlor rather than back in the breakfast room, his mother rubbing her hands together against the cold. A footman opened the door, and Evander had a quick word with him.

"I just asked James to bring a breakfast tray here for Mrs. Hayworth." He turned to her. "Bread with jam, I believe?"

She nodded. "And some coffee, if there is some."

"Of course there's coffee, silly child." His mother followed after the footman. "I'll have James bring some back with your tray. Excuse me while I make sure Lady Beatrix has recovered."

She left the room with one final glare to Evander, which was either to ensure he behaved himself or that Sarah did. He wasn't sure which.

Sarah sat on one side of one of the small tables that dotted the room. "Thank you." Her voice was steady, but her hands were shaking. "You seem to make a habit of helping me out of fixes."

When the footman returned with the tray, Evander took a piece of the thick bread, spread the butter and jam on it, and placed it on a plate, holding it out to her. "You won't thank me by the end of the week. Your stay won't be nearly so comfortable or luxurious in the cottage. But I will share Mrs. Green with you. She's my housekeeper."

It seemed that every time he felt in charity with her, she did something so foreign to him that he didn't trust any of the good feelings he had. He could normally trust his instincts about people implicitly, but each time he thought he had a fix on her, her character shifted, and he was left not knowing if she was good and misunderstood or bad and thoroughly aware of it. Either way, she was probably someone best kept at a distance. He would do his duty to his father by taking care of her, and nothing more.

"I did behave badly and, as usual, while I'm sorry, there's a small part of me that can't regret it. She told me to pack my bags and called me a trollop under her breath. Don't you see? If someone insults me like that, of course I'm going to laugh at them when they fall over in the most clumsy way imaginable."

She eyed the thick globs of raspberry jam with an eagerness that surprised him. She'd shown the same enthusiasm for her dinner the previous evening. He'd seen similar enthusiasm when he took food baskets to homes where there wasn't enough food. Adding yet another facet to her confusing personality. How could a person wear a velvet cape and yet be hungry? Cashmere shawls and slaver over fresh bread and jam?

"You made her words prophetic. Because now you *are* packing your bags."

She shrugged. "I'm not unhappy, Mr. Ambrose. Dinner last evening showed what a maze this place is. I'm better off in a sweet little cottage. Will this jam be there? It is so much like the one my mother used to make."

"With regard to that...." Evander started.

She looked up, polite inquiry on her face that didn't fool him for a moment. "Yes?"

"Who are your family that my mother would assume your manners would be more ladylike?"

"Ah. That is, perhaps, a story for another time." She took one last piece of buttered bread from the plate and rose. "I'd best pack my bags. What time do you think a carriage will be available for me?"

Evander smiled broadly. "Now there is an evasion of topic if ever I heard one. Suddenly scared of the truth, Mrs. Hayworth? Are you embarrassed by your family or for your family?"

"Both, if you must know."

With that, she left the room.

"Interesting," Evander said to the fire.

And that was the sad truth—he couldn't help but be interested, even though he knew there was no good end in sight.

CHAPTER 13

FINALLY AN EXPLANATION FOR WHY MR. AMBROSE CARES NOT A JOT FOR HER

It was a frigid afternoon, the frost never quite thawing from the morning and steam clouding every breath they blew. A sane person would be in front of the fire with a book. Instead, he was in the earl's third-best carriage, once again playing nursemaid to an opera singer.

Not that he minded. Instead, it was like fate, and her bad behavior had intervened to throw them together even more tightly. Sarah was like a little light relief in return for all his toil. Not that she should visit him in his own house, oh no. The last thing he needed was Mrs. Hayworth seeing the extent of the way his life was totally out of control. He had to keep her firmly at the cottage, carefully not getting involved in his life. She could be a little pool of calm for him to visit for the few days she was there.

"So," he said, in a bored drawl that attempted to hide his enthusiasm. "I suppose we must be happy that you lasted a whole twenty-four hours in the house before being booted out. So much for your vaunted ability to mix with people of all classes." He smirked just to annoy her. Which was very unchristian of him. But fun.

Her quiet self-assurance was impressive. She had stood up for

96

herself, and if they threw her from the house for it—that was no concern of hers.

"Yes, yes, Mr. Ambrose. I am a hideous troll who should not be allowed near people of quality," Mrs. Hayworth replied darkly, looking around at the scenery as they passed through the north gate of the earl's estate.

He nodded encouragingly. "Or bachelors, don't forget bachelors."

She blinked in feigned surprise. "And what of you? Don't you count? Or are you too far above us to infect?"

That amused him, too. He relaxed into the seat a little more. "No, no. I'm a widower. We're immune, you see."

Her gaze sharpened as if he'd told her something that came as a surprise. Probably his widowed state. People often were surprised. He was young. But you were never too young to die; that's one thing his vocation had taught him early. And it might cause a lurch in his heart to speak of being a widower so blithely, but there was nothing blithe about the grief he and the boys had endured.

"I'm sorry," she said simply and with definite sincerity. "Although it does explain why you are immune to my charms. You are still in love with your wife."

She looked so pleased by the observation that he smiled. So, she'd been wondering why he wasn't fawning over her? Interesting. And even better was the fact that she hadn't divined that he was as susceptible to her as every other man was. Just better at hiding it.

"I'm happy you could solve the riddle. I suppose part of me will always be in love with Eleanor. How could I not be?" He smiled softly, thinking of her. "But she died three years ago. It's getting better."

People usually spoke of Eleanor in hushed tones and never directly to him. It was refreshing to speak to someone who hadn't known her and wasn't tiptoeing around him.

"Was she lovely?" she asked, looking out the window as if she didn't want to see his face when he answered. Most people found grief hard to look in the face. But then she surprised him by turning back, watching him intently.

"I thought so," he replied. He could bring her face to mind now and only felt a small pang. And he found he wanted to talk about her. "We grew up together. She was the youngest daughter of Baron Lawler whose land adjoins ours, and the daughter they openly said they would keep from marriage so she could look after them in their old age. I didn't like that idea, even if she was accepting of it."

"So you married her?"

He nodded. "She was my best friend. They could hire a nurse to take care of them. It made me mad to think how blithely they planned her life. All that brightness and spark relegated to being a nursemaid." He stopped short. If he hadn't married her, and she *was* their nursemaid, she would still be alive. The heavy weight of guilt and sadness descended on him.

"Evander, do not think what you are thinking. When God calls people, he calls them, no matter who they are married to or what they are doing."

Was he so transparent? "It's the kind of thought I only have during the darkest nights. She died falling from a cart on her way to visiting old Mrs. Talbot."

Her gaze was a mix of empathy and determination. "Were you driving the cart?"

He shook his head. "No."

"Were you responsible for what happened?"

Now he frowned, seeing the direction she was going. "No."

"So you are withholding forgiveness to yourself for something you never did. Is that correct?"

"Well put that way..." It did sound slightly unhinged. He looked out the window as they entered the village. The streets were muddy and the wind bitter. Jem Thatcher leaned against the wall of the alehouse with a bottle like he had nothing better to do.

"Good Lord," he said, knocking on the roof of the carriage. It stopped in a few yards, and he opened the door. "Mr. Thatcher, don't you have somewhere to be?"

Keeping Jem Thatcher in employment so he could feed the five mouths at home was a constant occupation for him, much less Jem.

"Nah, they didn't want me," Jem said, and the slurring of his words suggested he'd been making good use of his morning.

Who knew what he'd done this time, but most likely, he had reported to work in a poor state. Evander was running out of places to employ him. "I will visit you later this afternoon, so get yourself sober."

"Right you are," Jem said easily, and Evander knew he would be no more sober then than he was now.

He closed the door and landed heavily on the seat. The carriage lurched forward.

"Parishioners," Mrs. Hayworth said mildly. "So drunk and annoying."

"Sometimes I have to accept I can't change everything. Although when I see his children, I have to keep trying." It was hard not to feel like he was wasting his breath. Every time he tried to make a difference to a family's life, after a short time, they ended up worse off than they were before.

"Understandable," she said easily.

"Eleanor would not say that. She would tell me to keep trying, that my efforts are never in vain. That I should persevere." He was exhausted with all the persevering.

"Goodness me," she said, her eyebrows raised. "She sounds annoying too. If people want to ruin their lives, there is nothing *you* can do to stop them."

"She often would though, that's the problem. She would find Jem a job he would love, like the time she put another drunken toad into a job in Father's stables. He loved horses, and the discipline of the stables was perfect for him. I cannot seem to strike that happy balance."

"I think you have all but sainted her," Sarah said. "Nobody is faultless."

He didn't want to answer that. It felt disrespectful to Eleanor's memory. Because while Eleanor seemed to understand the right thing to do for everyone else, she never quite understood him.

He fooled her for the most part. Did she know, now that she was in heaven, how he actually felt most of the time? Overworked, tired, desperately needing comfort. He often wondered what would have happened if he had told her how he was feeling. Would she have understood? Perhaps even admitted to feeling the same way? But instead, she had been a model of duty, and he'd been left, for better or worse, feeling like he had another curate rather than a wife. "Of course no person can be faultless. She would hate to be seen that way. She just liked to be useful, I think."

"Or maybe she just wanted to be married to you and took whatever horrible work came with it."

Her dancing eyes told him that she was jesting, but in fact, her words rang true for him. He had saved her from a duty she felt bound to, he had given her a life and her own family, and she was definitely grateful. But he couldn't help feeling that the union wasn't totally fulfilling for either of them. But who did have that kind of union?

"That's close enough to the truth," he said, closing the topic down.

But of course, Mrs. Hayworth would not let it go, at least not yet.

"I was jesting, silly man. Of course, she'd take you! Surely, you're a hero in these parts. The handsome vicar who is the son of an earl to boot? Women must have clamored after you."

Now he didn't know if she was serious or not. He assumed

she was serious. "Ladies tend not to clamor. Rather, they do things like leaving their pocketbook behind after services, so they have to come and retrieve it, or visit the sick at the exact time you do, displaying their empathetic depth."

"I shall have to remember that, next time I set my cap for the local vicar," she said sagely, her mouth set in a prim straight line, her chin lifted.

He sat up straight, feigning alarm. "Please don't. The Church has enough problems without making you a vicar's wife."

She laughed out loud. "Touché."

And just like that, she had him entirely in charity with her again. It was confusing how often he changed his mind about her. He should just decide and stick with it.

He either liked her or didn't. It was that simple.

Perhaps he'd defer that decision for a while. Decide not to decide, as it were. But he liked how she made him feel. It was like waking up on Christmas morning, knowing something exciting was about to happen.

Another long moment passed, the footfall of the two horses pulling them the only sound he heard. They both relaxed back a little, not feeling the need to speak. She didn't look for ways to fill that void. He was grateful.

SARAH ALIGHTED THE CARRIAGE, taking in the cottage that sat on the north edge of his property in full view of the main house. Even in December, it was pretty, with ivy crawling up the exterior walls and banks of roses that would be beautiful come Spring. The thatched roof still held a sprinkling of snow from the night before. It was probably smaller than a dog kennel, but she had no-one to blame for that but herself. She had enjoyed a perfectly fine room in the main house, but no, she had to spoil it all. Her damned temper. When would she get it in check?

So be it. This would be her week of plotting and planning. By the time she left Six Oaks and her enforced distance, she would have a complete plan, both for her finances and her career. It would all be mapped out. She could not afford to be exhausted just by the thought of it.

Their feet crunched along the gravel path that led to the door. "I think I will be happier away from the big house. Last night was tumultuous."

She watched as he fished a large key from his pocket. "I'm sure the big house will be happier away from you too."

He seemed to take great enjoyment from teasing her, and heaven knew she enjoyed finding his weak spots and returning the favor. She was used to dividing people. They either loved her flouting of social conventions, or they condemned her for it. But Mr. Ambrose seemed squarely stuck in the middle.

She knew what that meant—she challenged him but he couldn't get over his social outrage to appreciate it. Normally she didn't have time for that kind of indecision, but there was something about him, something that was dying to break free, that called to her. Made her needle him when she should just leave him be. Or it could be just his delicious chisel-cut jaw that made her do it.

She ignored his barb. "The countess said this was your grandmother's cottage?"

He nodded. "On my mother's side. She was a sole heiress from a family who was untitled but wealthy. My grandparents bequeathed this property to me through my mother's marriage settlement. This cottage was her dower house."

"And it sits vacant?"

He opened the door. The warmth inside beckoned them in. "It's handy. I once had my curate live here, but the current curate prefers to live in the village. You may see him walk past the cottage on occasion as he visits me. He's harmless enough, but I would not recommend inviting him in for tea."

"Why ever not? That seems most uncharitable." Oh but she loved to point out his shortcomings. It may make her a bad person, but bringing the militant gleam into his eyes was quite satisfying.

"Don't say I didn't warn you."

She quirked an eyebrow at him. "Surely the poor man is to be pitied. He likely does all your prayers and your sermons for a pittance while you live as a gentleman off the tithes of the land," she said lightly. It was the way of vicars who were also from noble families. But for some reason, even as she said it, she knew she was wrong. She scanned his face, looking to see if he registered the insult. Instead, he responded with an easy smile. Likely because what she had said was a long way from the truth.

"Mr. Pinlock does a lot of work, and yes, a fair proportion of what I should be doing. But he is well compensated and relishes his job. At least he has one, what with livings these days being so scarce."

"And good livings even harder."

"Do you know somebody in the clergy?" he asked, possibly wondering what informed her knowledge. Or possibly trying to guess at her background.

"Doesn't everyone?" she countered, not ready to tell him more. She walked through the small entrance hall.

The cottage was bigger than it looked from the exterior. It had a small entrance foyer with a round table. Behind that, there was a staircase with ferns hanging from baskets going up it, and a dear statue of a dog standing guard by the door. "Oh, Mr. Ambrose, it's beautiful," she breathed. "I shall greatly enjoy staying here."

He led her into the parlor. "I had Mrs. Green light the fires. She will bring you provisions and be in every morning to take care of the house."

Sarah nodded. The room had a comfortable sofa covered in a

floral pattern and a large rug in front of the fire that begged her to toast some bread in front of it.

Evander stood in front of it, warming his fine backside. He was wearing the buckskin breeches that so many men wore, but not as well as he was wearing them. He had the physique of an Adonis. She should definitely look away before she blushed.

"You are welcome to bring your father to visit here," she said, pulling her gaze away from his fine form.

He left the hearth and came back to her. "That's a good idea. He will be most happy to have you all to himself. Sing him a lullaby and he'll fall asleep by the fire."

She wandered from room to room, exclaiming over wallpapers and writing desks. There were fresh flowers by the window in the parlor that could only have come from the hothouse at this time of year. Another nice thought. His, or the housekeeper?

She found him in the kitchen, swinging a kettle over the range.

"The pantry is stocked," he said. "I'll make you a pot of tea and be on my way."

They were alone in the house, and the only noise she could hear was the swish of her skirts. It felt intimate. "Won't you stay?"

His brows drew together and there was a slight frown on his face. "Normally I would love to. However I must return to the fond bedlam that awaits me at home."

Now, what did that mean?

IN WHICH THE CURATE IS ROUNDLY
TROUNCED

The following day, Sarah was in the front parlor, taking her first sip of the steaming Ceylon tea Mrs. Green had made. It was barely ten o'clock but a message had already arrived to let her know that the earl would be coming to visit before lunch. So, she wasn't a complete pariah, then, and the earl obviously didn't mind her company, no matter that his wife had sent her away.

There came a knock at the door that made her look askance at the clock on the mantel.

It was entirely too early to be the earl, but then, perhaps he was up and about and saw no reason to wait. Thank goodness she'd dressed properly. Sarah patted her hair, tucking a loose tendril behind her ear.

She heard Mrs. Green open the front door and greet the guest very politely. "I'm afraid Mr. Ambrose is not here, Mr. Pinlock."

Mr. Pinlock? Ah, the curate. But why would he assume Mr. Ambrose was at the cottage?

The reply came swiftly, in a voice that carried in a clear if somewhat nasal accent. "Oh no, no, dear Mrs. Green. I have come to pay my respects to your newest guest. I would hate for her to see me riding up to Mr. Ambrose's house without knowing who I am."

"I'm quite sure she has no interest in the comings and goings of Mr. Ambrose's visitors." Sarah could imagine Mrs. Green now had her hands on her hips. "But very well. I will see if Mrs. Hayworth is receiving."

She came into the parlor, shaking her head. "It's the curate, Mr. Pinlock. You don't have to receive him if you'd rather drink your tea in peace."

Sarah shrugged. Whatever the curate wanted, Sarah could handle, no matter what Mr. Ambrose said. If he wanted to bore her, she'd have him on his way before the teacup was cold. If he wanted to insult her, as the clergy often did, he would be *wearing* the tea as he left. She smiled quietly to herself. She'd taken on bigger and nastier foes than the curate from a small village.

"Perhaps you could get me another teacup and saucer for this lovely tea and send him in," Sarah replied.

Mrs. Green bobbed a curtsy, her expression unreadable. "Certainly, ma'am."

A few moments later, he entered. He was a small man of perhaps thirty years of age, with a wide-brimmed black hat that he removed to reveal lank red hair. He bowed over her hand and leveled a superior smile at her.

Politely, he waited to be invited to sit, which she did. They both sat, whereupon he looked meaningfully at the teapot. Sarah poured him a cup, hoping she was doing it daintily as any lady.

He took it from her. "I am so pleased to meet you, Mrs. Hayworth. I hope you will forgive my intruding upon your peace, but I felt it important to keep you abreast of developments in this vicinity before things get out of hand. I would put the horse before the cart, as it were."

Sarah nodded. *This* was more like the clergymen she knew and loved, proving once again that Mr. Ambrose was the exception to the rule. "What exactly will get out of hand, Mr. Pinlock?"

"You probably don't realize it, Mrs. Hayworth, but the village is all agog with your visit, not just the main house but closer still, in our small village."

"Agog!" Sarah echoed. "How lovely of them to notice my arrival."

"Oh, they know all the details of your arrival, and I hesitate to pass this along, but they are all wondering how long it will take for our rector to succumb to your charms. The village is very protective of him, you should know. He may seem impervious, but being a fellow clergyman, I know only too well he is just a man."

She smiled sweetly. "How do you know he has not already succumbed, Mr. Pinlock?" She took a sip, watching him over the rim.

He coughed mid-sip and tea splattered on his leg. Sarah smiled into her cup. She did promise he would be wearing his tea before he left.

"I'm sure he's had no time for that as yet, Mrs. Hayworth. You only arrived yesterday!"

"I do work fast, though, Mr. Pinlock. But don't let me run on. What was it you wanted to warn me about the village? I assure you I will barely be here long enough to form a lasting impression. Your young women and men are safe from me."

"Oh." Perhaps foreseeing that whatever he had in mind was going to be met with amusement instead of the solemnity he had expected, he changed tack. "In that case," he drained his tea. "I would merely wish you a pleasant stay at Six Oaks and be on my way."

"Excellent idea," she said. "I'm sure you have a mountain of work to do. I have always been quite sympathetic to the plight of the curate. Often left to shoulder the main duties and responsibilities of his superior without the reward that comes with that higher position. You deserve to have your own parish, Mr.

Pinlock. The state of our church is a sin to waste the services of so many good men."

He sat again, and, for a moment, she rued that she'd opened her mouth. "It's true. Of course I look for my reward in the hereafter," he said solemnly. "But it would be nice to have a parish of my own, a flock of my own to guide. I try with the people of Six Oaks, but so often they merely repeat what Mr. Ambrose has told them, which is a completely lenient interpretation of the scripture."

"So Mr. Ambrose is a lenient shepherd of his flock? I'm surprised," Sarah said. He was certainly quite judgmental whenever he was around her. Although her time with him in the library showed he was capable of compassion and understanding.

"Oh yes. That's why I was so worried when you arrived. He's just as likely to befriend a Mary Magdalene as to try and reform her."

Sarah kept a straight face with great effort. "And before you know it, he would have fallen so far into impropriety that he would have to marry me, or some-such other nonsense, and then the entire village would be at sixes and sevens, with a lenient rector and opera singer for his wife and only the lowly curate to keep order."

It was so good it deserved to be an opera itself. And it was all in his head.

He thumped his fisted hand on his thigh. "Precisely! I don't know what made me think you would be a lady of small understanding. You have divined my thoughts exactly."

"It wasn't hard," Sarah said. It wouldn't do to start thinking on all the similar conversations she'd had in the past, with uncles, fathers, and once even a grandfather of a beau, begging her not to marry them or pull them into the oblivion of her lifestyle.

"Perhaps I have no ambition to improve my station in life. Perhaps I am content with what I have." It wasn't true, of course, but it would be enough to placate him. The upper classes, and more importantly, the cartoonists hated it when actresses and opera singers overstepped their mark. At the first sign of that kind of ambition, a very ugly version of your near-naked body was drawn with a coronet on your head and distributed for the entire populace of England to behold.

"A most becoming attitude," he said.

"Thank you, Mr. Pinlock. I do try to be sensible of my place in our fair society. After all, I am so far down society's ladder, I cannot even see the rungs."

Mr. Pinlock looked at her suspiciously. "So you actually haven't charmed him at all, have you? You were just funning."

"Making light of your assumptions," she replied. "And no, I have not charmed him. Quite the opposite, in fact. I think your fair and non-judgmental rector has reserved all his God-fearing judgment for me."

That seemed to make him happy, for he stood, placing his hat back on his head. "Shall I talk to him, Mrs. Hayworth? For the short time you're with us, it seems unfair for us not to be as welcoming as possible. We're honored, we truly are."

"Oh no, please do not. I would be mortified."

He turned at the door. "Will we see you in church tomorrow?"

She tilted her head, surprised by the question. "But of course, Mr. Pinlock. I wouldn't miss the chance to hear your sermon. I assume you do them and not Mr. Ambrose."

He scowled, his long red nose scrunching up. "Never. Come what may, Mr. Ambrose is in that pulpit on Sunday morning. He gives me not a scrap of time there." He sniffed loudly.

Sarah smiled, glad that despite being an earl's son, Mr. Ambrose did not really leave his responsibilities to someone else. "I'm sorry to hear that. But I shall look forward to the service in any case."

Sometimes it was a great deal of fun to show them just how well she knew all their hymns and prayers.

Once a vicar's daughter...

CHAPTER 15

THE EARL COMES FOR A VISIT

Wrotham insisted on taking a picnic basket on their visit to Mrs. Hayworth.

"I won't go empty-handed, my lad." He was as excited as a pup about to go on a walk.

"You're not empty-handed. You brought *me* along, and I can tell you on good authority that I amuse Mrs. Hayworth no end."

"Now don't you go falling in love with her too, my lad. Enough trouble pulling Marcus out of it without going straight back in after you."

Evander shrugged, vaguely annoyed that anyone would tell him who he could fall in love with. "And what harm would it do if I did fall in love with her? I hardly think she would set her cap at me. Quite the opposite, I believe. Watch and see for yourself."

Evander had finally decided that because she seemed to have no designs on him, his fixation on her was completely without risk, which meant he could safely indulge in it.

Mrs. Green led them through to the parlor where Mrs. Hayworth rose from reading a book. She had a blue knitted blanket over her knee that she pushed aside when she stood. A cheery fire burned in the grate and the room was toasty warm.

"Gentlemen! So lovely to see you." She made her curtsy and then led them into the dining room where the footman had laid out the contents of the picnic basket. Bread, fresh from their ovens, cheddar from the dairy and wine from Bordeaux. Mrs. Hayworth looked at the table with astonishment.

"That looks like simple fare for a peer of the realm," she said with a decided twinkle in her eyes. He liked that twinkle. It meant she was up to mischief. And nothing made the earl happier than mischief.

"Bah. I am a farmer at heart. Don't let the silk and lace fool you." Wrotham smiled back, his own eyes twinkling merrily too. For that alone, Evander would forgive her anything.

Father tugged at his old-fashioned lace cuffs and she laughed. "I like old-fashioned, my lord. And I like that claret you brought. I'm so glad you don't think I'm too much of a lady to partake of it."

Evander poured them both a glass. "We assumed," he said, handing it to her, "that delicious is delicious, no matter what."

"Indeed," she said, lifting her glass to the earl. "To your health, my lord."

"Thank you. And thank you for agreeing to stay here. I know it's not ideal, but I'm having the devil of a time bringing Marcus up to scratch, and I would dearly like to have him settled sooner rather than later."

"I'm sure he knows his duty, my lord," she said softly, obviously wanting to reassure him. "And we can both admit that perhaps I made my own bed here, so to speak. I have no intention of getting in the way of your plans."

His shoulders slumped with relief. "Ah, thank you. You're a good girl. I knew you were."

"That's refreshing to hear," she quipped. "I so often hear that I am a very bad girl! You divine my true spirit, I see." She sat upright with her chin raised and a beatific expression on her face.

Evander thought about it. The words had a ring of truth to

them. It must indeed be hard to be good when the corner of the world you occupied was living a dissolute life. "It's easy to be good when you are surrounded by good people and very little in the way of temptation," he replied. "It is, therefore, more commendable to be good under more pressing circumstances."

"And that is the closest you will ever come to complimenting me, Mr. Ambrose. I shall take it to my heart and keep it there under lock and key." The pious look on her face had them both laughing.

"What a minx you are," Father said. "But tell us, where to after here for you? Vienna? Naples?"

Evander noted her quick-blinking worried expression that was quickly covered by a bright smile. "Oh, I'm sure something will come along. I expect the letters will be waiting in London for me upon my return. But at the moment, I have no notion where I will be in a month's time. I would like to stay in England though. I have been too long traveling, and it is quite wearying to have to speak in foreign languages all the time when one's mind speaks in English."

Interesting. The first time they met, she told them she couldn't attend the musicale because she was going directly to Venice. A small fib to save face, perhaps? In reality, she had nowhere to go, and he was fast realizing that her circumstances truly might be desperate. Father leaned forward and refilled his own glass. "How many languages do you speak? I heard Angelica Catalini speaks four."

She tilted her head to one side. "Let me see. French and Italian, of course, German for the Mozart, Spanish because I like it, and a smattering of Russian from my time there. Conversational rather than written, you understand. Their alphabet confuses me no end."

Wrotham laughed out loud. "Ha! More than Catalini or you, Evander, with your Cambridge education. I should have sent you into the opera instead!"

"I'm sure Evander learned more than languages at Cambridge. He learned. . ." she looked thoughtful. "What *did* you learn?"

She had used his given name. How lovely it sounded. Did it mean he could call her Sarah? He would never assume, but it felt right to be on such an intimate basis, somehow. "I learned how to drink beer, how to bet on a horse race, and how to get into a mill." He shrugged. "What more did I need?"

"As I thought," she replied gleefully.

He motioned to his father. "You see? I told you Mrs. Hayworth has no high opinion of me."

"That's not the case," she replied. "How can any vicar truly empathize with his flock unless he has walked in their shoes, so to speak. I commend you."

Father looked from Mrs. Hayworth to him and back again, obviously trying to figure out the dynamic of their friendship. Evander would have to ask him what he discovered because he himself had no idea what was going on.

"Will you come to our local service tomorrow, my dear?" Father asked.

She darted a glance to Evander and then nodded.

Drat. The last thing he needed was Sarah Hayworth in the congregation. Bad enough the villagers and his family had to listen to him waffle on. At least they didn't have the unnerving habit of divining his true feelings with a single glance.

She'd be there for five minutes and the secret would be out. The thing that he worked so hard to hide. That the passion he had for his profession had followed Eleanor into the grave and his heart was as cold as the winter ground piled on top of it.

"Please don't feel you have to," Evander said easily.

"Nonsense," Father said. "Evander will be at the church, so we'll send a carriage for you, my dear. It will do my heart good to hear you sing the hymns in that heavenly voice of yours."

"There is no need to send for a carriage; I shall quite enjoy the short walk to the church."

Evander looked from Sarah to his father and back again as they beamed at each other in mutual admiration.

He let out a long sigh. Sarah was coming to church tomorrow.

CHAPTER 16

WHERE SARAH KNOWS ALL THE WORDS TO
THE HYMNS

The following morning, Sarah dressed for the December cold in a demure deep blue woolen dress and cloak and walked into the village. She hoped to blend into the congregation, but that would depend on how big the church was.

Too small and she would stand out no matter what and become the spectacle she was so desirous to avoid being.

When she reached the main road, her fears calmed a little. The church was a large gray-stone building, surrounded by evergreen holly, with beautiful red berries abound. People entered from all directions, and Sarah joined the throng. Once inside and seated behind a large man, Mr. Ambrose wouldn't even know she was there.

Unless the blatant stares and heads turning from the villagers alerted him.

Oh dear. The whispering started and the tone of it suggested she had quite the nerve coming to church. She inspected the buttons on her glove and the prayer book she found at the end of the pew, hoping they would lose interest. Normally she would attempt to brazen it out by smiling and waving but did not seem appropriate under the circumstances. Her cheeks were uncomfortably hot.

Soon enough, the organ played an introduction, and the opening hymn began. The church was full for this nine o'clock service, with children of all ages squirming in their seats and being artfully calmed by their parents.

Mr. Ambrose entered.

His eyes narrowed when his gaze landed on her and she felt her cheeks flame even more. What a terrible idea this had been. She was not a regular attendee at this church as she was at Curzon Chapel and it was obvious she was not expected.

Luckily, everyone sat in rapt attention the moment Mr. Ambrose opened his mouth; the young ladies, Sarah noticed, paid particular attention and sat very straight in their pews.

Well, she would have too if she had a strong and handsome vicar preaching to her each week from the pulpit. She would sigh and twist her skirts around her fingers. Never would church services seem so enticing or vital. A smile spread across her face, and she found herself enjoying watching the congregation from her position at the back until it came to his sermon and she gave him her full attention.

"Today," he said, his voice naturally projecting, "I want to talk about the Good Samaritan."

Sarah sighed inwardly. How many times had she heard her own father preach on this parable, taking some happening from the week in the parish to berate his parishioners for turning a blind eye when they could have been of help.

Her father used it because he was the one that had to fix the mess afterward and that annoyed him. Sometimes she thought her father needed the story told to *him.*

"The other day, I was walking down the main street..."

Here we go. Sarah lifted her eyes to the ceiling.

"...when I noticed," he continued. She waited for him to keep going, but he didn't. After a few moments, she looked up, only to find him staring at the ceiling the same way she had done only a few moments before. The congregation waited patiently for him, thinking perhaps that he was pausing for effect. He wasn't, Sarah was sure of that. He also hadn't forgotten what he was saying.

He leaned hands on either side of the pulpit and took a deep breath.

"Honestly," he said, shaking his head. "I come up here every week to encourage you to care for one another and be respectful to one another, and every week, one of you does something that makes me wonder why I bother."

There was a universal intake of breath.

"There's someone I have to visit in jail, or find legal representation for, or talk down from a fight. Is it the fault of the alehouse that you are drunken? No. Is it the fault of Mrs. Parker that she left her reticule in the haberdasher's and therefore deserved to have it stolen?" He took a deep breath and let it out. "I am somewhat tired of being your conscience when your heart and moral code should dictate your behavior. I have enough to do without that."

There was another general gasp of indignation, which was probably understandable since half of the congregation was likely law-abiding citizens.

He looked around the church. "And you gasp, as if *you* have never done anything to warrant such a declaration. Well, all you gasping ladies, please tell me how the knowledge of a certain opera singer staying in the cottage became common knowledge if you did not gossip about it? The slander of her character is as bad in my opinion as the petty crimes that would land you in front of the magistrate. You do far more damage than you know. Or perhaps you do know, and that is even worse."

He looked around the congregation, glaring. Then his gaze landed on Sarah, and he closed his eyes briefly. She knew he wished she was not there.

The entire church seemed to swing around to look at her, and she wished she wasn't there too. She lifted a hand weakly to wave at them.

Part of her wanted to smile at the very thought of a vicar telling his congregation he'd had enough of them, but the larger part was concerned that he had reached this point. Despite her teasing to the contrary, she knew he was a man who worked on keeping an even temperament, which meant something was very wrong. She hoped what was wrong with him was not her, that her presence hadn't somehow pushed him over the edge.

He sighed. "Now that I have outraged you all and said far more than I meant to, I hope you will forgive me and know that I only ever want what is best for you. Now let us sing something to uplift us and be on our way to a better week."

With that cue, the organist began Psalm 130, which began with 'Lord from the depths, to thee, I cried.' Not perhaps the uplifting tune he had in mind.

She watched Evander roll his eyes, and then she really did smile. He left the church, and she wondered if anyone would have the gumption to speak to him after a service like that.

Sarah didn't leave, instead, she picked the pocketbook and pencil out of her reticule and sat down as the rest of the congregation swarmed out, looking stunned.

She smiled to herself and wrote in the book.

'Lesson of today's sermon: Mr. Ambrose looks very handsome when he is angry.'

She put the book down on the pew. He would know where to return it.

CHAPTER 17

IN WHICH FANNY TURNS OUT TO BE A DOG

It had taken most of Sarah's evening to fill the bath she found in an upstairs room with delicious hot water. And since she'd climbed the stairs a hundred times with that bucket, her aching muscles were even happier to relax into it. As usual, she could feel how beneficial the steam was for her throat. Not that she'd taxed it today at church.

The cupboard in the room had revealed a treasure trove of lotions and oils. Maybe they belonged to Mr. Ambrose's grandmother. She liked that thought. There was even a stash of French-milled soap with the lingering fragrance of lavender.

The cottage was unusual enough to have a bath with its own permanent room, but the oils and soaps only confirmed that the lady was a great believer in the power of soaking oneself in waters for cleansing and relaxation.

Sarah had come to the same conclusion on her many visits to the hot springs in Tuscany.

She sank into the bath and let the warmth spread through her. The cottage was cozy and blessedly quiet. Living in the center of London had always been a noisy affair, but she'd loved the sound of the night watchman and the clop of horses along the road outside. Even when something woke her at five in the morning when she'd only fallen asleep at three, she just groaned and rolled over. She'd become a Londoner.

But the country had a quiet so deep it felt like a heavy blanket. She closed her eyes, allowing herself to relax. Just as she did, there was an almighty bang outside.

Sarah shot out of the small bath, splashing water everywhere. How on earth could something *sound* like gunfire without *being* gunfire? She ran to the window, but the candle on the windowsill stopped her from seeing outside, so she blew it out. There was nothing out there, nothing but a faint orange flicker in one window of Mr. Ambrose's house.

Then, shouting, stomping, and another flurry of loud reports.

Sarah gasped at the now unmistakable flash of orange light in the upstairs window.

Fire. No!

Even in the depths of winter, a fire could rip through a house without care for the snow or rain outside.

Eyes wide with horror, she pulled her plush velvet dressing gown on and ran downstairs to cover that with her cloak and then a scarf on her head. Then on went her boots, without doing up the buttons, and she was out the front door within moments. There was a definite smell of gunpowder in the air.

What on earth?

She looked up at the main house window in the distance, where the blaze was obviously in the drapes, and ran to the rear of her cottage where she'd seen a pail earlier.

What on earth was Mr. Ambrose doing? Was he an amateur scientist experimenting with gunpowder? She had no idea, but even as she flew across the cold and muddy lawn, she could see someone try to douse the flames with water.

Would anyone realize they needed help? The wind was blowing away from the village and the very situation of Mr.

Ambrose's house, on a large area of land with many trees, meant there was every chance the fire would go unnoticed.

The front door burst open, and a boy came out, pulling two smaller children behind him. One looked barely out of leading strings.

Children? Not his surely? He'd never even *mentioned* children. Her world turned on its axis. Everything she thought about him was wrong. And he had encouraged that.

"Alexander," the little blond one yelled. "We forgot Fanny!"

The boy they called Alexander put them under a tree. "Now you two stay right there!"

He spotted Sarah. "Thank God! Can you help us?"

"Is everyone out?" she panted.

"Papa is upstairs, and Fanny is inside too." His voice rose in panic.

"I shall find her," Sarah said. "Where would she be?"

"In the kitchen, near the hearth. That's her favorite spot."

Fanny was obviously a pet. "Very well. I trust you to all stay here while I go find Fanny. Hold a moment. What is Fanny?" For all Sarah knew, she could be a canary.

"Our dog, silly."

"Right. Of course."

Alexander ran back toward the house, picking up a pail of water that was sitting by the front door. "The pails are behind the house near the well," he yelled over his shoulder.

Calling out 'Fanny' as she went, Sarah ran through the bottom level of the house, which was not smoky as yet.

A small pug, much like the ones she had seen at the earl's house, wandered out into the hall. "Goodness, you're solid," Sarah said, picking the dog up and carrying it down the hall. When she let it out the front door, Fanny ran to the boys and stood guard, even though she was smaller than they were.

"Good girl, Fanny," she said, taking herself around the back of the large house to the well and the pails that were stacked next to it.

"I can do this," she said, pumping water as fast as she could, ignoring the burn in her upper arms and shoulders. She filled the bucket and entered the house, amazed that the smoke had not yet made its way into the hall. Perhaps Mr. Ambrose was doing a good job and the blaze was almost out.

She closed each door as she came to it, aware that the smoke could be just as damaging as the flames. She climbed the stairs with her bucket, following the shouting.

"Get more water," she heard Mr. Ambrose yell. At once, Alexander, his face now sooty, shot out from the room. He stopped when he saw Sarah, but she just pushed past him as he ran down the stairs. Sarah called after him. "You fill the pails and run them to the bottom of the stairs; you're stronger than me."

His chest puffed up with pride. "Good idea."

He didn't need to know she wanted him out of the way of danger. Being smaller, he would surely be more susceptible to the smoke than her.

Sarah followed the sound of water and the sharp crackling of the flames. Wrapping her scarf around her mouth, she opened the door. The heat hit her in the face far worse than a hearth. She tried not to breathe the smoke in, but it was probably useless.

The blaze was so much bigger than she expected. It had ripped up the wall and set the wallpaper aflame, sending off an intense heat. The drapes were lit, too.

Evander was yanking the heavy drapes onto the floor, probably to stop the fire creeping up the walls. He jumped back as they came down, creating a small bonfire on the floor. He turned and pulled the blankets off the bed, putting them on top of them in an attempt to smother it. Fire was an unpredictable beast and could move to the ceiling at a moment's notice. Mr. Ambrose must know that too, for he was fighting the flames from the base of the blaze.

The drapes *were* still on fire, though, and would eventually catch the rug and floor beneath them. Thank God she'd come. It was contained, but barely. In a few minutes, it would have been out of control and beyond either of them.

Sarah dropped the buckets at his feet. He didn't even turn, just picked them up and threw them at the top of the fire, bringing it back down and drenching the wall. He probably thought she was Mrs. Green.

Sarah didn't wait, but ran back, meeting the boy halfway down the stairs with two more buckets. She gave her empty ones over.

"Is it working?" Alexander asked, his face a picture of horror.

"Yes, I think so," Sarah replied. "Where are your servants?"

"They go home to their families every night," he said.

So there was nobody to make sure the younger ones stayed put. "Keep the younger ones safe, will you?"

He nodded and ran back down with the empty buckets.

This would take more than her bringing him water. She would have to fight just as hard as he was if they were going to save the house. Help, if it came, would be too late. This was it. Sarah picked up a spare blanket and tried to smother the flaming drapes.

The smoke was clogging her throat, making her cough, making her eyes water. None of it mattered. Evander must have finally figured out it was her and not Alexander helping him.

"Get out, Sarah!" he yelled at her. "It's not safe." He had soot on his forehead and cheeks, his eyes red with smoke.

"Unlikely, Mr. Ambrose," she said. She took his empty buckets and ran out, to return only a few moments later with full ones again.

They worked hard and in silence, the only sound in the room the crackling of the fire and the whoosh of them dousing it. She would collapse soon. It was too much. Her throat was burning. His must be worse.

Still, they fought on, and eventually, miraculously, the wall fire was out, and now the water could be used on the drapes. They were taken care of within four buckets, and it was over.

The flames were out and all that was left were puddles and char and the hideously strong smell of burnt fabric and wood.

Sarah wiped a hand across her nose. "Goodness me. Are you all right?"

He stared at her, the green of his eyes so much brighter, surrounded by soot.

"Yes." His voice was rough. "But my throat hurts like the devil. You?"

"I'm fine." It was a lie. The burning in her throat was intense, and her eyes felt raw. But there was no way she would burden him with that on top of all of this.

But she couldn't have been more wrong.

"Liar." He drew her to him, holding her, with one large hand behind her head and the other pulling her close. "Thank you, Sarah. Everything would be gone without you."

She felt his lips press against the top of her head.

"You're welcome," she mumbled into his chest. She looked up at him, at the soot smudged all over his face. "You're filthy."

He looked down at her. "And you're pristine. How do you do that?"

"It's my angelic nature."

That made him laugh. "I think not so, devilish Mrs. Hayworth. Come, let's go outside and make sure my rabble of children are in one piece."

"They were sitting under a tree when I last saw them, with Fanny guarding them, wondering aloud how many rooms would burn."

He shook his head. "They've probably stolen my horse now and taken off in fear of me."

"Of you?" She couldn't imagine him being a strict father.

"Oh yes. And they should be in fear. One moment I was

relaxing with a book, all the boys safely in bed, and the very next moment, I was fighting a fire to save their lives and the house because they decided they should try to set off crackers in their bedroom. Firecrackers you had no idea they had or where they found them. And they must have stolen my flint to do it. So, theft *and* arson. Yes, I'm angry."

"Good Lord! I don't doubt it. So you have no idea where they got them?" Sarah said.

"I'm sure that will come to light quite soon." He was grim, and Sarah knew the boys had likely crossed a line previously uncrossed.

"Are they always so ingenious?"

"Stupid you mean?" He took her hand and led her from the room. "Not normally this stupid, but yes, normally quite stupid. I only thank the Lord I purchased all those extra buckets after the last incident."

There had been another incident? Sarah had *thought* there were a lot of buckets at the ready.

"I owe you a debt of gratitude bigger than I can ever repay," Mr. Ambrose said.

"Nonsense," Sarah said. "But it will take days to put their bedroom in order."

He looked around them, at the disaster that was the boys' bedroom. "I'll get some men from the village to help me. They're always grateful for extra labor."

They went outside, where the older boy was standing guard over the younger two, still beneath the tree. They all looked contrite.

"We're sorry, Papa," the elder one said.

"So sorry!" the younger two said together. None of the children looked much alike, but that often happened, she supposed.

He was their father. He was a widower. His life was, in fact, so much different from the one Sarah had attributed to him in the carriage that she felt abashed. If he had a curate taking care of some of his duties, it was probably so he could school and take care of his boys, not so he could squire around.

"You can be as sorry now as you like; the fact remains that you set fire to the house and endangered our lives." His voice was shaking, probably with a combination of anger, fear, and relief. Then he coughed a deep racking cough that suggested he'd taken in more smoke than she.

"And the house reeks," Sarah added. Now that the flames were out and the smoke almost gone, the sharp tang of burned wood and fabric was strong even outside. "Why don't you come stay with me at the cottage? It has plenty of room, and nobody need know for only one night. You can leave at dawn if you like. But it's late, and the boys need to be in bed." *And I want to keep an eye on you with that cough.*

"No, I…" He took a deep breath, then thought the better of refusing her. "Thank you."

She didn't know what had changed his mind, but she was glad something did. She nodded. "Excellent. I'll take the boys to the cottage while you gather some clean clothes and supplies. I'm sure they eat a lot." That would get him out of their way for a little while, and hopefully his temper would calm by the time he returned. Not that she feared for them, it was just she could see the boys were on the edge of panic and everybody needed some calm.

Mr. Ambrose strode back into the house, and she watched the boys look at each other in alarm. "Now we're going to catch it. I've never heard him this angry," said Benjamin, the middle-sized one.

"Maybe he'll use the strap on us like that old man at the schoolhouse did that time," the eldest one said.

Somebody had taken a strap to Evander's boys? There must have been consequences for whoever did it. Some would say the boys 'needed' it, but anyone who had experienced the strap as a child thought otherwise. Herself included.

"No, Alex, Papa would never do that!" The littlest one started crying again. This was about to become chaotic.

"Let's make our way over to the cottage, shall we?" Trying to be the voice of reason when she was almost collapsing from exhaustion herself wasn't easy.

The littlest one started crying in earnest now. "I'm cold," he said. "I can't walk."

"I suppose you are cold without your dressing gown on. But we'll be over there in a moment, you'll see. There now, get on my back, and hope that I don't fall over, big lump of a boy that you are. While we walk, tell me your names."

"I'm Alexander. I'm eight," the eldest said. "My younger brother Benjamin is five, and the littlest is Isaac. He just turned four."

So little to know such loss. And Alexander was trying to be brave and lead them, she could tell. "Alexander, you make sure Fanny is coming with us, and carry her if she looks tired."

Many were the times she'd carried her sister on her back when they returned from the village, especially when her boots had developed a horrible hole in them. This she could do. But not much more, if truth were told. But little Isaac didn't seem to care, scuttling up her like a monkey and molding himself onto her back. Within moments, his little head was resting on her shoulder, and his warm breath tickled her ear.

It felt lovely. His warmth and his very littleness touched her heart in ways she didn't want to examine closely. But her heart had other ideas and regrets. She had missed five years of closeness with Rebecca. Someone else had held her close and comforted her when she was scared. Thank goodness that person was her own mother.

She couldn't live with herself if it had been an unknown person.

The trip seemed much slower than it was when she raced

toward the fire, but eventually, they made it back, and Sarah put him down and opened the door.

"Come upstairs. The bath is full, and you will each have a quick bath before bed."

They replied in a chorus of 'No!'

She turned to them, one brow arched. "Truly? You have done nothing but cause havoc this evening. I think it best if you do as you are told, and now."

"But we've already washed today!" Alexander said. "And we weren't actually in the fire, so we're nowhere near as dirty as you."

Sarah looked at her hands, which were sooted black. "True enough, I suppose. Very well, you can get straight into bed then. Luckily you were wearing your bedclothes when you decided to play with crackers."

She led the way upstairs to her bedroom, not looking back to see if they were following, but hoping they were. Inside her room, they stood watching her, with gimlet little eyes. Not moving.

"Well now, this is my bed, and of course I have had a nice warm brick in it all night to warm it up. I would suggest that getting into bed before your father arrives *might* be a good idea."

She saw the moment comprehension dawned on them.

They jumped into bed and pulled the blankets up over their head, looking like a bundle of wiggling worms in the process.

She laughed, despite how tired she was and how much her hands, eyes, and throat hurt. "There now, I'm sure things will look better in the morning." *For all of us.*

How on earth did people do this every day? She was exhausted after an hour.

She closed the door and was halfway down the stairs when she heard the unmistakable sound of glass shattering in the bedroom.

After racing up the stairs, she opened the door, and the overpowering smell of jasmine and rose hit her even before she saw the perfume bottle broken in two neat pieces on the floor, the contents pooling on the floorboards.

Naughty. They'd spilled a fortune worth of perfume that she had carefully rationed for months.

Grabbing the bottle, she loomed over them, knowing she must look a scary fright. "Who did this??"

They were bundled up in the bed, pretending to be asleep. If she ever thought about her and children, it was a misty daydream of the way they'd be golden-haired little angels who would love nothing more than to listen to her sing them to sleep. Not of children getting up to so much mischief that they feigned sleep not to face the repercussions of their latest escapade.

No doubt the moment they closed their eyes they were hatching their next plan for world domination.

Heaven help her.

"I know you're not asleep. Now, which one of you heathens dropped my bottle of perfume?"

Alexander snored loudly.

Sarah growled under her breath. "Very well."

There was a noise on the stairs. She went to the door to see Mr. Ambrose at the bottom of the staircase. "What's very well?"

It seemed like the kind of thing that should be between her and the boys, so she made a quick decision not to tell him. After all, he didn't need anything else to be upset about.

"Oh, nothing," she said.

But he looked from her eyes to the broken bottle in her hand and back up again. She saw the dawn of comprehension. He knew exactly what had happened.

"I'll replace it," he said as he slowly climbed the stairs. "Boys! It's time to talk!"

She looked back at the children in her bed, who were huddled together, squeezing their eyes shut. Picking up the candle, Sarah closed the door to face their father on the landing.

He opened his mouth to say something, but she put a finger up to her lips. "Shhh. They're very sleepy. They are exhausted."

His eyes narrowed. "They're not asleep." He moved to open the door, but she swatted his hand away, then opened it a crack so he could see into the darkened room.

"I have brandy downstairs; can I interest you in a drop?"

He shook his head. "I'm too charged for that."

She closed the door on the boys. He did indeed seem coiled for action. The excitement of the night was still flowing in his veins. He had almost lost his house and feared for his children's lives too. No small thing.

"I'd normally suggest a ride on your favorite horse." Or perhaps the answer was in her medicine box, where she had a lovely vial of Valerian that would take the edge off any number of hysterical conditions. "Or maybe a brisk walk, or a glass of warm milk…"

"Or this," he said, leaning in, one hand braced on the door behind her, the other curling around her neck.

"Oh!" A tremor went through her as their lips met, and she knew one thing—nobody had ever kissed her like this. He pulled her to him and drew on her mouth like he was drowning and she was air. The flavor of him, smoke, and something sweet was hot in her mouth, the taste of him like a drug more potent than anything she had in her medicine chest.

She heard a groan and realized in horror that the sound came from her. The sound only made him kiss her deeper and hold her tighter. Everything she had made herself forget about being with a good man came rushing back. And all she wanted was to keep kissing him until they both forgot who they were and why it wasn't a good idea.

And he was certainly thorough—kissing her slowly until her toes started to curl. She relaxed into the kiss, not thinking about anything but the way his lips were hot and soft while the rest of him seemed implacable.

She let out a long sigh without meaning to, her knees buck-ling underneath her. He held her with one arm around her waist and the other in her hair, running his fingers through it as he continued to weave magic into her heart.

She returned the favor, tracing her fingers along his strong jaw. The hint of growth on his normally clean-shaven face was just another thing to mesmerize her.

He pulled away and trailed his lips up her neck, behind her ear, setting a blaze of sensation across her skin. She felt heavy and sleepy. He nuzzled in the curve of her neck, and surely, he could feel the pounding of her pulse there; it was so loud it was almost drowning out all thought.

"Your heart is racing," he murmured in her ear. He pulled back, looking at her in a confusion that was both endearing and flattering. "So is mine. What on earth was that?"

"A kiss, I believe. It seems you excel at it."

"Humph." He searched her face, looking for who knew what. He wouldn't find what he was looking for, that she'd wager.

"I apologize," he said stiffly. "This night has gotten the better of me."

"I understand," Sarah said and wrapped her arms around him, burying her face into his shoulder. "I was so scared for you all."

He shuddered, his shoulders quaking. She pulled back a little to see that his cheeks were wet.

She held him tighter, this big man who was responsible for so much. "Hush," she said. "It will look better in the morning". She led him toward the second bedroom. It was cold, the door having been shut from the warmth that filled the rest of the cottage. She shivered, and he got to work on the fireplace.

"This house only has two bedrooms, you know," he said, conversationally, placing smaller sticks under the bigger log.

"Oh." She hadn't thought about it when she issued the invita-tion for them to stay. "I will sleep downstairs in the parlor, then.

I'm smaller than you and more likely to be comfortable on the couch."

The fire crackled and jumped to life.

He turned to her, his face weary. "We've put you out enough already. Please take this bed."

She shook her head. "No. I shall see you in the morning."

They stared at each other for a long moment.

"Thank you for everything, Sarah." His voice was deep and gravelly, probably affected by the smoke, as hers was. All she knew was that the sound of it seemed to hum inside her.

She stayed at the door with her hand on the knob. "And thank you. I'm not likely to forget a kiss like that in a hurry."

He didn't say anything, and she liked to imagine it was because he was thinking 'me either'. But that would be crazy. He'd kissed her because he was overwhelmed and had too much roaring in his blood to do anything else with it. Another man would have tried to carry it further. But not her Mr. Ambrose.

Her Mr. Ambrose?

He would and should never be her Mr. Ambrose. But in the aftermath of such a stressful time, it was hard not to think of him that way.

But all she wanted to do was hold him to offer him comfort. She wanted to forget all those 'never again' promises she made to herself. But never again meant never again. So instead, she turned her back on him and left the room.

CHAPTER 18

IN WHICH FANNY'S ROTUNDNESS IS
EXPLAINED

The next morning, Sarah found Mr. Ambrose in the kitchen, pouring steaming water from a black kettle into the blue china teapot and looking very domesticated.

The notebook she left in church sat in the middle of the table. Her eyes flew to his, finding him looking at her with an amused expression. "Yours, I believe? I had it in my coat pocket. I don't make a habit of being angry at my congregation you know."

He sounded defensive, perhaps misunderstood.

She shrugged. "I stand by what I said, fire and brimstone Mr. Ambrose is *very* fetching."

His cheeks flared with spots of red, a sure sign she'd reached him. "That you find me fetching when I am showing my worst inclinations...I'm not sure what to make of it."

She shrugged. "Perhaps that I see you as you are, not as others would have you? Honesty and no pretensions, as we agreed."

Fanny had found her spot on the warm stones next to the hearth. Her little tail thumping when she saw Sarah. She patted her, and Fanny snorted and snuffled, pushing her head into Sarah's hand while groaning in happiness.

"Isn't she funny?" Sarah said. "What a dear little dog."

"The boys adore her," Mr. Ambrose said. He was wearing a fresh linen shirt, tucked into buckskin breeches. The everyday clothing suited him well, the breeches hugging his long, lean legs, and the sleeves of the shirt rolled up to display muscular forearms. The kitchen was small but had a clean hearth that looked serviceable. How many afternoons had she watched her mother bake scones on a griddle just like it? How many songs had Mother requested she sing, even from the age of five, while she worked? It was unlikely Mr. Ambrose would ask her to sing for him. She smiled at the thought.

"Tea," she said. "It smells nice and strong."

"That's because it is, Mrs. Hayworth," he said simply and brought the teapot over to the rustic wooden table that looked as though it had served many a meal.

She sat at the table, her head in one hand. "Don't you think that after everything we went through last night, we might call each other by our given names?"

He stopped mid pour and considered her, his eyes twinkling. "You mean that battling a fire together puts us on more intimate terms?"

"I think perhaps kissing me into oblivion puts us on more intimate terms."

He pretended to ponder it. "I think you may be right." He finished pouring and placed the cup in front of her. "Your tea, Sarah."

"Thank you, Evander."

She watched as a slow blush crept up his neck. He quickly poured his own. "My grandmother always preferred to eat here, near the hearth. Do you mind?"

"Not at all. It's a lovely view into the back garden." She drank some tea and looked out at the view. Snow had fallen overnight and covered everything in sight. "Oh."

He put his teacup down. "What?"

"Look at the snow!" Large flurries fell as far as the eye could see and had settled over the garden making it look like it was covered in white fondant. "Do you think we're snowed in?"

He rose and looked out the window. "If not now, we will be soon," he replied. "This hasn't happened in five years, but it's not unheard of hereabouts. We could still make it, if we leave now."

He sounded reluctant. It could be because he didn't want to brave the storm or because he wanted to stay with her?

"You're not going out in that with your wee ones. You'll all catch your death!" The very thought of trying to travel even the shortest distance in a snowstorm was foolhardy. "You're not going anywhere this morning." If he needed an excuse to stay, she had just given him one. "I'm thinking of making a pot of porridge. Would your boys like that?"

"If you put enough honey and cream on it, yes. Mrs. Green certainly won't travel in this weather and neither should she." He seemed unconcerned by the snow problem or perhaps just ignoring the situation it put them in. He also seemed unfazed by the kiss, although it was all she could think about every time she looked at him. Or even when she wasn't looking at him. What was she supposed to do, ignore that it happened? Perhaps he thought that nobody need ever find out he and the boys had stayed over if the snow stopped them discovering it. Perhaps he saw this as a blessing.

She finished her tea and found a pot the right size, added water, and put it on the hook to warm.

It would feel good to stir something over a hot stove for a while. Very calming. And even *she* couldn't mess up porridge. She found everything she needed, which was really just oats and milk, and set about it.

It was just starting to thicken when there was a thumping in the hall.

"Get ready," Evander said simply.

They burst into the room like the firecrackers they'd set off the night before. The awkwardness was over. For now.

"Slow down," Evander said, and they instantly straightened.

"Benjamin was going to see if there were any biscuits or cake," Alexander said.

"Was not."

"Well there isn't," Evander said. "But if you come and sit politely at the table, Mrs. Hayworth might just share some of her breakfast with you."

She stopped stirring, turned, and smiled at them. "I make excellent porridge."

Alexander looked over at his father. "Sometimes Papa cooks for us."

She could imagine him cooking, funnily, which was not a notion she'd ever had about a man before. "What does he cook?"

"Toast," Benjamin said. "We love to sit in front of the fire and toast our bread and then put butter on it."

The image of them sitting around the fire eating toast together, maybe laughing, licking butter off their fingers was vivid. It was all very domestic and in a far less pompous way than he was probably raised himself. He was raising his boys the way he wanted to raise them, rather than the way their station would dictate.

"That sounds delicious," Sarah replied, letting the oats cook while the boys scraped back their chairs and sat at the table.

It felt...she wasn't sure what she was feeling. Warm? All the traveling over all those years, and nothing had felt like home until this very moment, in this little cottage in the middle of a snowstorm. Obviously, she was easy game for even the slightest family intimacies. Hopefully, they wouldn't try to enact the scene or she might pass out from overwhelm.

Sarah served their breakfast with a generous spoon of honey and cream on top of each bowl.

"And a big bowl for your Papa Bear," she said, putting a bowl in front of Evander.

"Papa Bear! Papa Bear!" the boys chanted, delighted by the pet name.

Alexander put his spoon in the porridge and tasted it. He screwed his nose up, but valiantly smiled at Sarah. "Delicious!" Then he considered her closely. "Maybe you could be our Mama and cook for us every day."

It was said with a tone of wistfulness that broke her heart a little. They were too small to know such loss.

"You're pretty, too," Benjamin added solemnly. "Papa, don't you think she's pretty?"

My goodness, they were laying it on as thick as butter on toast. A total onslaught. Almost as if they'd decided what they wanted on their way down the stairs and were now setting about it.

Papa needed a wife, and she had conveniently appeared, so she would do.

"Yes, very," Evander said, conversationally, and she would almost think he didn't mean it but for the slightly pained expression on his face. "But she's not for the likes of us Benjamin boy. Mrs. Hayworth—"

"Sarah, please, let them call me Sarah."

He nodded. "Sarah is a famous opera singer and spends lots of time in Italy and London."

"We could go with her!" Alexander said.

Sarah smiled at Evander, wondering how on earth he was going to extricate himself from this. Because one thing was definite, she would make a positively hideous mother—no matter how good her porridge was.

History could tell you that.

~

Evander looked at Sarah, sitting across from him with a smudge of honey on her cheek. He wanted to reach out and gently thumb it away. They were wrong. She wasn't pretty, she was utterly beautiful, sitting at his breakfast table with that glowing smile.

The problem was, who wouldn't want her to stay? Who wouldn't want her to be the Mama Bear, even if she was only with them a few months a year?

Maybe?

He shook himself. What a ridiculous notion. What would the parishioners, no worse, the *entire clergy* of the Church of England make of the vicar who took an opera singer to wife. An infamous one. A woman who might accept him, not because she wanted to settle down with him and his family, but because it would save her the trouble of looking for another paramour.

Desperate, desperate.

But at least it made him realize the source of his despondency. He was lonely. Madly lonely.

So he needed to leave the lovely opera singer alone and find himself a wife.

A real one. Not one who would only stay if she was snowed in and had no other choice.

"Ah yes, I'm sure you'd just love to miss all your lessons and traipse around Italy. No. You will stay here and enjoy Sarah's company while she is here, and write letters to her when she is gone. She might never be your Mama Bear, but I'm sure she would be open to being friends."

He glanced up at her in time to see her eyes were watery and her brows drawn together in something that looked suspiciously like admiration.

Don't look at me like that, Sarah. I want you more than they do.

"Plus," he added, "it will do you good to practice your script. I might even let you use my quill."

The boys argued about that for a few minutes, and he mouthed 'sorry' to her.

"I would love more friends, and especially ones who will write to me when I'm in Venice."

Alexander put down his spoon. "Where's that?"

"In Italy. One day when you are older, you will all go on a Grand Tour and visit."

"Will we see you there?"

"Only if I'm still singing. My voice will probably have given out by then. But if I am, I will give you all a box to sit in and watch."

Only Alexander didn't look thrilled, and Evander knew it was because he was still trying to find a way to get Sarah to stay right where she was. He, of all the boys, perhaps because he was the eldest, missed his mother the most. Evander had seen the way he looked longingly at mothers and their children when they visited the village.

He would have to try to find someone. Until this moment, he hadn't realized how much it was affecting them.

He looked at Sarah, who was now telling a story about a dog she found in Naples, a little black dog who was lost on the street without a collar or an owner in sight. She wrapped them around her story, with the dog's bravery dodging carriages and stealing a meat stick from the vendor at the marketplace. He was about to receive a beating for that offense when Sarah stepped in to save him, paying the vendor twice what he would earn in return for what the little mutt took.

"We had a brave dog too," Benjamin said. "His name was Clyde. He was the best dog in the world."

"Has he gone to heaven now?" Sarah said.

The boys all nodded. "Maybe," said Benjamin. And only Evander knew how much grief was behind those quiet words. "He ran away."

"But what is the good news, boys?" Evander said, trying to inject some levity to the breakfast table.

It worked; they all brightened. "Fanny is having puppies!"

"Puppies!" Sarah said. "That explains her large belly." Thank goodness she'd gotten the dog out early the night before. She wouldn't have been able to live with herself if she'd been hurt.

"When is that to happen? Do we know?" She would love to see a litter of those dear little pugs rolling around.

"In the next month," Evander said.

"We have Grandpapa's kennel keeper on alert to come and help Fanny, should she need it," Alexander said with pride. "I organized it."

"An excellent idea. I'm sure he has seen the birth of many pups. Fanny will be in good hands."

"I would point out that I have also seen the birth of many pups. If, for some reason, Arnold cannot attend, I promise you Fanny will be well taken care of." Evander's voice was the voice of authority, and each boy was in rapt attention, believing him, trusting him.

And, in that moment, Sarah knew that Evander Ambrose was not the kind of man who made promises lightly. And when he did make them, they were forged in his lifeblood. Whether it was about a litter of puppies or raising a child.

She shuddered. Men like him, made with conviction and honor, were not only rare, they were impossible to sway, impossible to lead. Not exactly the type of man she normally gravitated to. If *he* gave a woman a diamond, it would be real, and it would be forever.

Fanny was a lucky dog.

<h1 style="text-align:center">CHAPTER 19</h1>

<h2 style="text-align:center">WHERE ANY EXCUSE TO STAY TOGETHER
WILL DO</h2>

The snow continued, a gentle layering over the land, coming through in drifts that climbed further and further up the door of the cottage. Evander sat in the corner, reading Gulliver's Travels by the fire, and the boys had an old toy box they pulled from a cupboard and were very busy rediscovering its contents.

Sarah, on the other hand, was at a complete stop. What did one do with the whole day ahead and no activities planned, no work to do, no parts to rehearse and prepare for? This was the time most women would pull out a basket of knitting or embroidery.

She found herself oddly out of step with the world and decided perhaps she'd sit by the window and watch the snow. It was calming and peaceful, a soft white quilt over the entire countryside.

"I wonder..." Evander said. "...if you would teach the boys something to sing for my father at the musicale. Is that something you could do?"

"Oh, Papa, no," Benjamin said. "You will make us wear those

frilly things and those itchy breeches and those silly shoes with the buckles."

"Yes," his father said. "I believe I will."

All three boys started wailing and complaining about itchy breeches and frilly shirts.

"Your grandfather will love it, so complain all you like; it's going to happen. I'm sure Sarah knows a suitable song."

"We don't want to sing a girl's song." Alex looked at Sarah, bashful. "I beg your pardon, Mrs. Hayworth."

"No offense taken," Sarah replied.

"We like rude songs," Benjamin said.

"And where would you learn such songs?" Evander asked them, innocently.

"Jem. He tells us," Benjamin replied, over the whispered warnings of his elder brother.

That would be the same Jem who Evander had tried to find work for, who left job after job even with a large family to feed. She had an inkling things might not go so well for Jem if he was teaching the vicar's son's rude songs.

Evander's glare suggested the boys were going to get another talking to, very soon on the heels of the one she'd overheard earlier regarding the fire. There wasn't a dry eye that had come into the parlor after that.

"I shall have a talk to Jem. I hardly think that ribald songs are appropriate for the sons of a vicar."

His chosen occupation was hardly their fault. "Oh, did you never sing ribald tunes when you were a lad?"

"Never," he replied.

Sarah shrugged. "I know any number of rude songs. There is nothing especially interesting about them." It was like saying there was nothing interesting about a box of sweets; their ears pricked up, and suddenly, they crouched in front of her chair with eager looks on their faces.

"Will you teach them to us?"

"When you are twenty-one and no sooner," she answered with a smile. "I do not want to get on the wrong side of your father. The song I'm about to teach you is as pure as the snow sitting outside our door. You will sound like angels."

They all groaned in horror. She was fast coming to understand they were nothing like the little sisters she had left behind. "And in your pretty frilly shirts, you will look like angels too."

They groaned twice as loud, and she met Evander's annoyed glare with a sparkling smile.

"You're not helping," he said.

"I never said I was going to," she replied. She turned to the boys. "Very well, if we must sing a horrible frilly shirt song, we'll sing this one first. It has enough blood and gore in it to keep you happy, and I have an inkling that your grandfather would love to hear you sing it anyway. Most people don't pick up on the blood and gore. See if you can find it. It is called Down in Yon Forest."

It was a special song, probably from the renaissance, although it felt like it might be even older. It was slow and mysterious and never failed to capture her. She'd learned it from her first singing instructor, who'd said it was from the time of the crusades and knights of the round table.

She quietly started to sing it for them, pulling them into the story, getting them to think about the words and about the way the lilting rhythm added to the mystery.

Down in the forest, there stands a hall,
The bells of Paradise, I heard them ring.
It's covered all over with purple so tall.
And I love my Lord Jesus above anything.
In that high hall, there stands a bed,
The bells of Paradise, I heard them ring
Is covered all over with scarlet and red
And I love my Lord Jesus above anything.

All in that bed, there lies a knight
The bells of Paradise, I heard them ring
Whose wounds they do bleed with main and with might.
And I love my Lord Jesus above anything...

SHE KEPT SINGING THE VERSES, and for a moment, she was twelve again, standing in a dusty hall and singing the very same song as part of a Christmas choral group. She'd dreamed of that small hall, gray-stoned, in the middle of a dark green forest. It was so real she could almost hear the bells. And when she looked at those little boys, she could tell the words were creating something similar for them. The haunting tune, and the evocative words. It was powerful stuff for a child to sing.

"That's beautiful," Evander said, but the emotion in his eyes suggested he truly had been moved.

"Something for everyone," she replied and proceeded to introduce them to the lyrics, and then once she'd written them out, taught the boys to sing the entire thing in rounds.

It was one way to fill an entire afternoon without picking up an embroidery needle.

They were adept learners, their sweet high voices telling her they sang in church often. They had a natural harmony that was so appealing. The earl was going to love it.

Evander had stopped pretending to read his book about half an hour before, engrossed in their learning as much as they were. But the boys were tiring now, forgetting words and becoming irritable when they did. They had almost mastered it, but enough was enough.

"Boys," Evander said. "I'm very proud of the way you have focused on learning the song this afternoon. You have done well."

"Wonderful, aren't they?" Sarah agreed with a smirk.

"Papa," Benjamin ventured, probably realizing in his clever

way that now was the perfect time. "You know that we are truly sorry for the fire. We will never use crackers again without you."

"I know," Evander said.

"Can you love us again?"

She watched him take a deep breath and knew it was from them not understanding just how very much he did love them. "Of course. Let's not be angry with each other."

He knelt and drew them all into a big messy embrace. Legs and arms and heads knocked together. Sarah laughed. *Well, my work here is done.*

"Let's play hide-and-go-seek!"

And they did, romping around the cottage with more high jinx than should ever be had when the weather outside was so very miserable.

She hadn't played like this since she was a child herself and felt every bit as excited by it as she had then. And what was the harm in enjoying them while she was here? They were hardly likely to get attached to her after one game.

CHAPTER 20

WHERE NOBODY FORCED THEM TO STAY

Evander hadn't known what to expect when Sarah offered to teach the boys a song. But if anything, he'd assumed it would be something fun. Something he would have to unteach them after she left. Like an aunt that delighted in instilling naughty things.

But he'd done her a disservice because she'd taught the boys a hymn that would keep them happy with its adult lyrics but would also make his father cry, he knew, because it had brought tears to *his* eyes when he heard it. Somehow she'd done something to keep everyone happy, and the next thing he knew, he was reunited with the boys and feeling better with the world than he had in forever.

Days ago, when he'd been in her audience after dinner, he had attributed her skills to clever manipulation. But here, there was no reason for her to manipulate the situation. Nothing to win, no one to impress. Just the local vicar and his three misbehaving sons. And yet the result had been the same. She had touched them all and made them feel their hearts again.

The boys were exhausted after the hide-and-go-seek, which

carried on long after he and Sarah tired, and they had made a quick meal of ham with bread and cheese.

Isaac had sat on her lap and let her feed him custard in a way he'd not let Evander do in ages, and Benjamin asked her to read Gulliver's Travels to him. The boys sat in rapt attention on the bed while she read them the story. It was the chapter where Gulliver met the yahoos and she half scared them out of their minds even though he was sure he'd read it to them before. He stood at the door, leaning on the jamb, watching them, taking in the scene of the boys behaving like little gentlemen, scrubbed clean and in their nightgowns, with Sarah so engrossed in the story that she didn't even see him in the door.

He backed away quietly and went to the kitchen and the relative safety of washing up.

It wasn't hard to see what was happening. To him and his boys. And, he told himself with compassion, it was only to be expected. She was beautiful, too beautiful to be confined to such a small space. But to have her trapped here, even for a short time, was like having a butterfly in a glass jar. Mesmerizing, breathtaking, but not sustainable for either the butterfly or one's own moral conscience.

Evander went to the back door with the lantern, checking on the snow level. The night was quiet and calm, no snow or biting wind, just the kind of cold air that bit one's nose with its frost. He kicked the snow. It was soft and easy to move. He could go for a walk to the village early in the morning, tamping down the path on his way. He could. But he wouldn't. Instead, he would eke out every last minute of this little holiday. It was cozy and he wasn't afraid to admit that he liked it.

When he came back in, Sarah was there, picking up a cloth to help him.

"I think they'll go to sleep quickly," she said. "Or at least I hope they will."

"I'll check on them. Thanks for reading the story."

"Everyone deserves a little break now and then, even if it is only to do the dishes." She laughed at the pile he'd made.

He motioned to the back door. "I think we'll be able to get out about midday tomorrow if there's no more snow."

"Do you think they've been snowed in at the big house too?"

"Perhaps, but they have sleigh runners for all the carriages and plenty of staff to tamp down the snow to reach the outhouses."

"I've enjoyed the enforced quiet."

"Quiet? With those three tearing around?" He didn't really know what she thought of the boys. Were they fraying her last nerve, or was she as easy with them as she seemed? It occurred to him that he knew nothing about her and her feelings on any number of subjects from the most important to the most trivial. He did, however, feel like he was getting the real Sarah here at the cottage, not the opera singer, not the performer, and not the woman trying to catch a husband.

He was strangely complimented by the thought because he was quite sure not many saw it.

"Relative quiet, then," she acknowledged with a mischievous smile.

"Relative to what? A taproom brawl?"

She laughed, and that made him happy. Would he still be this happy when she left? Or would she take that happiness with her?

She put the dishcloth down and picked up a bottle of wine from the rack. "Burgundy?"

He nodded. "If it's not vinegar Who knows how long it's been there." He got two glasses from the cupboard. "Shall we adjourn to the parlor?"

She smiled naughtily. "Or shall we adjourn to the thick carpet in front of the fireplace and enjoy the glow?"

He could be naughty too when he forgot his responsibilities for a moment. And this night was probably the night he could do it. No possible visitors, children soon to be asleep and a beautiful woman sitting on a rug with him.

"The carpet it is," he said, following her to the parlor.

Once they settled, she hugged her glass, taking sips and looking into the fire. It was comfortable, but not quite comfortable enough. There was still a slight draught. He got a lap rug from the chair and laid it over her shoulders. She pulled it close, wrapping her arms tightly around her chest. "Thanks."

"Tell me all about your family," he said, because he'd been wanting to know since he'd seen her dangling from that moon, and this would probably be the best and last time he would have the chance to ask.

She glanced over, her eyes bright with something he couldn't interpret, and then looked back at the fire. The moment stretched out, and he wondered if she was ever going to say something.

"When I look back, I realize we were poor," she said, her gaze far away. "There was a lot of turnip and swede soup, and not a lot of meat unless we wanted to lose another chicken. We had eggs though, and Mother knew a hundred ways to cook them."

"Your father was a farmer?"

She raised her eyebrows in surprise. "No! Father was and still is a vicar. It's just that the living is quite a poor one. There are no lands attached like you have, and certainly no inherited lands."

A vicar! It was all he could do to hide his astonishment. She truly had been gently raised then, as his mother had suggested. But not in wealth. No wonder she had seemed to understand more about the clergy than a lady normally would.

"My mother seemed to know of your family when she said she expected better from you. How is that?"

She started a little. "She must have a very good memory. Yes, my mother was the niece of the Earl of Ravenhall. She had a season in London and would be the same age as your mother, I think. Perhaps they met? Then there was a small scandal attached to her name and an even smaller dowry that meant the only man to offer for her was the local vicar, much to the family's disdain."

He nodded in understanding. "But how did you come to sing opera from those beginnings?"

"I was sixteen when an opera company passed through our little village. They weren't performing, but came to church and heard me singing there. They offered to take me on and teach me to sing. Of course my father said no, but at the time, I could see no way out of our situation, and when they told me the money I might make singing opera, well, that made up my mind. I escaped during the night and planned to send money back to my parents and save my family." She picked some fluff from her sleeve, as though detached from the story.

He gleaned from her tone that the plan had not quite worked. "What went wrong?"

She shrugged. "Just everything. My parents disowned me, the opera company I was supposed to sing with was little more than dancing girls lifting their skirts, and there was precious little musical instruction." She laughed at her own naivety, speaking lightly, but something about the way her shoulders slumped told him the wounds were still there. "What did you do?"

She nodded. "I did the only thing I knew. I sang. And, wouldn't you know it, there is a market in London for young and pretty sixteen-year-olds who can sing."

"And who look and sound like ladies," he added.

"Yes. I left them in London and was lucky to come across the manager of the ensemble at Vauxhall before I came across any of the madams there. My story may have been vastly different otherwise."

She was opening up to him, perhaps as a consequence of the long hours they'd spent together, but he got the impression that this wasn't something she did lightly, if ever. The words were cautious at first, but the more he nodded and silently listened, the more she relaxed.

"So you sang at the Gardens? That must have been fun."

"It was." She took a sip of wine. "Fireworks and romance and hunger, because I never had enough shillings to buy food. I suppose if I look back, it was shallow entertainment, but at sixteen, it was like the moon and the stars all in one garden. I met Gianni five minutes after I arrived. He was a violinist in the orchestra and let me sit with them when he heard how much I loved music. He made sure I never went down the dark walks and got me my audition for the orchestra. When he was to leave England, he told me I wouldn't last a day in London on my own and took me with him to Italy."

"As his lover?"

She laughed. "He had no interest in English girls. He was more like a brother, I suppose. In fact, when he met me, he said I reminded him of his sister back home. It was the luckiest turn of events in my life. I was welcomed into his family, who are a prominent musical family in Naples. For some reason I'll never understand, they paid for my musical education, and well, when you can sing, the rise can be quite fast. I was playing lead roles in regional towns in Italy by the time I was eighteen, and La Scala by twenty-three. I stayed there for almost five years. I owe him everything."

It was hard to believe that her life in Italy had been that easy. More like she didn't want to let him into the struggles she'd faced. But perhaps it was true, and he hoped, for her sake, that it was. "That sounds like a blessed turn of events. Where is he now?"

She smiled softly, her eyes far away. "Still living in Naples, probably playing his violin, happily married with three children. We don't write as often as we used to."

"And your family?"

"Ah, my family. They are still in Upminster. I send money, all that I have to spare. I think they are doing well."

She sent them all she had to spare? It once again sounded like she struggled for money when he knew that she earned a great deal, and didn't seem the kind to spend it frivolously. "I don't understand how a singer of your repute can be struggling for shillings."

She sighed deeply. "Easily when you invest in the 'change' and it all goes bad. I had enough to retire, and I was a week too late removing my funds. The scheme collapsed, many people far richer than I lost more—but for me, it was everything. I had to start again. All over again."

And for a woman on her own, that must have been devastating. Little wonder she hoped to find a husband. Although he couldn't help feeling that might not be the right answer for her. "Couldn't your parents help you, after you have helped them for so long?"

She shook her head. "You can't expect them to own me. I am long since ruined. The vicar's daughter, an opera singer!"

"Actually, I do expect them to do just that." He knew, in his heart though, that it would be virtually impossible for a vicar in a perilous financial position to do anything that could alienate his patron. But he was still outraged on her behalf.

"Says the man whose position in society is set by the circumstances of his birth. Not everyone has that luxury, and I'm sure you know that. They have six other children to think of." She looked into her glass as though to find solace there. "They have made the right decision."

But Evander wasn't ready to let it go. "Then they shouldn't take your money. It's hypocritical."

"They have very good reason to take it. But what of you?" she asked, skilfully changing the topic. "You have obviously been struggling since your wife died."

"I'm perfectly fine."

But she wasn't happy with that, her eyebrow arching and a sardonic gleam in her eye. "Of course. Perfectly fine. Three children, no wife and, if I'm not mistaken, a crisis of vocation, no?"

He breathed in a shocked breath. Good Lord, she truly did see right through him. "What on earth would make you say that?" he said lazily. He couldn't take offense at her insight. He was too relaxed.

"I don't know. Maybe it was the way you told your congregation that they should be responsible for their own moral decisions?"

"And shouldn't they? I'm sure the Lord would have no problems with that statement."

"I have no idea what the Lord would think. I'm only saying that your vocation does not seem to be fitting you very well at the moment. Did losing her dent your faith in God?"

Ah, faith. One moment you have it, the same way you have an arm or a leg, never questioned, taken for granted. But then, just when you need it most, that soft firelight inside is drowned out by a storm, it's banks eroded by a river of grief. To think he'd thought his faith would get him through losing Eleanor. Now it was hard to tell if there was anything left at all. It felt hollow.

"Did losing your entire family dent yours?" he countered, because he'd rather not answer her question.

He stared into her eyes—they were deep blue with the flickering of the firelight dancing in them.

She looked away and shrugged. "I lost God so long ago I'm sure he's forgotten I was ever there."

"I doubt he has forgotten you. You're quite loud."

She turned back, and he was glad to see the sparkle in her eyes. "I am, aren't I?"

"But it's true." He put down his glass and pulled his knees up to hug them. She must have recognized the defensiveness of the movement because she pulled a pillow onto her lap and beckoned for him to lie down and lay his head on it.

Oh. He would *definitely* do that. He would spill all his secrets if she would just run her fingers through his hair a little. It was quite innocent, really.

Maybe he'd been wrong all this time, not pursuing a wife if this was how it felt. It would be wonderful if life could feel like this.

Because when she kissed him, the worries of his world dropped away and for those brief moments…

He lay down, his head on the pillow, her fragrance, light and sweet, wrapping around him like a blanket. And then her long fingernails raked through his hair in such an exquisite way he thought he might die.

"Now, what is true?"

"That perhaps I have gone to heaven," he said.

Her hands stilled. "That's not what you were going to say."

CHAPTER 21

IN WHICH THE COST OF A DEEP DARK SECRET
IS CHEAP

It was quite obvious that Evander had not had close contact in an age. She watched as the pulse on his neck leapt each time she touched his hair and could swear she felt his heartbeat hammering near her leg.

He was so different from the men of her acquaintance.

If she were silly enough to allow herself into a position like this with them, they would take advantage of her. Evander, she knew, was desperately trying to hide how she affected him.

And probably had been since they first met. But she did affect him; she was sure of it now. He had reached the point where he could not hide it.

Much like her, really. The urge to take him in her arms was strong but not to be indulged.

"After Eleanor died, my faith was so strong for a few hours, thinking God was close, that he was holding me and my boys, but then…"

He paused, and she realized she had stopped her light touch on his head. "Go on."

"I find I can only go on if you continue to move your hands."

"I see. How convenient. Very well, Mr. Ambrose—"

"Evander."

"Very well, Evander, I will rub your head, and you will tell me the extent to which you have fallen." She ran her fingers lightly through his hair, which was no chore. It was thick, dark, and wavy, as soft as ermine and as dangerous to her restraint as a box of bon-bons.

He closed his eyes again. "Then it was just gone. Thinking that Eleanor was in heaven was no comfort when I was so angry that she should be there at all. She should have been here. And God abandoned me, too. I used to feel a kind of companionship with him, like I was a trusted servant. Now. Nothing. Just me, wandering from day to day and trying to be a good father and failing, and trying to be a good shepherd of my flock, and failing. And then I look up and realize that all the belief I had was just fair-weather faith. At the first sign of trouble, it was gone. And it's very hard to be a vicar when you've been shaken like that."

"And it makes you wonder how strong it was to start with."

"Exactly," he agreed softly.

"Or," she said after a moment's thought. "Perhaps you have been struggling through grief just like any normal person would. You would have seen your fair share of grief, I'm sure?"

"True. It affects people differently and for different lengths of time. It's not predictable."

"So you could say that grief, one of the hardest things for a person to go through, especially when the person lost was so young and meant so much, could do strange things to a person."

He nodded. "Very strange."

"And that it would be perfectly acceptable to become lost for any amount of time, because such things are not predictable."

"But what if it is gone forever?" His voice was quiet and level, as though he were controlling himself.

How could she answer that?

"Then you shall have to go find it again. And it may look

different, and it may feel different, but our lives keep changing too. Does anything ever stay the same?"

"I suppose." He did not sound convinced.

"That is the wisest advice I have ever given and all you can say is 'I suppose'?" Sarah pulled the lobe of his ear, unwittingly discovering that it was velvety soft. "Outrageous. You know, many men in our fair church have little or no interest in religious matters or their faith. It's not like you would be alone."

He sat up. "They are not me. It's not about the job, Sarah, it's about me. I don't feel like me anymore."

His gaze was distracted by the log burning low on the fire, and he got up to add another and poke the logs around.

"You will *have* to be content with a new you. Those days before your loss are gone. You cannot recapture that innocence."

"Thank you for that happy thought." He sat next to her again, running a hand through his hair.

She took his hand in her own. "You cannot recapture them, but do you want to? Do you want to continue to live in that bubble where nothing bad happens to you without knowing how strong you are and what you are capable of?"

He looked at her, his hand still in hers, his eyes candid and devastated. "I am broken, Sarah. Her death broke me."

She shrugged, but squeezed his hand a little tighter. "Perhaps. Broken and lost, and nobody would blame you for that. But at your core," she lifted her hand and his over his chest. "Can you not feel that you are whole? That there is light inside you, goodness in you, no matter what happens to you and no matter how much you lose? I see it. Even in your kindness to me, me, whom nobody ever helps or supports. You came to my side and knew I needed help, no matter how brave my face."

"Well, I'm not sure if you know, but you have this certain expression when you are anxious…"

He was missing her point. "I most certainly do not. I am known to be a superior actress."

He smiled slightly. "You suck on your bottom lip, I'm sure of it." Having told her the truth of his situation, it seemed he was now trying to change the topic.

"That's hardly an unusual expression. Perhaps I do that all the time."

"I first noticed it with Morley after the opera, then at dinner, and most recently after your escapade with Lady Beatrix."

Goodness, he had been closely watching her since they met. That indifferent facade was just that–a facade. And it couldn't be true in any case. She was known for her calm expression, no matter what was happening. "Well, I don't know about that. I've never noticed that I do it, and you're the first person to tell me. In any case, I was trying to give you a compliment, to reassure you."

"Compliment accepted," he said and let go of her hand to lie on his side, resting his head in his hand. "Now that you know I have been watching you closely, will you tell me what the trouble is? I know there is the money issue, but you can surely earn more of that over time. So what is it?"

She turned to him and smiled so brilliantly that hopefully he would forget his question. "Really, Evander, I would tell you if there were something seriously wrong. There is not. I am merely contemplating my next course of direction."

He may have poured his heart out to her—but her secrets were so very lowering. He would look at her differently, how could he not? Pregnant by an Italian prince who didn't love her, didn't want to marry her, and wanted nothing to do with her child. Even Gianni and his family had distanced themselves from her when they realized she was with child. Then when she did get home, she knew nobody would employ her if they thought she had an illegitimate child waiting for her in the dressing room, so she gave the child up.

Gave her up. It still hurt to think about her sweet and trusting one-year-old face. Did she know to miss her mother now? At five, she was old enough now to wonder, to long for that connection. She would have longer hair now; it would be a riotous mop of dark Italian curls. How she ached to see it.

"Nothing wrong," he repeated.

"Not a thing."

He shook his head, possibly in frustration because he knew her well enough now to understand that she was keeping something from him.

He lifted her hand to his mouth and pressed a kiss on it. "Then I will bid you good night. Life is too short to charm the secrets out of a woman who will never be mine in any case." He stood, and without looking back, left the room.

CHAPTER 22

Sarah waited for Evander to come back.

He did not. She waited until the candle gutted, but the house was quiet, so he must have fallen asleep.

Was he upset with her?

And if he was, why did the thought make her stare at the ceiling instead of sleeping? The couch felt lumpy and hard tonight.

Certainly, they had become friends, but that did not mean she would make him privy to the most private parts of her life. And yet it had been so hard not to tell him everything about Rebecca and see if he could come up with any better ideas than she could. But she had silenced herself, and he knew it. He had left one of his shirts on the back of the chair, so she put it on, knowing it was wrong to do so, but was comforted by his scent and the thought he had worn the shirt. The linen was worn, soft, and so comfortable.

Perhaps because of that, she slept soundly, only waking when a bird started chirping on her windowsill at an ungodly hour. She threw a pillow at the window, but that only made it louder, in a slightly more outraged chirp.

But the gray morning light had clarified things. She needed to get Evander and family back to their house or up to the main house as soon as possible before she blurted secrets that would make him look at her with disappointment. She could bear anything, but not that.

She put on her dressing gown over his shirt, pushed her feet into her slippers, and went to the kitchen.

It was unfortunate that she was in clear view of the window when Mr. Pinlock's head popped up at the window, peering inside. He waved madly when he saw her, his eyes round with urgency.

She went to the front door and opened it, about to give him a very polite but pointed refusal of entry, when she noticed he was not alone, and the identity of the other caller, well known to her, was enough to have her quaking in her pink slippers.

Stay upstairs, Evander. Please stay upstairs.

EVANDER HEARD the doorknocker and pushed himself out of bed to go and see who was calling. *Please do not be Father.* He was partway down the stairs when he realized Sarah had already answered the door. His curate was standing behind another clergyman and not just any clergyman, but the Archbishop of Canterbury.

"Your Grace, it is an unexpected pleasure to see you again." Sarah curtsied deeply. She was wearing her dressing gown, velvet pink, with bows at the elbows. Her hair was up in a makeshift bun.

His heart fell into his boots. The Archbishop of Canterbury? *Of all the people to visit.* And Sarah knew him? Strange. Or perhaps not strange since opera singers certainly found their way into the highest of stratospheres.

"Not so unexpected for me, Mrs. Hayworth. This fool chased

my carriage as I was coming through the village. Then he proceeded to regale me with Banbury tales about a fire at Mr. Ambrose's house, and the fact that he suspected Mr. Ambrose had taken shelter with you." He turned to Mr. Pinlock. "Go, now. You've done your damage, but if I hear you spreading false rumors, I will become personally involved. Mr. Ambrose's father is a dear friend of mine."

Mr. Pinlock reversed course, bowing and scraping, his large wide-brimmed black hat plastered to his chest like a shield.

"Oh dear," Sarah said weakly.

She turned, her eyes wide when she saw Evander on the stairs behind her. She stood back, and His Grace, the Archbishop of Canterbury, entered the room, somberly dressed and regarding Evander from dark and narrowed eyes. His long face was paler than usual, but the tip of his sharp nose was bright red, likely due to the freezing day.

"Your Grace," Evander said, bowing deeply. "My apologies for the state of my reception. Between a house fire and snowstorm, things have been a little difficult."

Evander closed the door, noting the large carriage equipped with sleigh runners attached and magnificent white horses in snowshoes pulling it.

"I will prepare some tea," Sarah said. "I'm sure His Grace has had a long journey."

He smiled genially. "No, actually, Addington Palace is close by. But tea would be welcome. It will give me a chance to have a quick word with Mr. Ambrose."

Evander led him to the parlor, which, unfortunately, still had two wine glasses from last night's fireplace mischief. He groaned inwardly, knowing the archbishop had noted it too.

The archbishop sat, crossing one spindly leg over the other. The golden buckle on his shoe glinted in the firelight. "How long have you been alone with Mrs. Hayworth, Mr. Ambrose?"

"Not alone, the boys are here too," Evander replied. It sounded weak, even to him.

"How long?" The archbishop sat back in his chair and waited for Evander to answer.

"Two nights."

"Oh." He frowned. "I suppose there *has* been the snowstorm. But that makes little difference to a reputation. It cannot be a little lost, it is just lost."

"I wasn't aware we had been discovered. I underestimated Mr. Pinlock."

His grace smiled slightly, no hint of teeth showing. "The entire village likely knows by now."

And just to prove that things definitely *could* get worse, Evander heard the unmistakable sound of the front door swinging open again. The archbishop waved him away to answer it, and he entered the hallway to see his parents' groom standing in the hall.

"Joshua. How can I help you?"

"His lordship and her ladyship are in the carriage but wanted me to check you were here. We had word of a fire at your house, and not a moment to lose, they came straight as soon as they heard."

Of course they did.

"Bring them in. Don't leave them out in the cold." Evander went to the kitchen. Sarah looked up from the tray of tea she was assembling.

"Two more cups?" she asked. "I heard the groom."

"Two more cups, if it's not too much trouble."

"Oh, I think this is about to become very big trouble indeed," she said. Her mouth was set in a grim but determined line. His stomach twisted. It felt suspiciously like any semblance of choice was just about to be whipped away from them.

"I'll just check on the boys. Do you need a trolley for the tea tray?"

"No, no. I shall be fine. I love a good impromptu tea party before I have properly brushed my hair or dressed myself."

CHAPTER 23

IN WHICH IT IS DIFFICULT TO GATHER EXACTLY WHOSE REPUTATION NEEDS PROTECTING

Evander checked on the boys for a very long time. Or at least it felt like a long time. Long enough for Sarah to bring the tea tray into the parlor, set it down, and have the countess dismiss her from tea making duties.

"Take a seat, dear. I shall do it," she said, kindly, although Sarah couldn't help but notice the slightly assessing look the countess gave her.

Sarah sat on the chair nearest the fire and folded her hands in her lap and let the awkwardness of the situation wash over her. Who would speak first? It certainly wasn't going to be her.

In the end, it was the earl. "Tell us what happened, Mrs. Hayworth. We can see you are both in a compromising situation but can't do anything until we know the particulars."

"Should we not wait for Mr. Ambrose?" Sarah asked hopefully.

"He'll be back shortly, you may begin," the archbishop replied.

Thus ordered by the head of the church, Sarah had no choice but to begin. "Well, two nights ago, before the snowstorm, I heard a loud report, and after investigation, saw fire coming from the top window of Mr. Ambrose's house."

She looked up to see that the countess had turned pale at the very mention of the fire and was wringing a handkerchief in her hand. "Dear Lord."

Sarah continued, telling them honestly all the happenings of the past two days.

"And the house was too damaged to stay in?" the countess asked.

"The smell of the smoke was too overpowering to expect young children to sleep in it. This seemed the best solution."

"I must thank you for risking your life to help him, dear girl," the earl said. "I knew you were a good one." He reached over and took her hand, clasping it in his. "Isn't she a good one?" He looked around the room for agreement and only stopped after his wife and the archbishop nodded. He sat back, satisfied. "Liked her from the moment I saw her."

At his kind words, Sarah felt tears sting her eyes. She brushed them away and decided to continue her story before she gave into them and started crying in earnest. Why? Why had his simple compliment affected her so? "And, of course, our plan for him to return home at daybreak was foiled by the snowstorm."

"All very innocent and understandable," Lord Wrotham said.

The countess nodded. "We could all support them and this may well blow over. It's not like they behaved with impropriety," Lady Wrotham replied, then looked at Sarah closely, as if to check her reaction.

Evander chose that moment to enter the room. He looked at Sarah, appalled. "You told them? Why would you tell them?"

He must have only heard the 'behaved with impropriety.' Oh dear.

"Tell them what, exactly, Evander?" Lady Wrotham said.

"Why, that we shared a kiss."

Sarah's gaze flew to his in alarm, and too late, he realized he had betrayed them.

"Ah," the archbishop said. "So you have been a little less circumspect than we would have liked."

The earl laughed good-heartedly, but the countess glared at him. "And with the boys in the house! For shame, Evander."

"A simple kiss!" Sarah said, and she couldn't keep the bristle from her voice. How quickly the goodwill had evaporated. "It is so very unfair to be judged for something one could not help. We were both exhausted after the fire. Emotions ran high."

There was perfect silence, only relieved by the sound of the log crackling in the fireplace.

Eventually, the archbishop shook his head. "No. I cannot overlook it. You have an obligation to offer for Mrs. Hayworth. You have slept under the same roof, kiss or no."

"I..." Sarah found she had no words. She cleared her throat. "I do not believe Mr. Ambrose has harmed my reputation in any way, your grace. It is beyond harming."

His mouth set in a stern line. "Mr. Ambrose has a reputation as well. Think for a moment, how can he sanctify a marriage if all the guests remember is the scandal when he spent two nights alone with the most famous opera singer in England. I might even have to remove him from this living. Much as it would pain me to do so."

Sarah looked across at Evander, who was rubbing the back of his neck and frowning.

The tension in the room made her itchy. She just wanted them to stop talking about this, drink their tea, and leave her alone. But that wasn't going to happen. "I for one, do not think a man of his position should marry an opera singer. You couldn't ask it of him."

"You were a vicar's daughter before you were an opera singer," Evander said to Sarah. "I see no reason for you not to marry me. I am not against this. If you'll have me."

"This is what happens when I confide in people. They use it against me," Sarah said.

The archbishop sat back in his chair, frowning. "How am I not aware one of my clergy is the father of La Luminosa? Where?"

"Upminster," Sarah said quietly, wishing she could curl up in a ball and rock herself back and forth. Now her family would be pulled into this.

"Upminster," the archbishop said musingly as if trying to place the vicar in Upminster. "Browne?"

He needed to stop that. "Please, they have disowned me, your grace. Do not attempt to reunite us. I changed my name to Hayworth to avoid embarrassing them."

He shrugged lightly. "So no Mr. Hayworth? Very well. For now. But Sarah's father being a clergyman means despite her occupation, she is the daughter of a gentleman."

"But from the stage, Your Grace," Lady Wrotham said softly. "That fact is more difficult to overcome."

"For the wife of a vicar, or the son of an earl?" Lord Wrotham replied. "Because I seem to remember a young lady of my acquaintance who loved to tread the boards in the amateur productions in Kent some decades ago." He looked to the archbishop. "Incognito, of course."

"Wrotham!" the countess said in outrage, but there was a small smile playing about her lips. "The secrets of our courtship are not for general consumption."

"She was the most beautiful woman of her generation," Lord Wrotham mused. "Her Juliet was divinity itself." He glanced at the archbishop. "No disrespect intended."

"None taken." The archbishop smiled widely for the first time. "There we have it. The Wrothams have a history of marrying the most beautiful and talented women of their generation and giving them a job to do." He turned to Sarah. "You could have a job too, Mrs. Hayworth. It will be a hard job, but it will be a rewarding one. The loss for London's theaters would be a gift to Six Oaks."

Sarah drew in a surprised breath. Give up her opera because

she'd kissed a man? It seemed extreme. She might have been prepared to do that for a love match with a man who wanted to spend the rest of his life with her. But Evander didn't. Her shoulders slumped.

She snuck a glance at Evander, who looked mortified. "All that is lovely," he said through gritted teeth. "But we will not be rushed into this for propriety's sake."

The archbishop shrugged, as though whatever Evander said made no difference. "My lad, you will. I will not have you a laughingstock in the village and, with Mrs. Hayworth's fame, probably the country by the end of next week. Now it is known that I am here, and I will be assumed to be cognizant of the details. It is not just about *you*. Now what you do is a reflection of the highest office in the Church of England."

"Oh dear," Sarah said weakly. She had no desire to make Evander's life difficult or be at the center of the storm to be unleashed. True, it wasn't what she had planned, but it didn't feel wrong either, because her body was humming with excitement, quite without her approval.

It was obvious they would not leave until she and Evander had agreed to their hasty marriage. Well, agreeing to marry and actually marrying were two different things. She would not corner Evander into a marriage without telling him about Rebecca. It might change everything.

And if he couldn't spend a night under the same roof as her without the strength of the Church of England bearing down on him, how could he support an illegitimate child? Sarah's heart, which wanted to leap with happiness from the thought of marrying him, chipped a little more. Soon there would be no more of it left to break.

"You don't have to do this, Mrs. Hayworth. I will survive. The archbishop will survive, and so will the Church of England, believe it or not." Evander expression was solemn.

"Are you sure?" she asked. "Because after all the times you

have come to my rescue, I quite like the thought I can save *your* reputation. I could hold this over you forever."

Evander looked into her eyes, searching, then picked up her hand and pressed his lips to it.

"And I would let you."

"Oh dear," she heard the countess say while Sarah looked deeply into Evander's eyes.

"What's that?" the earl replied.

"This may be a love match after all," she said, sotto voice.

Were they in love? How could she be in love so fast? How could he? It wasn't love. But perhaps they could rub along well enough without it.

He picked up her hand and brought it to his lips, watching her over his knuckles. His gaze was heated, a promise. And the matching heat that bloomed inside her told her she wanted whatever it was he offered.

But Rebecca. She hadn't told him about Rebecca. And she certainly wasn't going to do it in front of both his parents and the Archbishop of Canterbury. A lady had *some* pride. She could always cry off if it went badly. Or marry him and disappear to the continent if she was making his life too hard.

She ignored the pang that caused and turned to the group. "But perhaps everyone would allow us some time to talk in private? We shall see you all at the musicale tomorrow evening."

"Excellent!" the archbishop said, taking that as agreement. "Then neither of you will mind if I marry you next week before I head off to Bath. It's not like a special license is a problem." He laughed quietly at his joke and then turned to the earl. "In all honesty, Wrotham, I think this is going to turn out for the best. You said he needed a wife, and I've long thought that Mrs. Hayworth was too good for London's fribbles."

Next week! "So soon? Surely it is enough if we are betrothed? I don't have my belongings with me." *I need more time to adjust.*

Evander put a hand on her shoulder. "We will confirm things

with you this evening..." He was telling her nothing would be organized before they'd spoken. *Good.*

The archbishop took his leave, and then it was just the countess and the earl, who were also preparing to leave.

The countess looked at Evander sternly. "Can I take the boys for you? I haven't seen the damage the fire did; however, it must need attention."

Lord Wrotham nodded. "Good idea. I will send you some men before lunch; they should be able to patch you up enough to move back in tonight," Lord Wrotham said.

"Thank you, and yes, that would be wonderful. Then I can take the boys home."

"That is also acceptable. But you will not stay under the same roof as your wife-to-be until you are married." She waited for his answer with eyebrows raised.

"Yes, Mama," he said dutifully, and she felt rather than saw the tension in his shoulders.

"I would like to reiterate that we actually did nothing wrong," Sarah said, feeling the need to come to his defense.

But the countess just smiled mildly. "No, and you are not being punished. But our actions do have consequences, and Evander knew this when he chose to stay with you and not take a horse up to the main house to call for help."

It was true, so there was nothing Sarah could say.

The countess took the walking cane that his father handed to her and nodded briskly. "Very well, this is not why I came to visit, but don't misunderstand—I am not displeased. You are to be married." She smiled at both of them, and her smile was genuine. "I wish you all the happiness your father and I have had."

Evander shook hands with his father, and the older man clapped him on the shoulder. "I also wish you joy," he said. "Although I am sure you will not need my wishes. Now where are those rascals? Let's be off."

CHAPTER 24

IN WHICH A MARRIAGE OF CONVENIENCE IS POLITELY OFFERED

Evander closed the door. Now he was alone with Sarah. His wife-to-be.

Wife.

Well, perhaps wife. It still felt like it might not happen.

Would the fledgling love he felt for her be enough when the reality of her situation hit her? When she realized her life was not completely her own, or when all the children were sick at once, or she was with child herself? Her life had been her own for so very long.

He could see the road ahead, and his infatuation with her did nothing to inform him as to what she would think of those things. He may love everything he knew about her, but he knew precious little, really.

So he had to go with the bone-deep feeling that this was right. And whatever it was she didn't want to tell him last night, perhaps now she would trust him enough to share it.

"This is all quite sudden, isn't it?" she said. She didn't sound displeased, and that gave him heart.

He took a deep breath and let it out slowly. "Yes, but it feels right to me."

She took his neckcloth and pulled on it teasingly. "I *could* offer you a marriage of convenience if you wanted me to disappear to the continent…"

A marriage of convenience? Is that what she wanted? To marry him and then go on her way? He picked up both of her hands and held them in his. They fit in his perfectly like they had been made for each other.

"No, Sarah. No fake marriages. No marriages of convenience. I cannot and will not lie to everyone and to you. When we marry, you will have my heart, my name, and my protection and whether you want it or not, my love."

"Your love?" she said with a squeak. "You do not love me. You *could* not love me." She leaned in and he inhaled her scent, rose and sweetness. "You just want me to kiss you again."

"Entirely true." But right now, it felt like the cage surrounding his heart had burst open, this glimpse of what life would be like with her in it, enough to blow the bars off it.

Withholding love was a waste of time. Trying to guard your heart was a similar endeavor. It was better just to give that love freely and wherever the heart willed it. And his heart was willing it for Sarah with stupid speed this morning.

But for Sarah, he could see that love was a complicated thing. It was tied up in a family that no longer loved her and men that loved her for the wrong reasons. Her lessons in love were all hard ones. So he would not bombard her with his feelings.

"But I care for you," he said, looking deeply into her eyes and taking a leap of faith he hadn't known he was capable of. "I think it started the moment you flashed that paste diamond in my face and told me that charity began at home."

"Oh." She seemed nonplussed, her mouth a confused frown. "I'm no saint. There have been decisions in my life that might change your intentions." Her brows were scrunched together, as if she was trying to find the right words but having difficulty.

"Just tell me, Sarah. You can't varnish the truth." He may have sounded easy-going, but his heart was thumping. He didn't *want* to hear anything that changed his mind. Didn't want to think that anything could.

She took a deep breath and closed her eyes. "In Italy, I had a child."

Such a small sentence to convey such a large event. He shook his head to try to clear the fog that was descending. In his wildest thoughts about what her secret could be, he had stupidly never thought of that. Where was the child?

"You were married to a Papist?" There was no divorce in Italy, only annulment that was almost impossible to come by.

He felt a surge of relief when she shook her head.

"Actually, no, I was not married." Her gaze was averted and seemed to be in a time and place far away, a small furrow across her brow.

"Good, good." He frowned and felt his mouth draw down in an unhappy line. It was *not* good. Where was her child? Could he go and get the babe? How would he do that without making another scandal? Then, above all that – he felt a bone deep sadness for what she had endured.

"It was a mistake to tell you," she said, edging away from him. "You couldn't possibly want to marry me now that you know I have a child out of wedlock. I understand."

He looked up from his scattered thoughts to see tears spilling down her cheeks even as she stood with both hands clasped in front of her.

"No, no," he said, taking her hands in his. "I'm not angry at you. Far from it. I just want to find the man that left you in such a position. Was it Gianni?"

"No, he was the one that warned me against it." She wiped her tears and gave him a watery smile. "It doesn't matter who he was. It was six years ago, and I'm sure I have quite forgotten all about him."

"And what of the child? Where is he, or is it 'she'?"

She turned back to look out over the garden again. Fanny was dragging a stick that was bigger than her across the icy lawn. "She. Her name is Rebecca. And she is with my parents, of course. You don't think I would subject a child to the life of an opera singer?"

That was a perfectly good reason for the child not being with her. Her life in London was not a good environment to raise a little one. "And that is why you send them money."

"Yes."

"And that is why you let them disown you." The questions were coming fast now. He couldn't know enough.

She nodded, happy to answer just as quickly as he asked like she was lifting a burden. "Again, yes. They have done enough for me taking Rebecca in. They need do no more than love her."

He stood, his heart hurting for what she had endured. "Do you want her with you?"

He must ask. It might make his life hard and might throw them deeper in scandal than they could get out of, but he would no sooner deny a mother her child than stop breathing.

"Of course," she said, but the brittle answer made him realize she held no hope of such a thing. Perhaps he should not encourage the idea if he couldn't do it.

He looked out over the garden, but not at anything in particular. Fanny dropped the stick, lifted her nose to the air, and barked her snuffly bark at something.

"Are you angry?" She asked like she knew the answer was 'yes'. Which it was not. In fact, even after a few short minutes, he would dearly love to see a little version of Sarah.

"At you?" He turned to her. "Of course not. My guess would be that this is the reason you are so protective of your virtue. I did wonder, given the nature of your surroundings and the temptation that must bring."

She shrugged. "I learned how easily a man can promise one thing and do another. It was a hard lesson."

"What *does* make me angry was that this man abandoned you in your time of need."

She shrugged one shoulder. "It was hard at the time, but he was young, like me. Italian. A prince. His mother visited me and told me all about his betrothal. I was horrified."

He blinked rapidly, trying to get his head around the fact her little girl was related to Italian royalty. One of the things he had loved about her was her steadfast rule, one that all society knew, that she didn't let married men dangle after her. He'd so admired that trait that he had forgotten to ask himself why she had it.

"Now I hate him even more," he said simply. "But that is not why I am upset."

"Then why? Tell me. I can't do anything about my past…"

He smile ruefully. "I know. I am upset because the first thing I want to do is go and find your little girl and bring her here with us." He shook his head. "But I cannot. There would be too many questions when our marriage is already covering a scandal all of its own. So I must keep this secret, just as you have, and that is unacceptable to me." He shrugged one shoulder. "I just have to remind myself that she is living in the heart of your family and has her grandparents and all your brothers and sisters with her. Does she look like you?" He shook his head. "No, don't answer that, of course she does."

HAPPILY, Evander answering his own question saved Sarah doing it. Because she didn't know. It had been years since she had seen her little girl. Back then, she had not particularly resembled Sarah. Who knew now? She had imagined how little Rebecca would look now a thousand different ways, and it didn't matter how often she asked her mother to send a miniature, it never arrived.

"I don't expect you to take her in," Sarah said. But that was a lie. Part of her truly hoped he would flout all conventions to bring Rebecca to her. But then, he thought Rebecca was perfectly fine with her family.

He pulled her into his arms. "I am honored you shared this with me, and I hope, when the time is right, we can decide on what is best for Rebecca's future. In the meantime, know that she will always be taken care of."

"That means the world to me," Sarah said. She raised her face to him, and he wiped the tears from her cheek. "Thank you."

So it wasn't a perfect world. But then again, when was it? The hard part was hoping like Hades that her daughter wasn't once again going to pay for her mother's decisions. That Evander would be as good as his word and continue to support Rebecca when Sarah had no income of her own to do it.

Trust in men wasn't something she had in large supply. But he had heard her darkest secret and still wanted to marry her. That was cause for hope. She would do it. It felt right, and that was all she could go by.

He pulled her into an embrace, lifting her toes from the ground. "So you will marry me?" he asked quietly in her ear. "I know it's rushed, but perhaps this is what we needed. Otherwise, you would return to London and forget how handsome I am."

"Yes, yes, I will marry you."

"Then come," he said. "Let's walk to your future home, so you can see if there are any changes you might like when the workmen come this afternoon." He cupped her face with his hands and kissed her, first on the left cheek, then the right, and then on the mouth. He drew back and smiled lopsidedly, and she saw his chest rise as he took a deep and not quite steady breath.

She took a deep breath too. "I would like that very much." There would be no thinking of running now. If he continued to look at her like he was, her heart would not allow it.

CHAPTER 25

AN UNEXPECTED VISITOR

Evander took Sarah's arm to walk the short distance over the snowy ground to his house. With her red velvet cloak billowing out behind her in the wind, she looked every inch the romantic opera heroine. So very out of place in the English countryside.

Franny trotted along in front of them, unfazed by her heavy belly.

He'd dressed carefully in the last of the clothes he'd brought to the cottage. His best buckskin breeches, boots shined to perfection, and his cravat a little loose around his neck. He had a feeling she'd like that.

And he wanted her to like that.

As she walked, taking in the house in front of her, he imagined what she would see. A pretty manor house, surrounded by a winter-bare garden with pruned back roses. Tall, elegant windows on the bottom floor and balconied windows on the second story.

If he was more critical, the shutters needed painting, and the boarded-up window where the firecrackers went off was an eyesore.

"

But it had potential.

Each step with her brought anticipation, now that she was his. Now he could stoke the fire of the attraction he'd felt for her from that first carriage ride, knowing it was actually going somewhere good.

They would be family. He felt a pang that came with the idea of starting again. More pieces of Eleanor would fade away as the months and years passed. In his heart, he hoped he could keep her memory bright even in the face of someone as vivacious as Sarah. He owed that to the boys.

He stepped ahead to open the door, turning back to smile at her. The tip of her nose was red from the cold, and a cloud of steam breathed out around her. Her gaze was lazy as she took him in from head to toe.

Now he was glad he had taken his time getting ready.

"You look very handsome," she said, inspecting the ground as though suddenly shy.

He felt himself blush, which would not be nearly so masculine or handsome, so he made a large to-do about putting the key in the lock. "Er, thank you. Let's assess the damage, shall we?"

They walked from room to room. A fine layer of soot lay where doors had been left open, and the boys' room was a complete mess, the sodden pile of burned drapes still on the floor.

"It could have been so much worse," Sarah said, taking his hand. She had pulled her mittens off in the hall and her hand felt warm in his. Instantly nothing else mattered.

"I'll have their toys and things cleaned if they can be salvaged. But come, let's look at the rest of the house. The undamaged part." Suddenly it seemed important she knew that he wasn't being coerced into marrying her. "You know, I would have chased you around the globe if I thought for one moment you returned my regard."

She winked at him, the minx. "I do not blame you. I am *very* attractive."

"I actually yelled out for you at the opera – told you to run for the hills."

Her eyes widened and her smile grew broad. "That was you? I loved it! I would never have found my line if not for that show of support. I thought everyone was laughing at my misfortune. You've been my champion ever since. One day, I would like to be yours." She placed her hand in his.

She was saying that she wanted to be his wife, his friend, his champion. It was all he needed to hear.

He pulled her close. "In that case, this is your new house, soon to be Mrs. Ambrose. I need you to tell me what is to be replaced." He held her close, then put her back down on her feet. "Most everything in here belonged to my grandmother, but she did have fine taste."

She twined her arms around his neck and closed her eyes. She had such a delighted and wistful expression on her face that it was impossible not to kiss her. He brushed his lips softly over hers and whispered in her ear. "I'm allowed to do that now."

He kissed her ear lobe. It was velvet soft. "And this."

He trailed kisses down her neck. "And this."

She shivered and pulled him to her and pulled his mouth to hers. None of those whisper kisses he gave her, but something much more urgent. She did not wait for him, but molded herself to him, raking her fingers through his hair and deepening this kiss until he felt his knees weaken. He staggered back to the wall, bringing her with him.

"And I am allowed to do that," she said.

He pulled back and opened his eyes, gratified to see her gaze look sleepy and slow-moving.

He swallowed hard.

"You are going to make dull evenings at the vicarage very exciting," he said under his breath. "Now, where am I?"

She did a bad job of suppressing a smile. "In the upstairs landing."

"Right. I was going to show you around the house. Come downstairs again." *Come downstairs while I desperately try to calm my thumping heart.*

She went down the stairs ahead of him. "It's so much prettier than I remember," she said. "Even with the soot."

"There was too much smoke to see that night," he said. "But we'll put it to rights in the coming days."

They walked through the hall to the dining room and then the sitting room. "I am so glad the wallpaper wasn't damaged," she mused, running her hand up the flocked floral wall. "I do so love this kind of wallpaper. My house in Curzon Street had one very similar." She let her hand drop and turned to him, a look of wonder on her face. "Those small tables look like Chippendale. Are they?"

He nodded. "Grandmother had lovely taste and the funds to indulge it."

She smiled, and her eyes looked equal parts surprised and happy. Or perhaps happy to be surprised. "There is nothing I would change here. You have a beautiful house, and it will be an honor to take care of it."

Oh. He had actually thought she would want to change everything and found himself nonplussed. "I want you to feel like it is yours."

"Ours," she corrected him and was rewarded with a smile.

The sitting room looked out over the back garden, which had rows of lavender leading out to an overhead canopy that was just twigs and sticks now but would be so much more in a few short months.

Sarah looked where he was looking. "Is that a wisteria briar?"

He took her by the hand to the window. "It is. It's very old and by far the most beautiful thing about summer here."

"I bet it smells divine."

"You will soon see," he said. "Summer will be here before you know it."

An image of them sitting under the wisteria together was so crisp and clear it was like a memory. *Maybe Sarah would be with child.* The little voice in his head came from nowhere but like everything else about her—felt right.

～

SARAH RETURNED to the house just before dinner, Mrs. Green letting her into the empty dining room.

"We'll be down shortly!" Evander yelled from above. Sarah waited, straining to hear the shouts, laughter, and thumping down the stairs. All was silent. Suspiciously silent.

She frowned.

A small knot of unhappiness tightened in her stomach. What if they weren't happy to have her as their mother now? She hadn't realized how much she wanted their approval and acceptance before that moment.

Time slowed as she waited.

She went to the kitchen to see if Mrs. Green needed any assistance with dinner. She did not. She tried to read a book, but the flickering light of the candle was making her eyes swim.

Then, finally, she heard the thump of little footsteps on the stairs and went out to meet them, her heart pounding with more nerves than it had when the Archbishop of Canterbury grilled her.

Bess, the maid, was the first down the stairs, rushing past her. She squeezed Sarah's hand on the way through. "Congratulations, ma'am."

"Thank you, Bess," she replied, and when she looked back up, they were standing on the stairs in a line from smallest to largest with their father at the back.

Alexander, Benjamin and Isaac were dressed in dear little matching navy wool coats and buff-colored breeches.

"Oh," she said, the air gone from her lungs. "You all look so handsome."

She expected them to at least smile and perhaps give her one of their boisterous hugs, but, instead, Alexander stepped forward and took her hand, kissing it so earnestly it made her heart squeeze. "We are so glad you are to be our Mama now." He looked to Evander for approval.

Evander nodded. "Excellent job." He ushered the boys to the table where they pulled back their chairs sat quietly, three sets of bright eyes on her.

After man-sized napkins were firmly in place to prevent disasters, Evander led them in a simple blessing. They had their eyes screwed shut while he said the prayer, their cheeks scrubbed and rosy red. Sarah noted once again how different Benjamin was from Alexander. Evander's wife must have been very fair, for his hair was almost white blonde.

So there they sat around the table, napkins firmly in place and showing her their best manners. Mrs. Green brought in their dinner and placed the platters on the table where they could help themselves, yet still, there was not a peep out of the boys.

It was unnatural, but touching. "My goodness, how well-behaved you boys are! I vow I am quite intimidated to live with you if this is the level of gentility I must aspire to!" Sarah winked at Evander.

"Oh yes," he said conversationally. "My sons are leaders in the ways of the gentleman. Indeed, I often take my lessons from them."

"You're both funning us!" Benjamin said. "Father knows this is our very best behavior because we don't want you to be frightened off and not marry him."

"Hush, Benjamin," Alexander said, glaring through his spectacles. "You aren't supposed to tell her."

"I know you will always do your best to impress me with your manners," Sarah said, smiling at them. "But if occasionally you fail, do not fear, I will still love you, and love that you are always trying."

She didn't know what she had said until she realized that all four men were blushing madly.

"What did I say?"

"You love us?" Benjamin said. "Papa, she said she loves us. Already and after we set the crackers off!"

Sarah felt the heat in her cheeks, especially since she had been unable to tell Evander that very thing not so very long ago. "Why should I not?" she stammered. "You are all wonderful boys. How could I not marry your papa when I get you in the bargain?"

There was a long moment of silence at the table, as the boys all looked at each other, then chairs were scraped back, and suddenly she had three boys all trying to sit on her lap, none of them quite succeeding.

"Boys!" Evander said. "Manners, please."

"It's all right, Papa. She loves us!" Isaac said. Being the smallest, he wiggled his way onto Sarah's lap first, leaving the other two to kiss her on either cheek and generally create havoc with her coiffure.

They were saved from the situation becoming either more unruly or awkward by Mrs. Green entering the dining room.

"Sir, if you will. We have a problem." She motioned for Evander to leave the room with her. Sarah stayed where she was with the boys.

"What do you think is for pudding?" she said, trying to take their minds off whatever their father was doing. "What is your favorite?"

It worked. They could apparently talk about the different kinds of puddings and which was best for particular kinds of weather and moods, forever. Or at least the few minutes it took for Evander to return.

With a bundle of baby in his arms.

"Goodness me, what happened?" Sarah put Isaac down and got to her feet. It was just a wee little one, definitely under one, wrapped in a soft pink rug and a knitted hat.

"The baby was left on our front porch," Evander said casually. "As sometimes happens."

"Sometimes happens?" Sarah felt her voice rising. "Should we find the parents?"

Evander smiled slightly at her, as though she had a mean understanding of these kinds of situations-which was likely true. "The village is prosperous enough, but some of the outlying areas can have a hard time over winter."

The boys were gathered around him in a trice. "Is it a boy or a girl, Papa?"

"Let's see," he said simply, sitting on a dining chair and plopping the child on his lap. "Now," he said to the babe. "What's your name?"

Sarah took a few steps toward them and raised the child's chubby right arm where a white ribbon was tied. A name was embroidered on it in pink thread. "Emily," she said softly, and the child gurgled, looking at her with enormous blue eyes. "How old do you think she is?"

But Sarah knew. She looked the exact age Rebecca had been when she left her with her parents. Old enough to eat solid food, young enough not to understand her mama was missing.

"I'd say she's about eight months," Evander said. "More than able to crawl herself around if I put her on the floor."

"How can you possibly look after her with three boys already and a house that needs repair?"

Other than an admonishing quirk of his eyebrow, he ignored her. "I never said I was keeping her. I'm sure they'll be back for her when they can and I'm known for taking children in. But we'll muddle along in the meantime, won't we, Emily? You are welcome here."

He was *known* for taking children in? She frowned. If he was, then how could one little Rebecca be such a problem? Perhaps she should just go to Upminster, take Rebecca and leave her on his doorstep and see what happened. Then he would have no choice.

He turned to her. "I will need to go to the attic to retrieve the nursery furniture. But we shall have to adjourn our dinner while we get Emily settled and a place to sleep. There is no note with her, so I have to assume she may stay some time."

"Or maybe forever!" said Alexander. "A sister! Imagine Papa!"

Yes. Imagine a sister. But that sister could just as easily be Rebecca. It felt wrong to think that when this little one obviously needed help, but it was so hard not to.

"We shall see. I know you will love her for however long she is here."

Sarah picked up her little hand with one finger, delighted when the child's fingers grasped hers.

Yes, little one, we will love you.

The baby started whimpering, not crying, but a plaintive sound that made Sarah's heart ache. "Is she all right?"

"Hungry, I would say. Mrs. Green will be organizing it, I'm sure."

He had barely finished the sentence when the housekeeper came into the room with a little bowl and spoon.

"There's a dear love," she said. "Let me take her, Sir, and give her this. I'm sure she needs it." She took the baby away, the sound of her gentle cooing growing fainter as she walked down the hall.

"Is this how I came?" Isaac said with his head tilted to one side.

Evander nodded. "This is just how you came, Isaac, and a blessed night it was for us all." He ruffled the boy's head.

Sarah's mouth dropped open, then looked at Benjamin and Isaac in a new light. Although Alex had Evander's dark hair and green eyes, the younger two bore no resemblance to Evander at all—how had she not realized? He had three sons, but had only actually sired one.

It meant, despite the current situation, that in all of England, she had happened by sheer luck to land on the very man who could bring her daughter into his house.

Why had he not just agreed to do it, if this was no big thing after all? Hope warred with frustration, leaving her feeling confused.

Hope was a dangerous thing, but she couldn't help herself.

"You amaze me," she said, struggling to keep the raw emotion from her voice. What was that emotion? Admiration?

The clarity hit her like lightning to the heart, making the poor organ grow twice its size like it wanted to leap from her chest.

She loved him.

This strong protector who gave his own love generously and freely. No matter that he came with a vicarage, and she would have to be a vicar's wife.

She loved him.

From thinking she was being forced into a marriage, suddenly, the very Mr. Ambrose who she'd sparred with for days was the answer to her lost dreams. It would be worth giving up her singing if it meant that maybe, just maybe, she could be the mother to Rebecca that she always should have been. With a respectable upbringing and a noble family behind her.

He turned, confusion on his face. "I amaze you? How so?"

"This child is welcome to stay here, for as long as she needs, no questions, no judgment."

He tilted his head to one side as though not understanding what point she was making. "I know they wouldn't leave her with me unless they were desperate."

"But they just left her on your doorstep!"

He shook his head. "No. Mrs. Green said her mother was hiding in the bushes to make sure she was taken care of. They didn't abandon her. I do what I can, and so does Six Oaks, and, most often, it is enough."

"But..."

"No buts. She is welcome here. I know they wouldn't bring her to me unless it was a last resort. Nobody leaves a child behind if they have any other choice."

She sighed. What did he think of her? Did he think she had another choice? If she thought back, it wasn't desperation that had made her leave Rebecca with her parents, more just knowing that she couldn't raise her alone without an income, and her income came from singing.

He looked at her keenly. "Are you plotting to leave a child on our doorstep one day?"

"What child?" Benjamin said loudly.

"Hush now," Evander replied. "I think I hear your pudding coming. Why don't you go and help?"

They scampered away.

She didn't want to tell him what she'd really been thinking. "How did you know?"

"It would be hard *not* to assume another could arrive here, as Emily did. But it is not the same. One day, sooner than you think, she will be the spitting image of you, and the entire story will unravel. Your position will be hard enough without someone looking closely and asking why the child looks so much like you. We need to let things settle. Once you have her living with you, you won't ever want to send her back to her grandparents."

Mrs. Green and the boys came in with the pudding, which was plum, much to the boys' excitement. They ate it like there was never going to be another pudding again. All that good food had Isaac looking sleepy, although Benjamin and Alexander had the look of two boys ready to stay up all night.

Bess soon came in and directed them to kiss Sarah and Evander good night. They did so reluctantly but with the same earnest endeavor to please that Sarah had to laugh.

"I know you'll revert to your impish selves tomorrow, but tonight has been lovely." The impulse to tousle their hair was strong, so she gave in to it, then pulled them all into a hug. "Sweet dreams, sweet boys."

~

SARAH HAD BEEN STARING at the fire for a long time, swirling a glass of sherry in one hand and taking sips from it.

Evander took a sip from his own glass, savoring the warmth of it in his mouth. "I wish I knew what you were thinking." He hoped she understood his reasons for not fetching her daughter immediately. It did not sit well with him not to have full knowledge of the child's situation. He would fix that just as soon as he could.

"Just that I could fall asleep right here." She closed her eyes as the log crackled in the fire. She had kicked her slippers off and her stocking toes curled into the rug at her feet.

"Then I had better get you back home," Evander said.

"Mmm," she said. "Can I sleep in this cozy chair? Nobody will know."

"Everyone will know. Let's not court more trouble." Evander stood and held his hand down to her. "I will ride you home."

"I am home," she took his hand and allowed him to pull her to her feet. They walked to the hall where he picked her cloak off the peg and wrapped it around her. "I shall be lonely."

He brought her hand to his mouth and kissed her knuckles. "You will be fine until the morning."

She snuggled into him in a most bewitching way she would not have yesterday, as though the telling of her secret had brought her to him in a way he would never have imagined.

He brought his mare, Diana, around from the barn, and lifted Sarah into the saddle, then himself behind her.

It was a very short distance to the cottage. But even so, by the time they arrived, he had the fragrance of her hair filling his senses like they had been empty for an eternity. It would be all he could do to deposit her inside the door and scoot back to his own bed before he self- combusted.

He slowed Diana to a walk and came to a stop at the front door, jumping down and hanging the reins on the pole.

Helping her down, she slid into his arms again, and then walked with him to the door. She opened it with her key, but did not invite him in, which was for the best.

He stood in the doorframe. "Thank you for coming to dinner." Very urbane, and you could hardly hear the tremor in his voice. "Before I go, do you think your father might like to help the Archbishop officiate?"

Her eyebrows drew together, and she pushed her hands into her cloak pockets. "I suppose he might, especially if the wedding is nowhere near his parish."

"I don't know your father, but I would like to ask him." It could be the first step to reuniting her with her family. It would be an unusual family that did not want a connection to the Earl of Wrotham.

"I will happily allow you to butt your head up against the brick wall that is my father. But you may have to prepare yourself for the fact they've told the entire parish I'm dead."

"What?" He was so aghast he lost his manners.

She took his free hand and then motioned for the one on the doorknob. He gave it to her. "Oh yes. It's why I had to change my name to Hayworth, so people wouldn't make the connection. The family name, if you remember from the Arch Bishop's visit, is Browne."

He nodded. "That's right. Sarah Browne. A good solid Saxon name."

"Hayworth is my legal name. I used a solicitor to change it. Not that I had to, I am perfectly entitled to use whichever name I wish! But Browne is hardly the stuff operatic dreams are made of," she replied. "In any case, my father may come here to marry us, he may even bring my mother, but I do not expect them to become part of my life just because I've made one respectable decision."

He quirked an eyebrow. "And am I to believe that *I* am your one respectable decision?"

"Of course! Who could be more respectable than you?"

He shook his head mournfully. "And I thought you saw that I never feel quite respectable. Instead, you see what everyone else does."

"Ha! Don't worry, I have a fairly good notion that the reason you were so easily persuaded to marry me has nothing to do with protecting your reputation and more to do with getting close to me and my person."

"In the most respectable way possible."

"Oh dear, that sounds boring."

"It won't be, I assure you."

She nipped his ear gently. "Oh good."

He moved his head so she would no longer be nibbling on his ear, but kissing him on the mouth. They stayed within their own bubble, kissing until they were both breathless and flushed. He pulled away from her with a deep, shuddering breath. "I must go. Poor Diana is waiting for me."

He left her reluctantly, but he couldn't trust himself for a single moment more in her company. There was plenty of time for this after they were married, but in the meantime, he would show her the respect she deserved.

CHAPTER 26

A SECRET MISSION

The next morning, which was the day of the musicale, Evander put the sleighs on the carriage and prepared to leave for Upminster.

If Sarah thought he was going to leave her parents' attendance at their wedding up to chance, she was about to be surprised. He had to try.

He stopped by the cottage on the way. Sarah answered the door with a smile and kissed him on both cheeks. "Whip in hand and dressed for travel. Where are you off to? I hope you will be home in time."

"Now that the roads are clearer, I have a short errand to run. I will be home well in time." He took her hand. "What time would you like me to escort you to the main house?"

"I will practice here today and perhaps visit your house to practice with the boys—so perhaps an hour before the musicale starts?"

He lifted her hand and kissed it. "I shall see you then." He took his leave, encouraged by the fact she looked a little disappointed.

The trip to Upminster took just under two hours, and he stopped at the inn to get directions to the vicarage.

The house was just as the lady at the inn had directed, sitting to the left of the church. The grounds of the church itself and the adjoining graveyard were well cared for, the trees shaped and rose bushes pruned back to bare sticks ready to bloom in spring.

The vicarage was also well kept. A shiny black carriage sat in what looked to be a specially built small carriage house at the end of the drive.

Which was quite at odds with the poverty-stricken childhood Sarah had told him about.

He knocked on the door, and it was answered by a maid. When he gave her his card and inquired after her master and mistress, he was shown into a charming parlor with thick carpets and a damask covered sofa. He ran his hand over the smooth wooden side table, with its intricate woodwork. The Brownes certainly weren't poor now.

A few moments later, a man with white hair and deep blue eyes entered the room, a look of confusion on his face.

"Mr. Ambrose? How can I be of assistance?"

His eyes and pointy chin were so like Sarah's that Evander found himself predisposed to like the man.

"Good morning, Mr. Browne. I am the vicar at Six Oaks in Kent. It's an honor to meet you. I have had the pleasure of your daughter's acquaintance and thought it time I ventured out here to meet you."

"My daughter? Jane?" His confusion seemed to grow.

"Why no, Sarah." Evander watched his reaction closely and was not disappointed. His pale cheeks flushed a dark red, and he lifted his hand to loosen his neck cloth.

"Sir, I'm afraid you are mistaken and have come all this way for nothing. I have no daughter called Sarah."

It was said so bitterly that it was obviously a lie.

Sarah was not exaggerating the situation.

"I suppose then, you would not be interested in the fact she is to marry soon?"

He stilled for a moment, then shook his head. "I'm afraid not, since I don't know the Sarah Browne you speak of."

The door opened, and a woman entered. "Did I hear you say Sarah is to be married?" Her hair was still mostly dark brown, like Sarah's, with becoming threads of silver through it. She wore a day gown so elaborate that it was obvious she did not intend to do any domestic work. She smiled tentatively at her husband, and then at Evander, obviously waiting for an introduction.

Mr. Browne groaned as his entire fabrication disintegrated. "Thank you, Mrs. Browne. This is Mr. Ambrose; he is the vicar at Six Oaks and is to marry Sarah to some unwary fool, I assume."

"Oh," she said breathless. "Do tell us who he is."

But now, some impulse that all was not as it seemed meant Evander didn't want to give them any information before he had answers of his own.

"I think Sarah would like you to come to the wedding so that you can see for yourselves and meet her husband-to-be. She mentioned that she didn't think you would attend, and I was so sure that couldn't be true, that I had to come here for myself."

"She didn't set you up for this then?" Mr. Browne asked, eyes narrowed.

"Why no. Indeed, she told me to stay well out of it and that she would write to you herself."

"But she hasn't written for months," Mrs. Browne said. "Not since the money stopped."

"Shush, wife," her husband said.

"Well it's true! What is to become of the child if the money stops? Perhaps this good man can tell us. Is she marrying a man of wealth?"

Evander molded his face into complete disinterest. "I am certain her future husband is self-sufficient. And as for the child, I'm sure Sarah would want to make sure she is taken care of completely. Are you telling me this is not happening? I'm sure she would want to know."

Mrs. Browne looked to her husband, whose mouth was set in a grim line. How had Evander ever seen Sarah in him?

"If the money doesn't arrive from Sarah, we have nothing to pass on to the family."

What family? "The family who is housing the child, I assume?" His voice was steady, but he was so close to getting his answers.

"Yes," Mrs. Browne replied. "They care for her very well, so there's no need for you to look down your nose at us."

"I'm sure they look after her better than you would yourself," Evander said.

She looked mollified, even though Evander meant it an entirely different way.

"Well, I do have some funds from Mrs. Hayworth for the child, so if you would be so kind as to give me the direction of the family, I can be on my way."

"That won't be necessary," Mrs. Browne said. "We can pass on the funds like we usually do."

Why did Evander get the feeling that only a portion of all the funds Sarah had ever sent actually reached her child? Time to find out.

"Unfortunately, she said the amount she is sending is a trifle short of the usual amount, but she wouldn't tell me how much she normally gives."

"Ten pounds a month," Mr. Browne said smartly.

"I see. Then it's true, for I only have five."

"Sarah has never sent less than ten pounds, and often sends more," Mrs. Browne said. "Maybe she will send more after her marriage. You can give it to us, Mr. Ambrose. We will see to it."

"Not this time," Evander said. "I must deliver it myself as I have promised her I will personally report on the child's welfare."

They both bristled. "I can assure you we see the child each week at services. She is well cared for."

Rebecca was old enough to be at services. Would she look like

Sarah? Would she have fathomless blue eyes that flashed with mischief? He certainly hoped so.

"How lovely for you to still have that connection with your granddaughter," Evander said, unable to keep the sarcasm from his voice.

"Now see here," Mr. Browne said. "We were not in a position to take her in. This village is very judgmental, and the Earl of Tisdale, whom I owe this living, would be horrified to know that any child of mine had produced a child out of wedlock."

"Much less that the child herself was alive and making her living as an opera singer," Evander said.

"We will not come to the wedding. I wouldn't officiate if it were with the Archbishop of Canterbury himself. We will not be giving you directions to the child."

Evander stood. "Very well. I thank you for your time. Good day to you."

They let him reach the front door before following. "Mr. Ambrose?"

Evander's hand stilled on the knob.

It was Mr. Browne. He spoke in a whisper. "You tell her if she comes back here, we will not acknowledge her or accept her here. Her chance for being respectable has long since passed."

He blinked in the face of vehemence. "No second chances, then?"

But he knew it was impossible. They'd lied themselves into a corner saying she was dead and there was no way for them to come out of it without admitting their dishonesty to the entire parish.

"No, Mr. Ambrose. I'm afraid not."

He stood, holding his hat in his hand. "I will make sure I tell the Archbishop that, as he is indeed officiating the wedding, being a close friend of my father's and having known Sarah for some years. My father, who is, of course, the Earl of Wrotham." He smiled broadly, enjoying the way their mouths dropped open in unison. "I thought I would be sad if you refused to attend our wedding, but indeed I am quite relieved!"

Mrs. Browne jumped to her feet. "*You* are marrying Sarah? My dear boy!"

Evander shook his head. "No, I am not your dear boy." He tipped his hat and left them, without telling them when the wedding would be or where.

Likewise, any notion of encouraging his father to gift a living he controlled to Sarah's father was forgotten.

They weren't worth the effort.

Evander rode thoughtfully through the town of Upminster, mulling over everything he'd just learned. They lived in comfort and wealth; the wealth Sarah had amassed while relegating their own granddaughter to be raised on a farm

He was quite sure he could discover Rebecca's whereabouts. It was a small town where everyone likely knew everyone. He entered the village pub and made a few discreet inquiries with the barkeep about who in the village had experience with taking in foundling children. There was only one, a farm a few miles out of the village where an older couple was taking care of a young girl who had lost her mother in tragic circumstances.

A few miles out of the village, he looked for the farmhouse, finding it easily. Nerves ate away at his stomach. He didn't want to find her here, neglected. It would break his heart to have to tell Sarah what he'd found.

The door opened before he'd even alighted his horse, a tall man with ruddy cheeks and wild gray hair walking up the path to meet him.

"Good afternoon, Sir. How can I help you?"

He had the definite twang of Essex, which Evander always found friendly and welcoming.

"A few moments of your time, if you have it. I am Mr. Ambrose, rector of the parish in Six Oaks, Kent."

"Pleased to meet you." He held out his hand. "Jedidiah Williams. Come inside."

Evander followed him inside and was soon ensconced at the kitchen table with a hot cup of tea and biscuits that were still warm from the oven. Mrs. Williams sat next to her husband, a well-rounded woman of about fifty years, if he were to hazard a guess. They both looked at him with closed mouths and wide eyes.

"I come on behalf of Rebecca's family."

"Oh!" said Mrs. Williams with obvious surprise. She stared at the table for a few long moments. "We hoped this would never happen. We consider her our family now." She said the last with a pursed mouth and watery eyes. She dabbed her handkerchief on her cheek.

Evander took a deep breath, coming to a decision entirely from his gut. "She has her own family and they would like to claim her. But first, please tell me how much money you receive for her upkeep. It will not be coming from your vicar this month, as I have just told him."

"One pound every month, and very generous it is. Peg and I would find things much harder if the little girl were to leave us."

What a tidy profit the Brownes made off Sarah. "When the family claims her, they will leave you with an annuity to compensate for it."

Jedidiah nodded, and his wife clutched her breast. "Goodness me."

Evander knew this to be true because he would be the man providing it. The years had made him a good judge of character, and he already knew he was going to find Sarah's little girl in fine form and beautifully cared for.

"May I see her?"

"Of course," Mrs. Williams said, without hesitation. "But don't tell her anything yet. She knows I am not her mama and calls me Aunty, but we are all she has known and is as precious as our own child. I don't want her to get her hopes up about having a family if nothing is to come of it."

She left the room and came back a few moments later with a little girl in tow. She was dressed in a simple blue dress, with olive skin and a mop of curly dark hair that was tied with a green ribbon. Her brown eyes were framed by glorious long lashes, curled and adorable. It wasn't hard to see why the Williams family loved her.

To the eye, unless you looked closely at her mouth, which had the same bow-shaped upper lip her mother had, she had inherited more of her Italian heritage than her mother's English one.

But despite all that—she was definitely Sarah's.

And like a surprise punch to the gut, he realized he wanted to reunite her with her mother more than anything he'd ever wanted. He hoped he would not wake up from all these decisions that just 'felt right' and regret them.

"Rebecca, this is Mr. Ambrose. Please bid him good afternoon."

She did not smile at him. "Good afternoon, Sir." She bobbed a tiny wobbly curtsy.

"Very nicely done," he encouraged her. "You will be a fine lady one day, Miss Rebecca."

She hugged the leg of Mrs. Williams.

"There, there," the older lady soothed. "You go back to your dollies. I'll come and see you with some jam tarts and milk in a minute."

The little girl sped away, but not before Evander noticed she wore blue-kid slippers and that her dress was a warm woolen one. The ten shillings a month had most certainly gone to her proper upkeep.

Mrs. Williams's eyes followed her out of the room with a small smile on her face.

"You would miss her," Evander said simply.

"Oh yes," she replied. "But I always knew she wasn't mine."

"When is all this happening?" Jedidiah said. "We'll need time to get her ready. And proof. I won't just give my little girl over to any man that shows up; I don't care what he's the rector of."

"Why don't you come with me? Then you can see where Rebecca will live, meet her mother, and establish for yourselves that she will be raised in a loving family."

Mr. Williams chewed on his lip. "You'll let the vicar know?"

Evander nodded. "I visited Mr. Browne on the way here and will settle all with him." *Through a lawyer.*

They looked at each other, coming to a conclusion without words after Mrs. Williams nodded imperceptibly.

"We'll come. Peggie, go and pack our things. Will we be staying overnight?"

"Definitely. I'm sure that Rebecca will feel better if you're there with her." It was the night of the musicale, and with so many coming and going, nobody would notice some extra visitors Evander might have. "Of course, if you decide you might like to move to Six Oaks, I can make sure my father finds some land for you to farm."

Mr. Williams considered him, eyes narrowed. "And who would your father be, Sir, to be able to promise such a thing so easily?"

"My father is the Earl of Wrotham. And I am marrying Rebecca's mother."

Mrs. Williams clutched her breast again. "Goodness, our little girl *will* be a lady!"

~

EVANDER'S HOUSE was bustling when Sarah arrived to run the boys through their last practice. Two men walked past carrying bundles of holly. They nodded to her and Sarah wandered into the house and up the stairs to the boys' playroom.

She stayed with them, playing and practicing until the afternoon when she followed the scent of baking to the kitchen where she found Mrs. Green with a bench full of cakes cooling on wire racks. "Fruit cakes?" Sarah asked.

"Yes," Mrs. Green replied. "Apologies for the mess here today. We are packing the Christmas boxes. I was just about to take these cakes through to Mrs. Dalrymple and her daughter who are in the library organizing it. They should be almost finished. I hope you do not mind, but I may have let slip that you are betrothed to Mr. Ambrose."

So this could be awkward. She supposed she had better get used to that. "Oh. Very well. Allow me to take these to them. Where is the library?" Sarah picked up the tray. It was heavy with the solid cakes and she suddenly felt awkward. Nothing surer, she would trip over something and ruin Mrs. Green's hard work.

"Down the hall on your left. Wait, I'll open the door for you." Mrs. Green led the way.

Sarah entered the library, a long thin room that had been set up with two trestle tables along the length of it. They were loaded with the bounty that was to go in the boxes.

Sarah glanced down to the room and almost dropped the cakes when the portrait of a woman met her on the wall above the fireplace.

She was in modern dress, a whimsical Grecian silhouette that accentuated her lithe figure. Her nose was pert and her mouth a perfect rosebud. Her brown hair was artfully upswept with loose ringlets lying on her shoulders. Her feet were tiny and clad in blue dancing slippers.

It had to be Eleanor. Sarah's heart constricted and sadness swept through her that so much beauty had left the world.

At her feet was a pug that looked suspiciously like Fanny. A much younger and thinner Fanny.

"The late Mrs. Ambrose, that is," said a voice behind her. Sarah whirled around to see a lady in a green gown with faded red hair and a soft smile. It must be the Mrs. Dalrymple that Mrs. Green mentioned.

Her daughter, a younger version with vibrant red hair, stood behind her. "She was an angel."

"She looks like one." The smile of the woman in the portrait was soft and dreamy, one arm tucked around a bonny babe on her lap, obviously Alexander. "I am sad not to have had the honor of her acquaintance."

This was the type of paragon Evander married.

"This is the third year we've done the boxing without her," Miss Dalrymple said. "She was always ever so generous, working months to knit blankets and jumpers. She even made dolls for all the little girls in the village. There are no dolls now."

"Oh." Suddenly, Sarah felt her spirit in the room. Or perhaps it was just the lack of her spirit where it was supposed to be. And the fruitcakes were heavy. She put them down on the trestle table.

"We were hoping whosoever Mr. Ambrose married would pick up where she left off." Mrs. Dalrymple shot a sharp glance at Sarah, looking for a reaction. "Someone with some notion of what duty is."

Not Sarah, obviously.

"Mrs. Ambrose worked tirelessly for the people of Six Oaks. Her father is the baron of New Haven and wanted her to marry into the earl's family, but she took to her duty like a duck to water. Tirelessly."

"I never knew ducks were tireless," Sarah said. She looked keenly at the woman, wondering where she was going with all this. Just trying to make Sarah feel out of place? Perhaps. "I'm sure Mr. Ambrose is marrying to please himself, and the rest will fall into place if you will just place your trust in him."

The ladies said nothing, obviously being too well-mannered to disagree with such an outrageous notion.

A few moments passed in silence, then Miss Dalrymple started packing again.

"I do miss the mince pies Mrs. Ambrose made," Miss Dalrymple said. "I don't believe we have the recipe quite right, Mama."

"No," Mrs. Dalrymple agreed forlornly. "And we also forgot to make the lavender sachets for each box. I always thought that was a nice touch."

"I'm sure the recipients will be overjoyed with the boxes. They are practical and useful." Sarah looked inside the box just to take her eyes off Eleanor because now it felt like she looked down at her from every angle, judging her, and questioning why Sarah was in her home.

It was the portrait of a woman who would never leave a child behind.

She left the room with a hurried goodbye, feeling no better when she saw Mrs. Dalrymple's satisfied smile. Sarah collected her cloak and took herself home to the cottage.

In case she was wondering, it had just become abundantly clear that she could never fill Eleanor's dainty blue shoes.

CHAPTER 27

IS BAD NEWS BETTER IF DELIVERED BY A GOOD FRIEND?

Later that afternoon, Sarah opened the door of the cottage, expecting to see Evander on the doorstep. Instead, it was Miss Jones, in rumpled travel clothes and bags under her eyes.

"Clarissa!" Sarah said, using her given name.

"Truly? I travel two days across counties on the stage and you call me by that monstrosity?"

Sarah ushered her inside, removing her cloak, which she noticed had a good ten inches of mud on the bottom. "And then I go up to Wrotham Hall only to discover that you have been banished to a cottage. I have left Morley at the main house, of course. He drove me."

Sarah blinked, trying to knock some comprehension into her brain. "Morley? Why would he be here?"

Her longest friend dropped her bag and shook her head in what looked like awe. "He had a man waiting at the opera house for either you or me to return. When I arrived to see if they had drawn up any new contracts for you, he pounced and took me back to Morley's townhouse in the most beautiful equipage you have ever seen.

"His betrothal has fallen through and he wants you back desperately. I was going to send a note, but he asked your direction and wanted to leave immediately! Only imagine how romantic it all was! He then proceeded to sing your praises for the entire trip and tell me how lost he'd been since that fateful night at the opera house. Oh, Sarah, he said all the right things and appeared to be a man in great distress. I truly think he regrets everything that happened between you and only wants you back." She leaned in as though to tell a secret. "In fact, I think he now has the most honorable intentions toward you."

A sick feeling bloomed in Sarah's stomach. "He had plenty of time for honorable intentions." Not that it mattered, just the thought of Morley was enough to raise the hair on her arms. She didn't want to be anywhere near him and certainly didn't want to sing with him in the room. Suddenly, the little cottage that had felt so cozy, felt isolated and lonely. He could appear here at any time, pushing himself through the door just as he had her dressing room. She only hoped Lord Wrotham would send him packing, but she knew in her heart that when a viscount landed on the doorstep of an earl, there could be nothing but welcome.

"But you don't look happy by this turn of events," Jones said, inspecting her friend's face. "In all seriousness, you should not hold it against Morley for a moment's passion. He was nothing but gentlemanly on the entire trip, and I truly believe he loves you."

"Yes, I can still feel the strength of his love in the faint bruising around my neck." Sarah shook her head. "I want nothing to do with him, and I wish with all my heart that you had not encouraged him to think he had any chance of reconciliation with me. For he does not."

"People can repent." She kicked her bag out of the way. "Come, get me out of this draughty hall and in front of the fire. This is not the kind of conversation we can have standing around. Is there any food here? I'm famished."

It seemed that for Jones, being connected to that level of money and privilege would be worth being treated badly. "The parlor is through there; make yourself at home while I find some food."

It felt like Jones was preparing herself for a longer argument. They had often been on differing sides with regard to Sarah's romantic life, with Jones thinking in her pragmatic way, that Sarah should take advantage of every single opportunity, whether good or bad, that came her way. It was often the case that suitors would try to find a way to Sarah through Clarissa, and heaven knew, sometimes they were successful. Sarah likes nothing more than seeing her dresser treated well, and any gentleman that did so almost instantly had a tiny part of her regard. But not in this case. Morley had shown his true colors, and they were not pretty. No amount of sweet talk could make amends for that.

Sarah went to the kitchen, cut Jones a large piece of plum cake, and was about to put the kettle on to boil when she decided that brandy would be much more warming. So she poured two glasses from the study and went back into the parlor with the tray, placing it on the table next to Miss Jones.

Clarissa reached for the brandy first. "That will go straight to your head if you haven't eaten."

"There you go, spoiling my fun again." Jones picked up the glass anyway and took a sip of the brandy. She inspected the golden liquid. "My, that's quite nice."

"Yes, this cottage belonged to my betrothed's grandmother and everything here was chosen by her." Sarah sat back in her chair and watched as a variety of expressions crossed Clarissa's face, from confusion to surprise.

"Did I just hear you say *betrothed*? Are you to be married in the week it's been since I saw you last?" She frowned. "Well, tell me all." And then she closed her eyes as if remembering something terrible. "And God help us all when Morley finds out."

"Which is precisely why he is a bad man. Any ordinary man would take the news and quietly leave, but I certainly don't trust Morley to do that."

Clarissa nodded. "I'm sorry."

"You only ever do what you believe to be in my best interest," Sarah said, putting a hand on her friend's knee. "Don't think I don't know that."

Clarissa took the plum cake off the tray and the tiny fork that went with it and slithered off a small bite. "I don't know how I can eat this because I feel entirely sick now." She nevertheless ate the entire piece of cake in half a minute, leaving not a crumb on the plate. "So tell me all about him. I can't believe I'm asking this."

"His name is Evander Ambrose, second son of the earl. He is the local vicar. You may remember him as being the person who broke Morley's nose. We were snowed in together, and the Archbishop of Canterbury himself decreed that we should marry post-haste. In fact, the day after tomorrow."

This time her friend was struck silent, and Sarah could almost hear the cogs of her brain turning. "Jones?"

"I think I have the right to be surprised. You. Married to a vicar? And with no betrothal time. What about your singing? Do you give that up? Why am I asking, of course you give it up. And Rebecca? Does he know about Rebecca?"

"He knows everything."

Jones shook her head. "And here was me thinking nothing could surprise me." She stayed silent, thinking. "I suppose if you are going to give up opera, I will find myself without a position, won't I? Perhaps I shall find a husband too."

"You won't stay with me?"

"As what, a general maid? You know that is not my style."

"No, of course not." Sarah would need a lady's maid perhaps, but not a costume designer and dresser.

Clarissa smiled at her. "Don't frown. I'm sure having that lovely man will more than compensate for not being on the stage.

Your voice was starting to crack in any case." She threw Sarah a cheeky smirk.

"It was not, you hoyden," Sarah returned without venom. "My voice is as strong as it was ten years ago."

Which was not quite true. It had changed since her last illness and never really recovered its former glory. But only the harshest of critics noticed.

"I do wish you would stay here for some time though," Sarah said. "I could use my only friend, and we can do a husband search for you."

"You make yourself sound like the saddest person in creation. I am hardly your only friend."

"Very well. Nobody knows how to get Madeira stains out of satin like you do. I can't live without that."

"That's more like it," Jones said. "But no, I will return to London after your wedding. I'm sure I will find employment quickly with the wonderful references you are going to give me."

"Not just references. I will use every contact I know to find you the best employment possible. Not that you'll need my help, but you shall have it, anyway."

"I must say, I preferred the outcome where Morley purchased your theater and installed you as its star and we kept working together for years to come."

Sarah shrugged. "Everything comes to an end and, if there is even the slightest chance I can have Rebecca with me, I would give up everything I had in the world."

Before Jones could say anything, Sarah smiled brightly, happy both to have had the conversation and for it to end. "But tell me, how is your sister? The baby?"

Jones sighed and took a sip of brandy. "A bonny boy, chubby as you please and feeding like a little piglet. She is fine and surrounded by so many supporters that I felt quite unnecessary within a few days. I took my leave."

"And she has recovered well?"

"Oh yes. It made me somewhat ill, to be honest. I know that if I ever had a child, I would be the sickliest and most whining woman that ever lived. Instead, she glows and coos and would generally take the prize for any mothering contest if only the local fair would run one."

Sarah laughed, trying not to think about her own short time as a mother and how maybe, just maybe, she was going to get a second chance at being a mother. "I'm happy for her. And remind me not to visit you if you are ever in a delicate way."

They both laughed, back to being in sympathy with each other. It never took long.

If only she hadn't brought Morley.

CHAPTER 28

IN WHICH EVANDER ALLOWS THE ENEMY TO APPROACH

Evander took in the glorious sight of the ballroom transformed into the hanging gardens of Babylon with ranks of white columns lining the room. Plants hung from them, and there were small trees in pots dotted all around. Being the middle of winter, the flowers were silk, but they were spectacular none the less. The chairs, which had always been plain, had been painted gold and the entire room looked like a dream come to life. The guests were already seated, most leafing through the booklet that had been created with the order of acts.

"I see Mother has been busy," he said, as he followed his father and the archbishop to their seats in the front row. The archbishop was on one side, then a spot for Marcus, who always arrived late, and then Evander took his own seat. The musicale was to start in five minutes, and the acts were assembled in the supper room, from where could be heard the sound of tuning strings and voices warming up. They sat and waited for the fun to begin.

Isaac appeared in front of him, his eyes bright. He twirled around so they could see the full glory of his ensemble. "Grandmama says I look as fine as a six-pence," he announced. "I said perhaps she meant a guinea because they are worth more, aren't they?"

"Indeed," replied Evander. "But 'fine as a guinea' doesn't sound quite so interesting, does it?"

"I suppose not." He put out his hand. "Can I have my six-pence now?"

"No rascal. Go to the supper room where your brothers are. Mrs. Hayworth will be looking for you."

"Come back, lad," his father said. He fished inside his pocket and took out a small leather pouch. "There's a six-pence in here for you and your brothers." He handed out the coins and Isaac's face lit up. "Thank you, Grandfather!" He raced back to the supper room.

"You've just made his night," Evander said, patting his father's knee.

"And you've made mine, bringing me Sarah. I'm so happy for you, Son. Even if Marcus never marries, I know you will both bring me more beautiful grandchildren."

"We will endeavor to please you," Evander said, managing to keep a straight face and avoid the archbishop's gaze.

They stayed quiet for a few moments, Evander thinking about Sarah. It was a subject his brain was happy to explore for hours.

"Do you know why your brother won't, then?"

Evander pulled himself out of his daydream reluctantly. "Won't what?"

"Get a wife." It was said pleasantly, but Evander could feel the tension behind the words.

He looked his father directly in the eye, so he would know he wasn't lying. "I have no idea. Honestly."

"Hmph. Find out for me, will you? Marcus has sent Lady Beatrix away with a flea in her ear and has asked us not to speak of marriage again."

"Yes, of course." He'd find his brother and pin him to the wall for causing his father anxiety. "As long as you accept whatever his answer is."

The earl frowned. "I don't want to, but maybe I can now that I see you happily settled."

The conversation was blessedly stopped when Marcus himself arrived, sitting between them. "Evening, gentlemen. If we're talking about marriage, let's not."

Evander turned to him. "Just tell us why you don't want to marry and we can stop talking about it."

His brother's mouth set into a grim line. He nodded as though coming to a decision that gave him no joy. "I am already wed. I cannot marry twice; I believe it is against the law."

Father leaned forward, eyes narrowed, examining Marcus as if looking at someone he'd never seen before. "Is that so?"

Marcus looked straight ahead, focusing on the stage where the quartet was taking their seats. "That is so."

Father continued to stare at Marcus, quite obviously weighing up whether to say more. "Very well. But she must be a fright if you won't introduce her to us."

Marcus continued to look straight ahead, but Evander could see the pulse beating in his clenched jaw. "In truth, *I* haven't seen her for years. Remember when you sent me to Scotland to buy the cotton mill?"

Father nodded.

"It was then. But, in short, her family did not approve and she left me. They were seeking an annulment." Marcus ran a hand through his hair.

"Best you go sort this out then, Son. You're either married or you're not. I'll last long enough for you to take a trip, if that's what you're worried about. This needs to be settled."

Marcus seemed to choke on something that sounded suspiciously like a sob. "That's what we're all worried about. I can't go anywhere while you're ill."

Father waved him off with a disgusted expression. "Bah, idiot. Go. Where will you start?"

"Scotland, I think."

Evander blinked rapidly, trying to process all the new information. Marcus, married. He pushed down the hurt that his brother had never confided in him. His anger would help nothing. "We are here for you. Let us know how we can help."

Marcus leaned across and clenched Evander's knee. "Thanks, Ev."

Alexander ran across the room, his little blue tailcoat swishing behind him. He really did look like a very grown up eight-year-old. The doors to the antechamber opened and Sarah's head popped around. When she saw Alexander, she smiled and beckoned him in with her finger. He ran a little harder. Evander looked around the room and noticed his mother frowning at someone at the back of the room. He followed her gaze.

Morley. "What's *he* doing here?"

His father looked straight ahead. "I don't even need to turn around to know who you're talking about. He arrived this morning, and as I didn't tell your mother about that whole nose breaking incident, she had no idea that he was persona non grata and welcomed him into the house."

Evander felt a pit of anxiety opening up inside. "He wants her back; I'll bet my last shilling on it."

"Well he can't have her, can he?" Father sat back like that was the end of the conversation.

Evander didn't say anything, lost in his own thoughts. He'd won Sarah's hand through a series of mishaps and misadventures. He would never really know if she wanted to marry him, truly. But if he allowed Morley a chance and, if they didn't announce their engagement tonight, Sarah would be able to make the choice herself. He would never want to hold on to her if she would prefer to go. Even if the thought of losing her made him feel physically ill.

"I know you were going to announce that Sarah was to become part of our family tonight, but could you please stay silent? Let's allow this charade to play out."

The earl narrowed his eyes and gave him a sideways glance. "I'm questioning your sanity."

"I have never been more sane. I need her to come to me because she wants to, not because she feels she has to."

"As you will, Son, as you will. But if I don't end up with her as my daughter-in-law, I'll break Morley's nose myself. Then yours. You have my promise."

A string quartet took the small stage to open the musicale, the opening chords of Beethoven's String Quartet number 14. It was beautiful but melancholy, not quite setting the tone Evander hoped for.

Evander watched the earl close his eyes, letting the music take him away, a look of bliss on his face. So really, as long as Father was happy, who cared what the tone was? He watched until the music drew to a graceful close some time later, so happy that with the ups and downs the year had brought, he'd made it to the musicale.

"That was lovely," the earl said.

"Indeed. Sarah is next, are you ready?"

The earl slapped his knee. "I should probably brace myself against the torrent of sentiment she always unleashes."

"It does seem to be her talent. Hopefully she brings us something a little more lively."

Sarah entered the ballroom, dressed in a mint-green gown caught under her bust by a ribbon. A froth of white lace cascading down the front of the gown. She wore no jewels, but shone nonetheless. The elegant folds of silken fabric draping around her slim figure, hugging her in a way that was impossible to ignore.

Knowing she must have packed it especially for this occasion in that old brown trunk did not lessen its effect. What many didn't notice was that behind her, dressed in perfect miniature evening attire, were his three sons. Alexander leading and looking very distinguished in his tailcoat and gold waistcoat, followed by Benjamin who was holding Isaac's hand.

"We have a special treat for the earl on this very special night," Sarah began, her voice carrying to the farthest corners of the room without effort. "The earl's grandsons have been practicing very hard with a small song they'd like to share with you."

She sat at the piano and played them an introduction. She played naturally, like a person who had spent their entire life behind a keyboard.

The boys looked at her as she counted them in and then opened their mouths and started to sing—their voices high and innocent. It was the same song she had taught them at the cottage, but now she joined them to sing in rounds.

Her voice, pure and true as ever, wound around their melody, supporting them, making them reach further. The simple tune was so haunting and beautiful, and he was so proud and so sad while being so elated that it was all he could do not to sag into his chair and start weeping. These little boys, so capable of mischief, were also capable of this great beauty. They must have worked hard and diligently when he wasn't looking, not to miss or forget a word.

As the song drew to a close, the notes hung on the air, and his heart stopped for a beat. Then the applause broke out, his father louder than anyone, and the boys beamed with pride. He thought they might run over to him, but instead, they bowed deeply to their audience, and Sarah led them from the room, where Mrs. Green and Bess, probably even prouder than he was, waited by the door.

The earl then got up from his seat. The night did not usually have a host, everyone always content to just follow the program. What was he up to?

"And now, we have a performer who I know for a fact is the reason most of you decided to attend at the last minute. I don't blame you; I would do the same thing myself. Sarah Hayworth has sung seasons at La Scala, and of course our own Kings Opera House. Tonight, she sings *Bester Jüngling* from Mozart's opera *Der Schauspieldirektor*. Please welcome her."

He stepped back, and after their very enthusiastic applause, the audience silenced until all that could be heard was the turning of a page by a member of the string quartet. Then it began, and Evander closed his eyes, ready for her voice to envelop him like it had at the opera in London.

But this was a very different piece. It was cheerful and definitely playful. He cracked open an eye to see her swishing around the room, teasing a gentleman in the front row by pretending to consider him, then shaking her head. Then the next man, and then the next. In between, she laughed with the ladies as though they were all in on the amusement. Soon the entire room was pulled into her realm, something she seemed to do as naturally as breathing.

Soon, they were all on her side, their rapt attention pushing her to sing even more exuberantly.

His heart fell. Would she want to give this up if given an alternative? He wanted her to have the choice, but oh, the heartbreak if she didn't choose him. Under their gaze, she sparkled like the champagne in the glass he was clutching a little too firmly.

Then she walked down the aisle and was in front of Morley.

Evander's heart leaped to his throat and his breath disappeared entirely.

Please, God, I don't ask for much.

For Morley, she didn't waggle her finger or pretend to consider him. No. Instead, she raised an eyebrow and did what must be the operatic version of a scoff.

He breathed a sigh of relief. *But she hasn't spoken to him yet. It's too early to celebrate.*

Then she glided to the front and stopped in front of them.

He translated the lyrics in his head with his very rusty German. It was about giving your love to a man, discovering happiness, and the final line he translated quite well.

"Full of the purest love, I give you my heart in pledge!"

Then she looked at him, her gaze heated and full of meaning. He knew the meaning. It meant she chose him. He allowed himself to hope.

Marcus, sitting on his other side, turned to look at him. "By Jove," he said under his breath, "I think she likes you."

"Shut up," Evander replied. "I'm going to marry her."

"You always were a lucky chap," Marcus said affably.

"We'll see," Evander replied.

SARAH STUMBLED over her phrasing when she saw Marcus lean in and say something to Evander that left him looking sad.

The one time when she needed to win a man over with her voice, when the magic trap of the notes was not a lie but the truth in her heart—and he still looked crestfallen.

A thousand curses on Morley's head.

She had no idea if he had spoken to Morley or if he thought she had invited him; she had been too busy before the musicale calming the boys' nerves to seek him out. All she could hope was that if she sung to him, he would understand her heart.

The aria finished, and the applause rained down on her. She curtsied deeply, expecting it to make her feel better, as it always did.

But nothing happened. Their applause slipped away like water from a well-oiled coat because all that mattered was Evander.

After two more arias, she made her way to the supper room, where she was sure she would count down the minutes to supper when she could find him.

Footmen went to the trestle tables lining the sides of the large room and lifted off the muslin sheets that were covering the food and drink.

She tapped her foot in agitation, but soon enough, the large doors opened and the audience flooded into the antechamber and swarmed the supper table. It was amazing how listening to a concert could apparently give one an appetite.

Sarah was besieged by the same group of ladies who had treated her so coolly at dinner only last week. They greeted her as a long-lost friend pulling her into their group. "My dear, such a beautiful performance." Another, Lady Hitchcock, leaned in conspiratorially. "We also hear that you are to marry Wrotham's youngest, the vicar?"

Sarah curtsied to the group and then nodded. "I am indeed. I intend to be the happiest woman in all of England." Then she decided to add a little more gossip to the conversation. "It is a little-known fact that my own father is a vicar, so I feel I understand the life a little more than the average person might."

She tried to search for Evander around her, but while she saw nothing, she heard Morley's lazy tone directly behind her. She steeled herself not to whirl around but instead continued to chat to the ladies, suddenly grateful for their presence.

But her luck was not to hold. Morley pushed himself into their little group and offered his arm to Sarah. "I do believe you promised to have supper with me this evening, Mrs. Hayworth?"

"I did no such thing," she said, searching for Evander a little more frantically.

"Come now, we are old friends. Share a cucumber sandwich with me; it's the least you can do."

The ladies actually moved away so he could take her away

from them. Sweet charity, had none of them heard how he humiliated her in London?

He tried to take her arm, but she pulled it away.

"Hear me out," he said, his voice a whisper.

She stopped, put one hand on her hip, and eyed him critically. "Certainly, go ahead."

"You're not going to make this easy, are you, Sarah?" He had the air of a man much put upon.

"I will make it impossible, but please, continue."

He took a deep breath, managing to look nervous, although she was sure that was impossible for a man of his vanity. "Very well. Since we last met, my life has been in tumult." He led her away from the supper table and back toward the ballroom.

Everyone was in the supper room, but they were still in view through the large open doors, so there was no risk in letting him talk. Then she would set him on the right path. Away from her. "Do continue."

"My betrothal was never going to last, not when she discovered how besotted I am with you."

Nothing says true love like an Austrian crystal and trying to throttle me. Sarah held up her hand. "I will stop you right there, Lord Morley. I am to be married by the Archbishop of Canterbury who is in attendance tonight."

His eyes widened and his mouth dropped open. "This is ludicrous. Who could you be marrying within a week of leaving me?"

"I am marrying, Evander Ambrose. I think you know him."

"That thug who broke my nose?" He lifted his hand, which was still somewhat swollen. "You must be crazy. Call it off. He's not the man for you. What can he do for you?"

"Not really the right question," Sarah said quietly.

"It's always the right question for women who earn their own living. Let me tell you what I can do for you." He raised his hand and started to count down his fingers. "One, I plan to purchase the Star Theater in London and have you be its resident soprano.

Two, I also purchased that townhouse in Curzon Street you were leasing." He paused for effect. "I will put the title in your name."

She wasn't really listening. It was all flotsam. "How gratifying. But thank you, no." She could only imagine how ecstatic she would have been by these declarations only a scant few weeks ago. Before she'd entered a carriage with Evander and argued her way to Six Oaks.

"No? Are you crazy?"

"I have never felt more sane." It seemed the process of owning what she was doing made her more adamant about the decision. It felt right, deep in her stomach, the source of her power, a place that never lied.

His mouth closed in an unhappy line, and he blinked furiously, as though trying to make a decision.

Sarah looked around the room, not wanting to give him any more attention than she had to.

Moments passed. Moments she could be speaking to someone interesting instead of being monopolized by this bore of a man.

"Very well," he said, after a few moments.

"Good," she replied. "Thank you, and I bid you good evening." She turned to leave, but he grabbed her by the elbow.

Sarah looked down at her elbow, caught in his hand, with all the disdain she felt for him even *attempting* to touch her.

"I mean, very well, I have come to a decision."

"Unhand me, my lord."

He looked down at where he was gripping her and his look softened. "Dear Sarah, will you do me the honor of marrying me? Lord Derby married Elizabeth Farren..."

"And was a laughingstock. No, I must decline. Please believe that this is my final word. I hope to be married before the archbishop leaves." Sarah curtsied and pulled herself away from him.

Who knew what Morley's response would have been because Evander chose that moment to step out from behind one of the large potted fig trees. "I can't tell you how glad I am to hear that."

He was listening? So ungentlemanly, and yet she was glad he'd heard it all and she didn't have to retell it.

"If you had half a heart, Ambrose, you'd let her go so she can live the life she is supposed to live."

Sarah stood beside Evander. "No, Morley, I have already lived that life. I yearn for a change." Another thing she didn't realize was true until she spoke it.

"You can't live without the applause, don't fool yourself."

She turned to Evander. "Actually, I think it's the love I can't live without. Please excuse us."

She held her arm out for Evander to take, and he did, pulling her close. They walked toward the supper room. "If you'd wanted to leave, you know I would have let you."

"Stop talking, Evander. I've already wasted enough time on him, and I'm sure all those nice lobster tarts will be gone now."

"Never fear, I have secret contacts in the kitchen. We can raid it later. For now, I think we should see if the archbishop will marry us in the morning. I can't wait another day."

CHAPTER 29

A SMALL SURPRISE

After the festivities were over and the guests had all wandered upstairs to bed, Sarah wrapped herself in her red velvet traveling cloak and waited on the steps with Evander for his carriage to come around. The night was as cold as a Gunter's ice, and you could see no further than fifty feet for the fog. Sarah pushed her hands into the voluminous pockets of her cloak, trying not to breathe too deeply. Cold air was always bad for her voice.

"I do hope the fire is still alight," she said.

The carriage came into view, and Evander took her hand in readiness to help her into it. "I have a small surprise for you, but it is at my house. Would you come up just for a few brief moments so I can show you?"

Sarah stepped into the carriage, sat down, and pulled the rug onto her lap. It had been warmed by a hot brick that was now on the floor, gently radiating heat. She'd never been so happy for something in all her life.

"Of course, I never say no to a surprise." It must have been the reason he went out on errands today, to buy her something. The way he smiled at her with such excited expectation made her excited too. "What a lovely way to cap off the evening. You are very sweet."

"I hope you think so. I must admit a moment of horror when I saw Morley at the musicale, but after wrongly eavesdropping on your conversation, I must admit to feeling better than ever about everything. You sent him on his way better than I could have."

"Which is not saying much considering your way of sending him on his way would be to punch him in the nose again."

"I thought I controlled that urge quite admirably tonight."

They reached the house in companionable silence, holding hands as she rode forward, and he backward. A lamp burned at the front door, welcoming them home.

"We must be quiet now," he said. "I don't want to wake anyone."

He took a candelabra from the hall table and led her upstairs, every step creaking along the way. She giggled. "I must say it feels like the only surprise you are going to show me is a bedroom. And I was quite sure we had decided against that."

He stopped on the stairs and turned to look at her, and even in the soft candlelight, she could read his amused expression. He stopped in front of a bedroom and gently opened the door, beckoning her inside. What on earth was he giving her?

The room had a bassinet on one side where little Emily lay in a small sweet bundle and a bed on the other where there was a larger child sleeping. The child had a mop of dark curly hair, and even without Evander saying anything, a lump formed in Sarah's throat, and tears sprung to her eyes. "Rebecca?"

Evander nodded.

She rushed to the side of the bed and knelt beside it, like the child herself was a prayer.

Evander came closer with his branch of candles. What the soft light showed made her heart clench in what felt like an explosion of joy. Long dark eyelashes fanned out over soft sweet cheeks. Little fingers curled around an old worn dolly made of cloth. Her mouth was a perfect cupid's bow, her nose a sweet little dollop.

She was perfect.

Sarah reached out and touched her down-soft hair, running a curl through her fingers. She felt tears tumble down her cheeks without being aware she was crying them.

This was too much.

Too much to bear in such a small room when everything inside her felt large and uncontrolled.

Sensing her emotional overwhelm, Evander placed the candles on the mantle and came and knelt beside her. He said nothing but pulled her into an all-enveloping hug, bracing her as she sobbed so quietly it hurt her chest. She should be overjoyed, not melting into a quivering lump on the rug. But he seemed to understand and spent his time alternating between murmuring soft endearments and stroking her hair.

She had so many questions, but instead, she hiccupped on her tears and knew that this crying would not stop soon and was about to get ugly. Evander knew it too. He whispered in her ear, "Come, she isn't going anywhere. Let's go downstairs. You'll feel better in a moment."

He hugged her close again, then, after a few long moments, he stood and held out his hand to help her up. They left the room quietly, and Sarah couldn't take her eyes off Rebecca and felt infinitely sad as he closed the door as gently as he had opened it.

SARAH'S REACTION to seeing Rebecca was the best gift anyone could give him. Once down in the parlor, she took the small glass of brandy he offered and sat in the cozy chair by the fire, looking as though her entire world had exploded.

"Today? How? That's quite some errand." She could barely

form a coherent sentence, and it made him laugh to see her try. He told her the whole story. She was outraged.

"What do you mean Rebecca was on a farm?"

"Your mother gave her to a lovely farming couple, who are, by the way, sleeping in my guest bedroom. They were given one pound a month to take care of her."

"Raised by strangers? For twenty shillings? What madness is this?" Her hands were shaking as they clutched the glass.

"Let me see," he raised his hand to start counting off his fingers. "There is a new carriage house and stable with two lovely bays and a shiny black carriage. They have redecorated the vicarage with an abundance of new furniture and carpets. Your brother had his colors purchased for him, in the Dragoons no less, from the picture I saw above the fireplace. There was also a painting by Leighton in the hall, if I'm not mistaken."

She shook her head. "I don't know whether to feel stupendously angry, horribly sad, or both. They didn't want her. They didn't love her. I've been wrong about everything."

"Good Christians that they are," he said. "Eventually, I convinced them to speak to me about Rebecca. Once they had established that I wasn't believing the story about them not knowing you."

Sarah lay back in the chair, frowning. "In truth, I gave them that money, but I never told them what they had to do with it."

Evander shook his head. "You will not make excuses for their inexcusable behavior. If it makes you feel better, she was well-loved on the farm. I'm sure she was better off there than with your parents."

"But how will we explain it?"

"We'll embellish the truth. In your mysterious past, you were married, now widowed. You knew the opera was no place for a child, but now you are settled, you have brought her to you. Simple."

"She *will* call me Mama," Sarah echoed, and then promptly burst into tears.

"Blast it," Evander said.

Sarah looked up. "What is the matter?"

"Now I have made you cry again.

"This is the best wedding present in the history of wedding presents," Sarah said, closing her eyes and allowing the tears to gather on her cheeks. "It's good, crying."

CHAPTER 30

IN WHICH THE NERVES ARE FAR WORSE
THAN BEFORE A PERFORMANCE

The day of the wedding dawned with a clear winter blue sky, but Sarah couldn't feel cold. Her entire person was buzzing with anticipation.

Mr. and Mrs. Williams brought Rebecca to the cottage to share breakfast and Sarah was relieved to find them treating her little girl with kindness and care. She wore a sturdy but well constructed little coat of green wool and the sweetest brown boots.

Rebecca herself didn't like to stray far from Mrs. Williams even after Sarah had been gently introduced as 'the mummy who had to go overseas and left you with me all those years ago.'

Sarah just wanted to pick her up and hold her close, but it was not the right time and her hunch paid off, with Rebecca talking to her more and more over their tea and toast.

Sarah smiled at the Williams couple. "Will you come to the wedding this morning? We would love to have you there." She hoped it were true, there not having been any time to speak to Evander.

But the older lady shook her head ruefully. "Now we didn't bring anything fancy enough to come to a wedding with the

227

Archbishop of Canterbury himself, but Mr. Ambrose insisted, so we'll just be as inconspicuous as possible."

"Half the village will likely invite themselves." Sarah reached out and put her hand over Mrs. Williams hand. "I appreciate it more than I can say." It felt somehow like having Rebecca there would bond them as a family. It was too important not to have her there, not now that she was with them. "And I also hope you will take Mr. Ambrose up on his offer for your future. Nothing would make me happier than to keep you both close."

She did not know the details of what Evander had offered the couple, but she hoped it was enough to entice them to stay.

Mr. Williams spoke for the first time since breakfast started, his voice gruff his grey eyes keenly bright. "Well it is good farm land. We'd be fools not to. And we're not fools." He scooped Rebecca up and put her on his knee. "And how could we go without seeing this little one grow up, I ask you?"

"My sentiments exactly." Evander replied.

After a while, they took their leave and Sarah went upstairs where Jones was putting the finishing touches to her dress.

Together they had stayed up late sewing seed pearls along the hem and sleeves of her pale purple gown, turning it from a simple evening gown into something truly worthy of the chapel at Wrotham Hall. She had also produced a veil.

"Where on earth did you find this?" Sarah picked up the fine lace and placed it on her head, admiring the way the lace cascaded around her shoulders in graceful folds.

"Her ladyship," Jones replied. "The pearls are from her, too. It is a veritable treasure trove in their haberdashery cupboard."

"I'm amazed they dragged you away from it." The lace was old and soft, from a time when ladies wore panniers and hoops. "I love it."

"I was picking out the seed pearls in a box of loose ends when the countess brought it in to me. She said it had belonged to her mother and that she had worn it for her wedding. It feels like they are accepting you into the family, Sarah."

"To her credit, she is giving me a chance. I'm not sure I would give me a chance. I'm grateful."

Sarah inspected the beadwork Jones had done. All those tiny pearls individually sewn had taken them hours. "I'm also grateful for the time you have spent to make my dress look so beautiful." She pulled Jones into a messy hug. "Thank you."

"It is my wedding gift to you. I also whipped up something for you that is far too frivolous for this cold winter in a package on your bed."

"Oh, that sounds naughty," Sarah said. And the thought of wearing it for Evander was even naughtier.

"Naughty or nice, you decide. Now, sit in front of the looking glass, and I will dress your hair. Did you put the curling irons in the hearth?"

"Yes, they will be hot."

Jones proceeded to do wonders with her hair while she got more and more nervous as each minute passed.

Her dresser looked her in the looking glass. "Nerves?"

"Nerves."

"Deep breaths then. Just like a performance, they'll be too busy being blinded by your beauty to notice if you miss a note. Everything is going to be perfect."

Sarah lifted her hand to her shoulder so that Jones could clasp it. "Thank you."

"It has been my pleasure and honor."

The carriage arrived to pick them up at quarter to nine, and it was only then that Sarah remembered that she had no posy of flowers to hold. Which was bound to be the case when one got married in such a rush.

It was the middle of winter, and there would be nothing to be found in any case. Well. She would just have to hold her hands in front of her. At least the countess had sent a message to say she would drop by on her way to the chapel to give Sarah a gold ring for Evander, one that belonged to his grandfather.

As though summoned by magic, Sarah looked out the window to see the countess being handed down from the carriage carrying a small posy of lilies and a box that looked suspiciously like an old jeweler's box.

"My dear," she said, smiling. "I know I am late, but I had a thought you might need flowers. Do you?"

"I just had the same late thought! Yes, I do!"

"I have picked these for you out of the greenhouse and I hope you like the arrangement. I see you have the veil. It looks lovely. I am so glad it is getting used once more." The countess passed the flowers to Jones, who inspected the wide white ribbon with approval.

Then the countess reached into her carriage and took out two boxes, one small and dark blue, the other a little bigger and made of black leather. She opened the small box and handed Sarah the gold ring, smiling. "Thank you for agreeing to give Evander my father's ring. It means the world to me." As though Sarah wasn't entirely grateful to have the ring provided.

"It is I who appreciate such a valuable gift." She took the ring with a smile and put it on her thumb where it fit. "Safe keeping."

Then the countess busied herself with the black box, drawing out a necklace with a large sapphire pendant. It was such a deep blue; it was almost purple and had matching earbobs.

"Evander thought these would look well with your eyes," she said. "He picked them out for you last night. It is yours to keep, with our blessing."

"Oh," said Sarah, quickly removing the simple necklace with a cross she was wearing. "It's lovely. I have never seen anything so beautiful. Thank you. I am truly blessed to be joining such a wonderful family. I will never forget your kindness to me."

"What, in sending you away from the main house so you could be closer to my son?" She smiled a mischievous smile. "You are most welcome." The older lady searched Sarah's face. "You will make my boy happy now, won't you?"

"I will try with all my heart."

"Good, let's go, shall we? The groom is waiting for you."

They traveled to the chapel, arriving to the sound of bells ringing out over the snowy hills of the Wrotham estate. The chapel was covered in ivy, its large wooden doors open to welcome her. Villagers gathered outside to see her, clapping as she alighted the carriage. It all seemed perfect.

Except, she had no-one to give her away.

This had all happened so fast, and it had been such a long time since she'd been to a wedding that simple things like flowers and someone to walk her down the aisle had been forgotten.

But Evander had not forgotten.

The earl was standing at the entrance of the chapel, leaning on his cane. He smiled as he saw her. "I hope you don't mind, my dear. I heard your father could not make it on such short notice. It would honor me to stand in his stead."

Unbidden tears sprang to her eyes. "I would be honored, too. Thank you." It seemed all she did was thank other people for their kindness to her. It seemed she did have a family or was about to become part of one today, after such a long time out in the cold. Just by standing up with her, this man was more of a father than the one she had in Upminster.

Taking his arm, Sarah braced the earl, and he braced her. It was dark inside the chapel, but lit by so many candles that the air itself became hazy and warm. Soft chamber music floated through the small chapel, and Sarah looked to see where it came from, only to find a small group from the chorus of the opera house singing her down the aisle. They were accompanied by some members of the string section of the orchestra. Surprised and gratified, she smiled and waved at them.

How they had found out, she had no idea. Then she saw Jones' satisfied smile and knew immediately her friend had swung into action to make her wedding special.

Evander waited for her, with his brother Marcus by his side. The three boys stood in the front pew, and Sarah watched as the countess slid in with them. Rebecca was standing between Mr. and Mrs. Williams and waved shyly. Sarah waved back, knowing she would not be able to see her smile through the veil.

The earl presented her to Evander and took his place with the countess. Through her veil, she watched his expression. It was soft and tender as he picked up her hand and kissed her knuckles. She squeezed his fingers, and they stayed that way, with their fingers entwined until it was time to say their vows. The ring he placed on her finger, a shining band of gold that looked far newer than the one she had for him, but they meant the same thing. *I will love you*. Evander's dark eyebrows drew together in concentration as he slid the ring onto her finger, like someone desperate to get an important moment right.

Oh it would not be hard to love this man.

CHAPTER 31

IN WHICH BARGAINS ARE MADE AND DEALS ARE STRUCK

Perhaps he had just had the best night of his entire life. The most exciting, intimate, and loving night a man could have. A dream come true.

Perhaps it made him wake at dawn in excitement. Because Sarah slept like an angel, some better part of him had taken his horse up to his mother's hot-house to pick some flowers for her.

He came in through the back door to the smell of fresh cake that Mrs. Green had just taken out of the oven.

"I baked a treat for your breakfast. Raisin cake. No need to ice it, just eat it warm with some butter." She cut a few slices and put it on plates that were already on a tray. "Just a minute while I get the kettle for the tea."

"I'll get it." Evander picked the kettle off the range and poured the tea into the waiting pot.

"Mrs. Ambrose is still abed," Mrs. Green said with a small smile. "It was a big day yesterday."

And a bigger night. "That it was."

"And the little girl's guardians are returning home today to pack, I understand?"

"Yes, Rebecca will be staying with us now."

"Hmph," said his usually outspoken housekeeper.

"Please be open, Mrs. Green. Say what you will."

"I heard them say that Mrs. Ambrose was the little girl's mother."

"Her name was *Mrs.* Hayworth, if you remember." He left it at that.

"Oh. I suppose it was." She appeared to think on it a little more. "I suppose she was widowed at a young age, the poor thing, and had to do the best she could to raise the girl."

"Please don't spread this information around, I beg you," said Evander.

"Wouldn't dream of it, Sir," Mrs. Green responded. "Just you see what I'd say to anyone that gets in the way of my three boys' happiness. And she makes them happy, I can tell you that now."

"I feel the same way. But you can add me into that equation." He picked up the tray. "This cake smells like a slice of heaven. What is the secret ingredient?"

"I'd like to say love, but really it's cinnamon," she replied. "Away with you now. Go and visit that bride of yours."

Evander smiled as he left the kitchen and climbed the stairs with the tray, trying not to tip anything over. They never had fresh cake during the week like this. It was always a treat for Sunday after church.

As he got closer, he could hear murmurs behind his bedroom door. It was Sarah, talking.

"Of course I will read you bedtime stories."

Alexander murmured something.

"Yes, and I will take care of you if you're sick."

Oh dear. It sounded an awful lot like Alexander was negotiating terms. Their terms. Or perhaps just trying to figure out what having a new mother meant.

"And will you make jam tarts?" The small feminine voice could only be Rebecca.

She had the same sweet Essex accent Mr. and Mrs. Williams had.

"Of course," Sarah answered.

"And will you make me a new dolly?"

"We could sew a new dolly together. I'm sure. Miss Jones might be able to give us some instruction. She is a superb seamstress."

"Excuse me," Alexander said. "I had not finished asking my questions."

"Alexander, we have all afternoon to answer as many questions as we need."

Evander nudged the door open with his foot. He entered the bedroom to find all three boys and Rebecca on the bed with Sarah. Fanny was on his pillow, getting her large belly rubbed by Benjamin. "Best be careful what you promise. If I know anything about children, it is that one promise invariably leads to a hundred more. I have tea and cake."

She looked at him, laughter in her eyes. "Perfect. Alexander was just trying to figure out what it means now that we are married."

His son grimaced, not quite meeting Evander's eyes. "The others want to know too. You haven't told us. I don't want to do the wrong thing."

Maybe this was what everyone meant when they said he needed a woman's touch in the house. Alexander's desperation to get it right made Evander ache with sadness. He'd so tried to be everything for the boys, both mother and father, and obviously, he'd failed a little. It was impossible to be everything to everybody, a fact he was slowly coming to grips with in his stubborn, pigheaded way.

"I stand corrected. But in my defense, I was going to speak to you all over dinner tonight."

Sarah took Alexander's hand. "He has beaten you to it. We have so far discussed my ability to play cricket, or at least field in the absence of any bowling skills. Then we moved on to reading and what kind of books I think are good. Now, I think we are moving on to my nursing skills. Which are woeful, as I think you could expect. I can find good medicines in my chest, but as a nurse, I will have much to learn."

Alexander nodded solemnly. "We accept that. We have Mrs. Green and Father who do very well. Once, I lost the contents of my stomach all over Father, and—"

"That's enough, Alexander. Your new mama will not want to hear your most horrid stories when she is about to have breakfast."

He bowed his head. "Yes, Papa."

"Now, off you all go and wash your hands so that you can come back and share this cake with us."

"Yes, Papa," the boys said with more enthusiasm, jumping off the bed.

Rebecca stood on the bed instead and put her hands around Evander's neck. "Papa, my hands are clean. I can have cake now?"

She already called him Papa and looked at him from under long lashes that melted his heart.

He kissed her on the cheek and swung her onto the floor. "I hardly think so! No washing hands, no cake. That's the rule."

He quirked an eyebrow at Sarah. "And you thought she'd be *nothing* like you. I was ready to die for her the moment she called me 'Papa'. Little does she know that if she pushed a tiny bit further, I'd give her the cake and my slice too."

Sarah nodded, obviously trying to hold back a smile. "Don't get between your girls and their cake. I think that's the lesson that needs to be learned here." She picked up a slice and took a big bite out of it.

"Do I need to apologize for Alexander?" Evander asked, sitting on the side of the bed and taking over patting Fanny. "I hope he didn't upset you in any way."

"Oh, no. In fact, I like to know what is expected of me before I take on any role. It makes it so much easier. What about you? What do you expect of me?"

It felt like one of those rare times life sometimes offered, where you could be honest with no repercussions because nothing had been decided and the sands were still shifting. Much like their very first carriage ride.

"Well," he started, "I say this with no idea of what you are willing to offer, and with every likelihood that you will decline to accept any of it, but— "

"Yes?"

"I should like you to love us. To think of us as your support and your affection, as your rock and your safety. And if you could look at my boys, as I will look at your girl, as if she were my own and cherished beyond compare, then I will be a happy man."

"Then you are bound to be a happy man, because you are already all of those things to me."

"Truly? You will love us?" He smiled with mischief. "In between singing assignations, of course."

She almost choked on her raisin cake. "Singing? Goodness, I have given that up entirely."

He looked confused, his head tilted to one side. "I thought at the very least you would have a farewell performance. You cannot leave the opera without that, surely?"

She'd never spoken to him about it for the obvious reason that the idea of the vicar's wife continuing to sing the opera was mad.

In truth, in the whirlwind of the past few days, she hadn't put much thought into her singing future. Her only thoughts had been for Evander, their boys, and her little girl. That was the future now.

Once she had needed to be La Luminosa, but now, Sarah Ambrose—was more than enough. But it felt strange leaving that world without a farewell.

"Your Miss Jones may have let slip to me yesterday that she

had contracts for a three-week performance of The Marriage of Figaro." Evander raised one eyebrow to Sarah. "Interested?"

She nodded, feeling the tears spring to her eyes. "To say goodbye would be lovely. You don't mind?"

He shrugged one shoulder, looking unconcerned. "You'll come back to me after the three weeks?"

"Or better yet, will you come to London with me?" She lay back on the pillows and took another bite of raisin cake. "After all, if you find a man who's willing to fight peers of the realm for you and warm your feet at night, it's best to keep him close. Why do I get the feeling you are going to be a superlative husband?"

He leaned to whisper in her ear. "Because I will be. In every way."

THE END

Thank you for reading A Song of Secrets.
I hope you enjoyed it and I would love to hear what you
thought. If you could leave a review where you purchased
this book or any review site you enjoy, it would make my
day. Your opinion goes a long way to helping others decide
if a book is for them.

BUT WHAT HAPPENED TO MARCUS?

FIND OUT BY JOINING MY NEWSLETTER!
I'm currently writing a short story about Marcus finding
his errant wife that I will send to my newsletter
subscribers. Join me here!
https://www.robynchalmers.com/newsletter

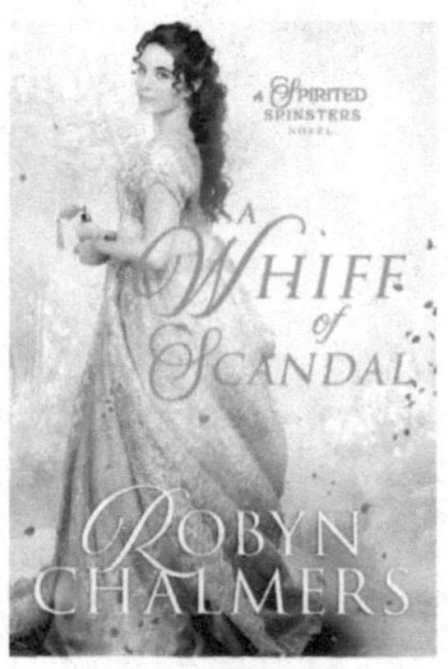

A Whiff of Scandal

To save her family, she'll risk ruin

Most ladies dream of finding a husband, but Daphne knows no knight is coming to save her and her sister from genteel poverty. She plans to make and sell perfumes to the Ton using the persona of Lady Spellwater to create allure and protect their reputation.

But when she discovers a devilishly handsome man is hunting her, all her well-laid plans unravel.

To catch a thief, he'll risk his empire

Hugh, Earl Mandeville is hunting Lady Spellwater to recover a rare and expensive ingredient she uses that is being stolen from his family business, before that business collapses. He has her scent and is determined to have her lead him to the thieves.

But when Hugh finally tracks her down, he finds the beautiful and spirited perfumer irresistible.

Now that he has caught her, he must figure out how he can keep her forever. Especially when he thinks it is her father who is the thief. Is it possible to choose between justice and love?

A Whiff of Scandal is a sweet regency romance.

On sale February 25th 2021

https://www.robynchalmers.com/books/a-whiff-of-scandal/

Robyn Chalmers is an emerging author of sweet regency romance.

She lives in a country town in southern Australia with her family and a white fluffy dog. She reads a lot, walks a lot and gets caught on Pinterest too much.

When not reading, you can find her writing her favorite kind of novel – Regency romance.

This is Robyn's first book.

She loves hearing from readers and you can find her on Facebook and Twitter.

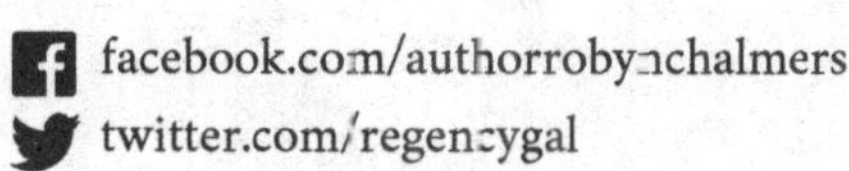